AN OMINOUS BEGINNING

General Ignatiev looked down with empty eyes at the chemical warfare expert. "You poisoned me," he said softly.

"I beg your pardon?" Pollock said, stunned.

"Yes, we thought you had come over to our side, but you have always been the enemy."

"General Ignatiev!" protested Pollock, backing toward the door. "Really, you must—"

"I'm the one you poisoned," Ignatiev thundered, "but it's you, Pollock—you scummy American spy—who's going to die."

He pulled a pistol from beneath his tunic and shot Pollock once, through the heart, before walking calmly to where the American lay and administering the *coup de grace*.

Then he put the muzzle of the Tokarev beneath his own chin, pointing toward the unseen Russian sky, and pulled the trigger.

By Daniel da Cruz
Published by Ballantine Books:

THE AYES OF TEXAS

THE GROTTO OF THE FORMIGANS

F-CUBED

TEXAS ON THE ROCKS

F-CUBED

Daniel da Cruz

A Del Rey Book
BALLANTINE BOOKS • NEW YORK

A Del Rey Book
Published by Ballantine Books

Copyright © 1987 by Daniel da Cruz

Library of Congress Catalog Card Number: 86-92037

ISBN 0-345-33644-5

Printed in Canada

First Edition: June 1987

Cover Art by Barclay Shaw

To
Owen A. Lock
Good friend—and a pretty good editor, too.

CONTENTS

1. ANNABELLA
2 MAY 2015

KEEFE MCCANN HAD JUST TURNED TO A HEADING OF 278 degrees, calculated to bring him into Wheeling in exactly twenty-three minutes, when the engine quit. He put the Cessna 425 STOL into a shallow glide, keeping the plane a niggardly few knots above stall speed, and hit the starter. The prop windmilled, the engine coughed, sputtered a few times, and finally started. Two minutes later it again fell silent, this time for good. To Keefe McCann, the problem appeared to be water in the fuel line, but understanding the problem wasn't going to help him solve it.

The Doppler altimeter read 4,340 feet. Below him stretched broken clouds as far as he could see, and below them, he knew, were several thousand square miles of West Virginia razorbacks and hollers. He briefly considered radioing Mayday, but realized it would be a waste of time. If he survived, it would be through skill or dumb luck.

He decided to give skill a chance. The flight path monitor showed his position as twenty-two miles from the nearest airport. Duck soup for an albatross. On the other hand, if the clouds parted long enough for him to spot a stretch of fairly flat cow pasture, he might be able to grease the plane in.

The plane descended through two thousand feet, one thousand feet, five hundred feet, as McCann kicked over the engine to no avail. Through occasional breaks in the low-lying clouds he could see hilltops with their stunted growth of scrub trees, fog-shrouded gullies, and a spiral of smoke winding up from an isolated farmhouse caught in the grip of a valley greedy for the human presence. At 220 feet, his heart was hammering so hard that he almost failed to notice a stream sliding by beneath his wing. He made a shallow turn to line himself up with the stream, broke out of the clouds, and saw to his horror that the stream doglegged. He was headed, not for water, but a dense copse of scraggly trees on its bank.

He wrenched the nose up, cinched his shoulder straps tight, and tried to tell himself that men had survived crashes worse than this was going to be. The trees atop a low hill brushed his wheels and suddenly a dirt road appeared at a thirty degree angle just ahead. It wasn't much of a road, but it was fairly level, fairly straight, and more than long enough to accommodate the Cessna. He fishtailed the craft, hit the ground with a mighty *thump*, bounced once into the air, and rolled to a stop with two hundred feet to spare.

For some time McCann didn't move, giving his trembling limbs time to unwind. Sweat from his brow ran down his nose and dripped on his flight jacket. He wiped it away with the back of his hand, and saw that it was mixed with blood. He had struck his nose on the ledge above the instrument panel when the plane hit, and hadn't even noticed. Breathing a huge sigh of thanksgiving, he released the harness, pulled back the canopy, and stepped shakily down on the dirt trail.

"Are you all right?" The voice came from a young woman standing beside the wingtip. She brushed back straight brown hair, reaching almost to her waist, to reveal a freckled face rather pleasant than pretty. A tight gingham dress revealed even more: the well-contoured body of a healthy country girl on the threshold of womanhood. She was barefoot.

"I'm fine," said McCann. If the girl was Country, the man was City. He had the well-conditioned body of the young executive who spends his lunch hour playing racquetball, and weekends lifting weights. Except for his broken nose, which was now swelling painfully, disturbing the symmetry of his face, he might have been a model for ads for men's shirts. He had thick eyebrows, high cheekbones, deep-set eyes suggestive of Indian forebears, and a wide, sensuous mouth fixed in a perpetual half-smile. It was the expression of a man who knew that something memorable was going to happen any minute now and was ready to savor it to the fullest. He was the kind of man people instinctively warmed to and trusted — soft-spoken, with an open and slightly self-deprecatory manner, and an air of complete sincerity.

The young woman examined him for a moment, then smiled. "Don't you go away, now," she said. "I'll be right back."

Keefe McCann watched her go, probably to assure her folks, watching from the window of the weathered little frame house at the edge of the woods down the road, that his was a simple forced landing, not an invasion from Mars. Dismissing her from his thoughts, he turned his attention to the engine. He soon discovered that water in the gas line was, indeed, the problem. In the air, the problem had almost been fatal; on the ground, he would simply filter the gasoline through chamois and be ready to go in half an hour.

The girl returned. In her hand was a small square of gauze. "Your nose is still bleeding," she said, and began gently to rub away the clotted blood.

Up close, as she dabbed at his nose, McCann found himself discovering that she wasn't at all the woman she had first appeared. The difference was impossible to explain. She looked precisely the same in every particular, but by some subtle feminine alchemy had suddenly become transformed from an innocent, barefoot country lass into an object of the most intense sexual desire he had ever experienced. Looking into her eyes, he saw that the rustic innocence had vanished. They were the eyes of a woman famished for sex, a man-eater whose libidinous appetite could be satisfied only by the exertions of a regiment of Marines shipwrecked for two years on a South Pacific atoll. McCann was not a Marine, and he had never been shipwrecked, but he recognized the call to service. His arms reached out to envelope her...

Her name was Annabella Ames. Orphaned by the death of her father two years previously, she had lived on alone in the simple cabin, but not in hardship. The cabin was furnished with a king-size water bed, soft lighting, a thirty-four-inch television set and satellite dish, videotape player with a substantial library of country-western cassettes, lithographs of horses over the fireplace, and electric heating, powered by a generator. Incongruously, Annabella also owned a single-sideband transceiver, which she said was her main contact with distant neighbors, although, again incongruously, she never spoke with them while McCann was around. As to her income, she was vague, and McCann was alternately too busy or too exhausted to wonder how she lived so comfortably with no obvious means of support.

Six days passed in a blur of furious concupiscence. The only occasion McCann got out of bed for any length of time was on the morning of the second day, when they pushed his aircraft beneath the limbs of a spreading oak. McCann knew that by now he'd be reported missing, and didn't want to risk a rescue party descending upon him to blight an erotic experience beyond his most fevered imaginings.

Despite the passion which consumed him, he couldn't quite bring Annabella Ames into focus. He'd made love to women with bodies just as exquisite as hers and features considerably more attractive. She had no conversation beyond what related to their mutual carnal desires. The range of imagination she brought to sexual gratification was like the Mississippi in springtime—broad, deep, and in constant spate, but in no way distinguished from that of any normally uninhibited woman. And yet, her physical magnetism was overpowering. He couldn't explain it; furthermore, he didn't even try, content to wallow in her caresses and forget that he had ever drawn a breath that wasn't infused with the ineffable scent of her body.

"Your ribs are showing," she said on the seventh day. "You've got to eat."

He leered at her, and lunged.

"Food," she said, slipping out from under him.

It wasn't among her better ideas. In a contest of arms —and legs—Annabella Ames was without peer, but put a skillet in her hand and she was a menace to humanity. He tasted, exactly once, her rubbery fried eggs, greasy bacon, soggy hash browns, and rancid coffee, and took the pledge. Nevertheless, he recognized that if he kept it up—that is, if he *could* keep it up—at this rate he'd be dead in a fortnight from malnutrition and exhaustion. Somehow, it didn't seem to matter.

"And then there's your airplane," Annabella Ames went on. "It's rented, isn't it?"

"Screw the airplane."

"Why not? That would make it unanimous."

He laughed, hollowly.

"Besides, if it's rented, they're going to be looking for it. And if they look hard enough . . ."

"There you go, talking sex again," he said.

She slapped him lightly. "If they look for the plane—and they're bound to sooner or later—they'll find it."

"Probably. Who cares?"

"*I* do. They'll accuse you of having stolen it. What else can they think, its being missing six days and all, and parked out there under that oak tree? They'll put you in jail, and I'll never see you again."

There was something in what she said. It *would* be wise to get that plane back to its owners. At the same time, he could stoke up on some decent food, put some flesh back on his anemic frame, and auction off his worldly goods. He wouldn't be needing them once he came back to the warm embrace of Annabella Ames, never to leave again. "I guess you're right, at that."

He made a mental computation: two hours back to Falls Church, Virginia, just outside the nation's capital, two hours to settle up his bill and get some decent food inside him, and two hours to get back to Annabella Ames's arms in an aerial taxi, there to remain for a long, long time, if not forever.

She kissed him fiercely, put a fresh Band-Aid on the bridge of his nose, and watched him bounce his plane down the dirt road and into the air.

The flight back to Falls Church, Virginia, on the outskirts of Washington, D.C., was routine. Once airborne, he obtained clearance for a visual flight plan from air traffic control, then radioed the private airport where he had rented the plane that he was on his way in. The tower said to come ahead. Any other time he would have remarked on the airport operator's singular lack of interest in what had happened during the week he had been missing, but McCann's thoughts were on Annabella Ames.

He landed on the 033 runway, taxied to the rental

hangar, and cut the engine. As he climbed out, four men in business suits walked across the hangar to greet him.

"Captain Martin T. Haversham?" said one of the men pleasantly.

"That's right," replied Keefe McCann.

"You're under arrest."

"Yes, well, I can understand that you've been worried about the plane, gentlemen," said McCann affably. "But the fact is, I was forced down last week with engine trouble in a remote part of Pennsylvania and had to walk twelve miles to the nearest telephone to order spare parts. Then a couple of teenagers in a car saw me walking back down the country road, and . . ."

"We're not here about the plane, Captain."

"You're not?" McCann was disappointed. He was just getting warmed up, and rather wished he could continue, so he'd learn how the lie he was improvising was going to turn out. "Then what's this talk about my being under arrest? Arrest for what?"

"That's something we thought you might be able to help us with, Captain Haversham—also known as Jeremy Powell, R.N., a.k.a. Dr. Julian R. Hartshorn, M.D., a.k.a. Professor Wendell Free, a.k.a. Russell Grebe, attorney-at-law, a.k.a. Fireman First Class John J. Henderson, a.k.a. Father Ronald Bellingham, and so on and so forth. Do I need to go on, Captain Haversham, or whatever the hell your real name is?"

"Not really. I think I've grasped your drift."

They cuffed him, read him Miranda, took him to the county courthouse, and recited indictments from seven states on a lengthy list of charges of fraud, on all of which he pled guilty in order, as he put it, "to save the court a lot of time." The presiding judge was equally accommodating, giving Keefe McCann as much time as the law allowed: thirteen sentences of ten-to-fifteen years, to be served consecutively.

2. THE ROSOVY FACTOR
12 JULY 2016

AGRICULTURAL EXPERIMENTAL STATION No. 23 WAS something of a mystery. The U.S. Army Map Service Satellite Survey showed it forty-miles due west of Nar'yan-Mar, northwest of Moscow and well inside the Arctic Circle, in the most bitterly cold, remote, and hostile area of the Soviet Union. In its labs beneath the permafrost, AES No. 23 conducted research on grass-seed germination in cold regions, aimed at increasing production of forage crops in Siberia. The American Mutual Inspection Team (MIT), which made bimonthly tours of the installation, gave it a clean bill of health: no weapons research was in progress. Still, an American agent had managed to obtain a copy of the Ministry of Agriculture budget summary for fiscal 2015, and it showed an allotment for AES No. 23 approximately nine times larger than the research there justified.

Something fishy was going on at AES No. 23. The Americans didn't know what it was, but they were working on it.

Klementiy Pavlovich Sheremetiev knew exactly what was going on at AES No. 23: grass-seed germination research. But funds concealed in AES No. 23's budget allotment were indeed being diverted. They were being spent on machinery, materials, and staff for Project Rosovy, of which Sheremetiev, chief of the Ministry of Agriculture's Chemical Pesticides Directorate, had been in charge since its inception.

On the afternoon of July 12, 2016, Sheremetiev was handed a message which he personally decoded. It was from Ornstein, his personal informant on Project Rosovy's scientific staff. The message read: "Tests indicate total success."

That same evening Sheremetiev took off from Moscow alone in his two-place Torg-11. He headed southeast.

After a flight of nearly an hour, he landed at an army airfield outside Pinsk, on the banks of the Dnieper in the Byelorussian Soviet Socialist Republic. Although his chief-of-directorate rank entitled him to a Zil, he was not surprised to find a mud-spattered Volga waiting for him when his plane braked to a stop at the far end of the field from the control tower. He climbed in. The chauffeur, an army lieutenant-colonel wearing the cloth cap and grease-streaked leather jacket of a provincial taxi driver, drove off.

Though there was little likelihood they'd be followed, for the next twenty minutes the driver randomly crisscrossed deserted country roads with his eye on the rearview mirror, alert for trailing lights. Finally, satisfied that they were alone, he veered south. Ten minutes later he turned down a bumpy lane and pulled up at a sagging barn on an abandoned collective farm. The wooden door swung up at his approach and he drove inside. A minute later a hovercraft appeared from the other side of the barn. Its high-powered engines in silent-running mode, it lumbered down the grassy slope to the marsh, glaring twin headlights giving it the malevolent appearance of a saurian on the prowl.

The ground-effect vehicle disappeared among the tall reeds, its passage marked only by the swarms of mos-

quitoes which fanned out on either side like a wake, and
the rank stench of diesel oil overpowering the fetor of
the marsh. After a minute or two the engines quickened
as the pilot slowly brought the machine to speed. The
whisper of the wind and the flutter of wings and night
birds pursuing their insect prey were no longer the loud-
est sounds to be heard across the 500-mile-long Pripet
Marshes, Europe's largest swamp.

Guided by inertial navigation, the craft rocketed
through the reeds and tall grasses for what always
seemed to Sheremetiev an eternity, but was scarcely
forty-five minutes, before slowing to a hover at the margin of a matted copse. The craft's iron companionway
swung out across the still waters.

Sheremetiev nodded to the vehicle's captain.

The captain flicked on the IFF unit and punched in his
personal identification code.

A moment later a black cylinder rose from the marsh
like the conning tower of a surfacing submarine. With
the whirr of an electrical motor, the six dogs gripping the
steel hatch rotated in unison to the vertical. The hatch
gaped wide, revealing a red night-light, and Sheremetiev
stepped inside. The hovercraft moved off into the night.

Sheremetiev was now dressed in low-cut felt boots
and a zippered coverall. He entered the day's five-digit
verification code on the key pad, and the lift slowly descended to the top deck of Project Rosovy's research
laboratories some thirty feet below the marsh's rotting
vegetation. The lift door slid back and he found himself
surrounded by a dozen smiling men in white coveralls
waiting to bid him welcome to Project Rosovy.

"Klementiy Pavlovich!" said Stanley Pollock, a bald-
ing, thickset man in his fifties, coming forward and
grasping his hand. "What a pleasant surprise!"

Sheremetiev chuckled. The presence of the entire senior staff to greet him on such short notice, when nor-

mally the morning watch would still be sleeping, told him they had known he was coming. Ornstein had somehow blown his cover. Still, it wouldn't matter now, provided the tests had really proved out. "I just happened to be in the neighborhood," said Sheremetiev with a sly smile. "I had a feeling that you might have some good news for me. I thought I'd drop in to hear it firsthand."

"Not good news," burbled Stanley Pollock. "*Momentous* news: we've made the breakthrough. The Rosovy factor works." Pollock's Russian was very good, but flavored with an East Side New York accent.

"I hope you're right," Sheremetiev said solemnly. "It's getting harder all the time to evade the hordes of American spies who seem to infest every hotel lobby, train compartment, and country crossroads these days, and I wouldn't have come unless I thought you'd finally done it. The Presidium attaches great importance to this project. Premier Zadov himself regards your work on the Rosovy factor as the Soviet Union's single most vital defense project of this—possibly *any*—generation."

The AES No. 23 researchers' smiles broadened. The pleasant implications of the director's words went a long way toward compensating them for the years of drudgery and heartbreak in this sunless crypt deep beneath a pestilential swamp developing the weapon which would, once and for all, bring America to its knees. Great rewards beckoned—honors, promotions, vacations on the Black Sea, and, most welcome expectation of all, soft jobs amid the luxurious surroundings of Boston or San Francisco or Chicago. After all, now that their work had been blessed with success, the conquest of America would be only a matter of time. When it was complete, Russia would dispatch administrators to root out the last vestiges of capitalism and indoctrinate the Americans in the benefits of communism. And who was more deserving of rich rewards than themselves, whose Rosovy factor had made the conquest possible?

"That is," Sheremetiev was saying, "*if* it works."

"Works?" Stanley Pollock chuckled. "Ever the skeptic, aren't you, Comrade?"

"With good reason. Twice during the past six years you've reported success, and each time rigorous tests have blown your 'secret weapon' out of the water. There's even been talk in the Presidium," he went on, looking at Pollock with studied guilelessness, "that you might be a plant sent by the CIA to lead us down the garden path of—if I may use the expression—sterile research. Not that I," he went on smoothly, when Stanley Pollock recoiled as if he had been jabbed with a sharp stick, "ever put an ounce of credence in such rumors."

"I should hope not," said Dr. Pollock, his moon face reddening. "After all, I abandoned an extremely promising career to come over to the Soviet Union. I left my wife . . ."

"Who had already filed for divorce . . ."

"And three children . . ."

"To whom you were so devoted that you couldn't, during our preliminary debrief, even remember their birthdays. But that is neither here nor there, my dear doctor. The remarkable chemical weapons you created for us during your first two years with us proved your loyalty beyond question. What confirms it is that you and your team have now devised a weapon which will destroy the United States utterly. If—and that is of course the operative word—*if* your tests hold up and the weapon works."

"Oh, it works, all right," said Pollock, with massive self-assurance.

"You asked me down in order to demonstrate that assertion, I believe?"

"Right this way."

Pollock led the procession down a low-ceilinged, un-painted corridor of rough-finished concrete, past the in-stallation's administrative offices, senior staff quarters, lounge, and cafeteria, to the robing room. There they donned bubble helmets with throat mikes, backpack res-pirators, and one-piece plastic suits that covered their bodies from helmet to felt slippers. They then passed through an air lock into the research area.

No expense had been spared to supply the complex with one of the world's top libraries on molecular biology and genetic manipulation, the best-trained men, and the most lavish equipment and laboratories Russia could buy. The floor was immaculate white tile, and the walls a restful blue. The centrifuges, autoclaves, incubators, walk-in refrigerators, and other equipment had been pur-chased from the United States and Japan, and the labora-tory staff who paused in their labors as the inspection party approached had studied for advanced degrees in their specialities in Germany, England, and the United States.

Pollock escorted the party through the laboratory area to a room with a row of easy chairs facing a double-paned, shatterproof, one-way glass that formed the en-tire wall. On the other side of the glass was what appeared to be a workman's cafe, with wooden benches along two walls, and bare wooden tables occupied by a dozen men playing cards or chess, listlessly drinking vodka—and not seeming to notice when it dribbled down their chins—leafing through magazines, or just staring vacantly into space. Tears ran down the cheeks of one of the men; nobody paid him the slightest attention.

The men appeared to be in excellent physical condi-tion, judging by their thick peasant necks, muscular arms, and ruddy complexions. And yet it was obvious that the spark of life had been extinguished in that dreary room, for their eyes were empty of expression, the

voices that filtered through the room's loudspeakers
were leaden, and the slump of shoulders those of men
without hope.

"Three weeks ago," explained Pollock, "these men
were in the prime of life. They are representative Russians from every geographical area and from many walks
of life—mines, elite regiments, olympic teams, universities, farms, and fisheries. On paper, each enjoys robust
health. But look at them—you can see for yourself that
these are doomed men, men without the slightest desire
to live. This is the third cohort we've tested, and the
results, I am happy to say, emphatically confirm those of
the two earlier studies."

"And what happened to the others?"

Pollock shrugged. "To them we made available a
painless alternative to a future without hope. You see,
each test subject is provided with a 'happy pill.' One
bite, and there's an end to suffering."

"Do you mean to tell me that all the rest have taken
their own lives?"

"No, no, Comrade Sheremetiev," apologized Pollock.
"I'm sorry I gave the impression. You see, at first most
struggle to preserve the will to live. After all, that's
human nature. They think—hope—their condition is reversible. Then, after eight or nine days, typically, they
lose heart. At this point occur most of the suicides, and
mostly among the younger men. Suddenly, out of the
blue. The others continue to slide gently downhill into
apathy. They lose their appetites and their interest in
what goes on around them. They neglect personal hy-
giene. Eventually, they must be force-fed. Several
have..."

"Figures, Pollock."

"Of the third cohort of thirty-three exposed to the Rosovy factor three weeks ago, the twelve men you see
here survive. Of the second cohort of thirty-three,

seven; and of the third group of thirty-three, two are still living. It appears likely that no more than three men of the original ninety-nine will still be alive two months from today."

"Lethal stuff."

"Quite. And those three will, we confidently predict, eventually be persuaded of the folly of continued survival and bite the bullet."

"And if they don't?"

"Well, they'll wish they had," Pollock said matter-of-factly.

Sheremetiev's eyes looked intently at the men in the room beyond. "Still, they *look* healthy enough . . ."

The inspection party was under the hot-acid bath, the hiss of water and live steam muffling their voices as they shouted into the microphones of their bubble helmets.

"The substance is, I gather," Sheremetiev was saying, "odorless, tasteless, and colorless."

"Colorless when completely diffused in the air. In concentrated form, it's a light pink."

"Therefore, as a very diluted aerosol, quite undetectable."

"Quite."

"But if, by some freak chance, the enemy discovered that it had been exposed to this agent?"

"It would be too late to matter."

Sheremetiev persisted. "But have you tried every conceivable means of reversing the effects of your new substance?"

"Exhaustively—even exhaustingly, I might say." He chuckled.

"And?"

"Results negative—100 percent negative."

Sheremetiev, in spite of a professional skepticism, began to believe that Pollock was on to something useful, after all. "And the dosage needed to produce the desired effect?"

"Approximately sixty-five nanograms. The molecules involved are rather gigantic, with a molecular weight on the order of 220,000. It doesn't take a lot of them to inflict the damage."

The chief of the Pesticides Directorate was willing to be convinced. But first he would have to see documentation with reputable scientists' names signed at the bottom, so in case anything went wrong he'd be covered. He'd have to inspect the Rosovy stockpile to make sure that it was sufficient to blanket the United States tenfold, so that not a single man would escape its devastating effects. As to the transport of the pressurized steel cylinders of the substance to the launch site in the Georgian SSR, already being prepared to receive them, that was something else he had to discuss with Project Manager Major-General Viktor Aleksandrovich Ignatiev.

"And where *is* Viktor Aleksandrovich, by the way?" asked Sheremetiev, who expected his old friend and colleague would have put in an appearance by now.

Pollock coughed apologetically as they emerged from the acid bath and sloshed through the distilled-water shower. "In Moscow, I'm afraid, Comrade Director. He went home to celebrate the breakthrough with his wife. Until yesterday, the pressure of work had kept him here for seven straight weeks. They've only been married a little over a year, you know."

"Yes, I know," said Sheremetiev, wryly. "I know just about everything there is to know about that randy old goat. Of course, had I alerted you about my forthcoming inspection tour, he'd have been here. That's precisely why I didn't. Advance notice would have afforded you the opportunity to cook the paperwork I am going to want to see the minute I get out of this damned straight jacket."

"Maybe we should wait for the general so I can make the full presentation and answer whatever questions you both may have," suggested Pollock. "You know, he's an even greater skeptic than you. So far, despite a review of all our reports, he adamantly refuses to concede that our success is complete and irrefutable. Typical, I'm afraid, of the military mentality when faced with scientific hypotheses beyond its understanding."

"Oh, for God's sake, don't be so stuffy, Pollock," said Sheremetiev, walking into the dressing room and stripping off his dripping suit. "Ignatiev believes only in what he can see. Like me. And don't forget, he's got a lot riding on this project; if it fails, he'll be lucky to command a PRP on the Uzbekistan border."

Sheremetiev's own position, thankfully, was more secure. The failure of the project would probably slow, though not halt, his ascent through the hierarchy. On the other hand, its success would practically guarantee that he'd be promoted to minister and be in line to fill the next vacancy on the Politburo. The vision of those fairy plums dancing before him, he settled behind Ignatiev's desk to review the results of the studies.

When he took a break for a coffee and a sandwich after five hours of reading, little doubt remained. Pollock's discovery *was* the breakthrough he had been promising ever since he defected from the United States nearly a decade earlier, the weapon that used no explosive yet was guaranteed to destroy his homeland utterly, the weapon he liked to call "a smaller bang for the buck."

By one o'clock in the morning, the mass of evidence seemed to Sheremetiev incontrovertible. To be sure, he was only a former mechanical engineer with no knowledge of biotechnology. He would still have to submit the dossier to his scientific staff for analysis and vetting. But unless Pollock and his crew were insane enough to try to fudge the facts and figures, the Rosovy factor was the ultimate, the breakthrough, weapon.

It was while Sheremetiev was pouring yet another cup of coffee in Ignatiev's office that the general himself stomped in.

"Ah, Wild Bull himself," said Sheremetiev jovially, coming out from behind Ignatiev's desk and giving the huge, square-built man a bear hug. The general stiffened in Sheremetiev's embrace.

"Where's that son-of-a-bitch Pollock?" said the general. His voice was flat and without emotion.

"I'd prefer, 'Hello, Klementiy Pavlovich—where's that son-of-a-bitch Pollock?'" replied his superior, suddenly cooling.

"Come on, where *is* the son-of-a-bitch?" repeated Major-General Ignatiev.

Sheremetiev pressed a button on the intercom and instructed the watch officer to have Comrade Dr. Pollock report to General Ignatiev's office at once.

The two men stared at each other. Ignatiev looked right through his old friend, his eyes seemingly focused on a point a thousand miles behind him. As for Sheremetiev, he had never seen Ignatiev look so awful, worse than after the prodigious three-day drunks during their days at the polytechnic institute. And yet, he didn't appear drunk, and certainly didn't have the characteristic odor of alcohol-cum-vomit that he remembered so well. What the hell was eating him?

Pollock rapped gently at the door and was told to enter.

He nodded to General Ignatiev and looked questioningly at the director.

General Ignatiev looked down at Pollock with empty eyes. "You poisoned me," he said softly.

"I beg your pardon?" Pollock was as stunned by the general's haggard appearance as by the accusation.

"Yes, it was you. It must have been you. You are the enemy. You have always been the enemy. I think I've always known that."

"General Ignatiev!" protested Pollock, backing toward the door. "Really, you must . . ."

"My beloved Natalia," said Ignatiev distractedly, clutching his face in his hands and sagging against the desk. "May she and God forgive me!" He straightened, his face suffused with hatred. "I'm the one you poisoned," Ignatiev thundered, "but it's you, Pollock—you dirty American spy—who's going to die."

He pulled a pistol from beneath his tunic and shot Pollock once, through the heart. The American reeled back and fell in a heap against the wall. General Ignatiev walked calmly to where Pollock lay and administered the *coup de grace*.

Then he put the muzzle of the pistol beneath his chin, pointing toward the unseen sky, and pulled the trigger.

3. McCANN
11 AUGUST 2016

DURING HIS FIRST FIVE MONTHS IN PRISON, KEEFE
McCann made three attempts to escape. For each of the
first two he earned thirty days in the hole. On the third,
in chaplain's garb, he got as far as the outer gate while
escorting a weeping widow in black who turned out to be
an airline stewardess, former girlfriend—and single.
After that, although his crimes had been nonviolent, they
put him in the maximum security wing.

There he got violent. He attacked another prisoner in
the mess hall without apparent provocation. On a shake-
down a spoon handle sharpened to a needlepoint was
discovered wedged under the rim of his towel bowl. On a
night of the full moon when, as scientists have confirmed, prisoners *do* become more restless, he set fire to
his mattress. Within minutes half the mattresses in the
cell block were afire, and in the confusion that followed
as the prisoners were driven into the exercise area
McCann nearly escaped again, wearing a homemade
guard's uniform and a stolen cap. Back in the hole he
went for yet another month.

"I've had it with this guy," said warden Erik Howard
to the prison's consulting psychologist. "He's one of
those weirdos who can't abide confinement. Some of
them go quietly stir crazy. Not McCann. Every chance

he gets he tries to bust out, and we throw him in the hole for thirty days, and the minute he comes up for air he asks for another helping."

"I see," said Dr. Karine Collier, a statuesque young woman whose white lab coat was about three feet short of covering legs that half the prisoners dreamed about and that was always on the verge of failing to restrain a firm, swelling bust that occupied the night visions of the rest. "You believe he needs help."

Warden Howard grunted. "If it was up to me, I'd weld the bastard's cell door shut. But that's the trouble, you see. He's a celebrity—you must have read about him—the papers were full of the man-with-a-thousand-faces bilge a year or so ago."

"I remember."

"Well, he was sentenced to so many years that he'll roll out of here in a wheelchair, if at all. Nevertheless, the publicity has brought a steady stream of women visitors from his former incarnations, most of them nubile and some with money and influence. Well, why not? Fraud is his stock-in-trade, and he's always been pretty good at making people believe what he wants them to believe. But I've got to admit he's a charming son-of-a-bitch, and I gather he likes women every bit as much as they like him."

"I fail to see your problem, Warden. He's a felon. He's been duly sentenced. You are merely doing your duty."

Warden Howard knocked out his pipe and pushed back his creaking chair. He walked to the window overlooking the yard. He pointed at the hundreds of men milling around in the exercise area. "There's my problem. McCann's giving all those men ideas. They say to themselves, 'Look at McCann—he nearly busted out of here four times. So why don't I give it a try? All I've got to lose is thirty days of sunlight on half rations, and if my luck's in I'll make it.'

"So I've got a security problem, Dr. Collier. I've got a morale problem. And I've got a disciplinary problem. If I keep on throwing McCann in the hole, those females on the outside are going to put so much heat on me for 'brutality' there'll be an investigation. *That* I don't need."

"Oh, *now* I see," said Karine Collier with an icicle smile. "You merely want to pass the buck."

Warden Howard shook his head stubbornly. "Part of your job is to help maintain the mental health of the prisoners so that they can accept their punishment philosophically and without making trouble that causes extra expense to the state."

"Maybe you'd like me to give him a little needle full of happiness. Is that what you're getting at?"

"Look," said Warden Howard, "I'm in a bind. I don't care what the hell you do so long as you can get that troublemaker off my back. I know your contract calls for only ten hours a week, so you can fulfill your commitments at the university, but can't you see your way clear to concentrating on McCann for a while instead of spreading yourself thin? If you could get him to accept the fact that he's going to be in here for a very long time, it would make things easier for me, not to mention McCann himself."

"I don't know—"

"Think of it as a challenge."

Warden Howard had said the magic word. Dr. Karine Collier was an overachiever who could no more resist a challenge than the prisoners she worked with could resist thinking up excuses that would put them in the same room together with her for five minutes, or even two.

She had been a beautiful child. She had been a beautiful girl. She was now a beautiful woman. And she hated it, because the world expected that, having been given beauty, she should be content. Quite early in life she decided that she would so excel in some field that her accomplishment would eclipse her looks, and she'd be recognized, not for what she was, but for what she had become.

By age eleven she was spending all her spare time practicing diving from the ten-meter platform. At seventeen she became NCAA champion, and the first comment she overheard was, "You oughta seen that Karine Collier coming off the high board—Christ, what a gorgeous body!" She never dived in competition again.

Instead, she immersed herself in her university studies, graduating *magna cum laude* and a few years later getting a Ph.D. in clinical psychology through an Army Reserve Officer program. At twenty-seven she was a captain, U. S. A. (Reserve), assistant professor of psychology at Pennsylvania State University, consulting psychologist at the state prison in Harrisburg, an associate at Telos, Inc., one of the nation's most prestigious think tanks, author of sixteen papers in learned journals, and sometime guest on TV talk shows. She wasn't married, but she was looking—for a man who would love her for her mind instead of her body. So far, she hadn't come close.

She approached the McCann case with circumspection. She knew he'd be true to his lifework and try somehow to take advantage of her. So she studied his file and the sheaf of newspaper clips which accompanied it, seeking the key to his character which she could turn to contain his propensity for flight.

McCann was apparently no ordinary flimflam man. He had the confidence man's knack of instilling instant and utter trust, but he also seemed to possess an intellec-

tual dimension uncommon in his profession. Money did
not seem to be the force that drove him. Nor was the
shallow satisfaction of bamboozling the innocent.
McCann seemed to live for the sake of wrapping himself
in an identity so totally that, in time, he himself came to
believe it. He was more Method actor than con man, and
the real world was his stage. On the other hand, he
seemed to enjoy improvising bit parts as catharsis for the
stress of developing his major roles.

In Washington, D. C. he had starred in a typical one-
night stand. Short of ready cash, he put on a black wool
necktie and leather jacket and willed his features into a
cast of the basilisk, that legendary serpent which could
kill by its breath or its glance. He entered the Senate
Office Building and walked into the office of the senior
senator from New York. To that silver-maned pol, with a
voice full of sadness he recited the dire consequences
that could befall the honorable gentleman for accepting
an unnamed union's political action committee funds and
then failing to come through on the vote. He was just
getting warmed up when the senator uneasily produced
his checkbook and wrote out a check for $10,000.
"Wrong union, friend," said McCann, coldly, and glee-
fully departed a few minutes later with a check for
$25,000 payable to "cash."

McCann considered himself neither confidence man
nor imposter but a man in love with the myriad roles life
offered anyone clever enough to master them, for
wasn't, as Shakespeare pointed out, all the world a
stage, and all the men and women merely players? As far
back as he could remember, like any imaginative boy
he'd been given to daydreaming and make-believe. A
boring accountant father and a stolid, colorless mother
drove him to escape into the realm of fantasy. In his
private world, he single-handedly fought off Russian
tanks with rocket-propelled grenades while holding fast to

the flaxen-haired girl swooning in his arms, discovered the cancer virus while laboring through the night in his laboratory, explored the far reaches of the Amazon in a leaky canoe, through brilliant defense won exoneration for a client unjustly accused of serial murders, and trudged alone, bent against the gale, up the snow-shrouded slopes of a Himalayan mountain to rescue a Sherpa lost in the storm.

The kids at school laughed at him, of course, and their laughter cut deep. Still, he pitied and despised them. How could they be content with a single identity, a single personality, a single outlook, when the diversity that was the world lay before them, when they could choose this persona today, that profession tomorrow, and another on the day after? He did his best to ignore the ridicule, and when he couldn't he retreated into the castle of make-believe where Keefe McCann was king.

Or, when he finally scraped through high school and decided college would be four more wasted years, if not king, then real estate salesman, or civil engineer, or heart specialist, professor of archaeology, Force Reconn Marine, private detective, diamond cutter, newspaper reporter, or civil servant. He'd read long ago that an individual was as many men as the languages he spoke.

That made him three men already, for in 1992, the year Russia and the United States signed their epochal cultural exchange agreement, Russian was introduced into the American school system as a language of instruction starting from the first grade. McCann was then five. When he was seven, due to ever-warming cultural and economic relations between the United States and China, and the huge influx of cheap Chinese labor to replace increasingly expensive illegal Mexican immigrants, Mandarin Chinese was introduced on the same basis. So, like every American under the age of thirty

who graduated from high school, McCann was almost
equally fluent in the three languages.

That was enough for most, but not for Keefe
McCann. He not only wanted to *speak* like other people
—he wanted to *be* other people. He got a head start at
the age of eleven when he was recruited by a counterfeiter to pass bogus money. Paying $4 for each phony $20
bill, McCann made an art of hitting theaters, drive-ins,
snack bars, magazine stalls, and other establishments
with fast-moving queues. He experimented with identities—sandlot football player with a ball under his arm,
newsboy carrying an armful of papers, mother's boy
with clean collar and hair slicked down, and runaway
with ragged clothes and smoldering butt hanging from his
lip.

As the most successful of the counterfeiter's helpers,
he graduated to the basement print shop, where he
learned about photo engraving, paper, inks, lithography,
holography, calligraphy, and other tools and techniques
of the forger's trade. Later, when he became doctor or
lawyer, merchant or chief, he was able to fabricate convincing documentation—letters of recommendation, diplomas, awards, newspaper clippings, testimonials, and
licenses—as required. He never traveled without fake
papers for a dozen identities, in the event the one he was
using went sour and he had to make a hasty departure.

Keefe McCann took great pains to elevate his performances to professional levels. He made friends with ease
and often went to work as assistant to someone skilled in
the occupation which he would later adopt as his own.
His quick ascent from hospital orderly in St. Louis to
staff psychiatrist at a prestigious Houston hospital was
typical of the way this M.D.—Master of Deception—
worked.

In St. Louis, it took just two days for orderly Lester
R. Williams to graduate from mopping hallways and

emptying bedpans to making patients' beds and assisting
the floor nurse in changing dressings. He absorbed the
technical terms and cliches of nurse-speak, observed the
instruments and techniques of the nursing trade, read
nursing journals voraciously, studied nursing texts and
sample R.N. examinations, and set up housekeeping
with an attractive head nurse ten years his senior to mine
the knowledge of her vast experience. In ten weeks he
felt that he was ready. He quit his job, bade farewell to
his sleep-in mentor, and boarded a plane for Billings,
Montana.

At Billings General Hospital, Jeremy Powell, R.N.,
was hired as a general-duty nurse, but because he was
hard-muscled and tough at twenty-four had no problem
transferring to the mental ward, where he could observe
psychiatrists at close hand. Again, he listened, observed,
devoured psychiatry texts and literature, learned the jargon of the trade, frequented bars where psychiatrists
talked shop, and formed a live-in liaison with an older
woman—a thirty-one-year-old Australian psychiatrist
with flaming red hair and an exquisite body. This time he
lingered some weeks beyond the four months it took him
to feel comfortable in the profession he was about to
ornament, for Dr. Rosalyn Bonham-Smythe was a lot
harder to give up than Billings.

Finally, after a medical apprenticeship of some seven
months, Dr. Julian R. Hartshorn, armed with a thick file
of excellent diplomas, state boards, and recommendations, all of which he had personally printed and signed,
obtained a posting as staff psychiatrist at Midvale Sanitarium near Dallas, springboard to the same position two
months later at the 200-bed Harley Hospital in suburban
Houston, patronized only by the rich and superrich.

He practiced with caution, speaking with weighty deliberation until the psycho-speak flowed naturally, and
prescribing no medication or course of treatment until he

had—under the guise of double-checking with both a
nurse and a doctor—assured himself that he was not
breaking Hippocrates's oft-violated first commandment
of medicine: "First, *do no harm*." Periods of intense
study to perfect his con-of-the-moment had developed in
him notable powers of concentration. He could glean
what he felt important from a thick medical text in three
or four nights of unremitting study, and he put in many
such nights until he had covered the literature a resident
psychiatrist was expected to command. He memorized
obscure passages from Freud, Jung, Menninger, Adler,
Horney, and other psychiatric saints, and was always
ready with an ambiguous quote to intimidate his colleagues when rational explanation failed, as it usually
did, to convince them. In treating his patients he relied
on acute observation, analysis, and common sense, qualities no more abundant among physicians than lesser
mortals. When he was in doubt, which at first was often,
he did not hesitate to flatter his seniors by calling upon
them for advice. He was, as a consequence, considered a
bright young star in the Harley Hospital firmament.

He lasted at Harley barely three months. When doctors began coming to *him* for advice, the adventure lost
its charm. He could probably have stayed at Harley forever, treating hysterical matrons better served by being
better served, advancing from resident to consulting
status, co-authoring dull papers for duller journals, dab-
bling in real estate, and amassing a fortune of Texan proportions. But what for? The noose of everlasting security
beginning to strangle him was the fate Keefe McCann
had resolved to avoid. Getting where he was now had
been an uphill struggle on slippery slopes, where a false
step would have sent him plunging to the bottom, to
prison and the road gang, It had been dangerous and fun;
now it was neither. Dr. Hartshorn resigned and took the
first plane west.

It landed in Los Angeles, where to the list of previous incarnations—fire fighter in Denver, *chef de cuisine* in New Orleans, assistant professor of sociology at the University of Chicago, investigative reporter in Kansas City, and an assortment of other amusing but mentally untaxing jobs—Keefe McCann added that of attorney-at-law. Again, he read voraciously, spent days in musty courtrooms watching expert advocates at work, set up housekeeping with a female criminal lawyer, and took voluminous notes at bar examination cram courses. Such was his diligence that he didn't have to forge the document calling him to the bar, but passed the state exam on his first try.

When Los Angeles was exhausted of its charms, he went back east, sold oil wells, won ordination as an Episcopal priest, then moved to Miami as an undercover agent of the FBI. He lived to the hilt, spending what he earned and a good deal more by kiting checks whenever short. However, he used only cash to purchase the bank drafts that paid for leases on his safehouses. His life of deception was a constant high. It was going to go on like this forever.

It did, until he went to Tampa to learn to fly. It was the easiest thing he had ever done—and the hardest. He had only to follow his teacher's instructions and he could not go wrong. On the other hand, he had to proceed step by tedious step; there were no shortcuts. He spent three-and-a-half months at it, earning his Private Pilot's License, Multi-Engine rating, Instrument and Commercial licenses—among the few papers he had ever come by honestly. He then forged an entirely new set eleven years old, supplemented them with coffee-stained fake log books crediting himself with 12,055 flying hours, glowing recommendations from several airlines, and a spurious document from the Department of Transporta-

tion appointing Captain Martin T. Haversham an FAA
check pilot.

The assigned crew did all the flying. Captain Haversham merely occupied the jump seat, giving sage advice
he had picked up from authentic check pilots, entering
his critique of their flight deck procedures and emergency drills on the evaluation sheet he would discard on
landing, drinking coffee, and chatting up the hostesses.
He was flying high until one day a new first officer, who
had been an instrument instructor at McCann's Tampa
flight school, happened to be dead-heading in the first
class section. On landing, he observed a familiar face in
the cockpit wearing the four stripes of captain and noti-
fied the FAA and FBI. By the time they got to the airport, Captain Haversham was gone. Nine days later he
returned to Falls Church with his rented plane. This time
they were waiting for him.

It made quite a splash in the press, because some
careless people in high places had egg on their faces for
unwittingly abetting Keefe McCann in his peccadillos.
He defended himself in court, and thanks to his background at the bar did a creditable job of it. But once the
prosecuting attorneys had drenched the jury with details
of his one-man white-collar crime wave, enough charges
still clung to him to warrant consecutive sentences of
ten-to-fifteen years for forgery, grand theft, impersonating an officer, fraud, practicing various professions without a license, and everything else they could hang on
him, including a number of crimes he didn't commit
which the police were happy to clear from their books.

Since the Parole Rationalization Act stipulated that a
prisoner must serve a minimum of half his sentence before reaching eligibility for parole, Keefe McCann was
going to spend the rest of his natural life behind bars.
Well, why not? Dr. Karine Collier reflected, as she finished reading the dossier—that's what prisons are for.

4. KARINE
6 AUGUST 2016

THE SMALL ROOM WAS FURNISHED WITH A WOODEN table, two chairs and Keefe McCann—who was waiting with folded arms and a thoughtful frown. As Dr. Karine Collier entered, he rose and held her chair, then resumed his place and smiled professionally.

She sighed as she placed her clipboard and pen on the table. "Okay, who is it today?"

Keefe McCann placed his elbows on the table and his chin on laced fingers. He examined her with the absorption of a biologist confronted with a new species of insect. "As you are obviously a woman of some intellectual attainment, Dr. . . ." he enunciated the word as if hard-pressed to keep a straight face, ". . . Collier, I will dispense with the bedside manner and discuss your problem as if we were, well, shall we say—colleagues? It would insult your intelligence to beat around the bush, so I may as well tell you straight out that the affliction from which you apparently suffer—mind you, my diagnosis is still provisional—is a condition that used to be called *dementia praecox*, New Latin for 'premature madness.' Today we prefer the term schizophrenia.

"Please do not be disturbed," he hastened to add, "by the pejorative implications of the word. After all, in our modern society, we are subjected to so much unpleasantness and stress that it is only natural that any sensitive being wishes to take refuge from time to time in a flight from reality, in an identity of his own happy creation. Indeed, the literature suggests that we all—normal and aberrational alike—occasionally indulge in this type of escape. But where do we draw the line between an old gentleman's daydreaming of knights and damsels in distress and a Don Quixote who actually mounts a swaybacked nag and rides forth to tilt at windmills? Usually that determination is a function of the time one spends in the world of dreams. A pleasant whimsy before one drops off to sleep is considered normal; the whimsy stretched out to occupy all of one's waking hours is considered insanity.

"And that, Dr. Collier, I believe is the crux of your problem. You have fashioned a world of gossamer fantasies. You believe, twenty-four hours a day, that you really *are* a prominent clinical psychologist. Building on this fantasy, you conceive yourself a latter-day Jeanne d'Arc whose mission it is to solve the ills of man. And in this fantasy you have had the misfortune to become enmeshed. But there is no cause for alarm. You have had the wisdom to consult me before any lasting harm came to you, and I shall do my very best to draw you out of your, shall we say—persistent hallucination?"

Karine Collier answered her own question. Today he was Dr. Julian R. Hartshorn, eminent consulting psychiatrist.

"If I may interrupt this fascinating monologue, Mr. McCann, I would like . . ."

"McCann?" McCann's eyebrows arched in mild surprise. He picked up the pen and scribbled a note on the yellow pad. "The name is not familiar. Is this McCann a man from your past—friend, an employer, a lover, perhaps?"

"None of the above," said an exasperated Dr. Collier.

"Keefe McCann is a notorious con man who has assumed many identities, one of which happens to be Dr. Julian R. Hartshorn."

McCann leaned back in his chair, for a moment speechless. "Well, some people have a lot of gall," he said finally. "The least he could have done was choose a fictional identity. How could he ever think he could get away with impersonating me?"

"He didn't. He was caught, convicted, and sentenced to what amounts to several lifetimes in prison, and by the wildest of coincidences, *Dr. Hartshorn*, he not only bears an uncanny resemblance to you, but wears a shirt with the identical number."

"Thank God for coincidences. Without them, our novelists would have to fall back on imagination." McCann shook his head. "But I think we'd better get back to your problem. This McCann person—just what role did he play in your life? Was it because of him that you conceived the rather original conceit that *you* are the doctor and *I* am the patient? If so, then I think we are onto a potentially rewarding line of investigation. You see, there was a case similar to this quoted by Arnholt in the *New England Journal of Psychiatry*, around 2008, I seem to recall. What Arnholt discovered was that his patient, a bright young fellow named Prendergast, had somehow come to believe that the clerk at the shop where he bought a holofi set should pay *him*, Prendergast, for relieving him, the clerk, of the merchandise. Typical sudden-onset role reversal, one would say, but when other factors are taken into account . . ."

Karine Collier tuned out. When McCann really got going, there was nothing she could do to shut him up or snap him back to reality.

No doubt about it, McCann was certainly the most fascinating case that had ever come down the pike. In eight sessions she had never once been able to shake

him. Whoever he had decided to be, he acted the part to
the hilt. Moreover, his performance was anything but su-
perficial. He was good. Whether playacting the lawyer,
or investigative reporter, or airline check-pilot, or fire
fighter, or sociology professor, or any of his other alter
egos, his command of the relevant body of knowledge,
no less than the jargon of the trade, was impressive.

She had taken on the McCann case as a favor to Warden Howard, but now it had taken on a life of its own.
The prisoner was an elective schizophrenic, inhabiting
his identity-of-the-moment with persuasive effect. Was
there some inaudible voice of consciousness she could
not hear that told him he was just acting, or did he, for
the moment, really *believe* that he was that assumed persona? There were a thousand such questions, but with a
life sentence hanging over him she had plenty of time to
get the answers. And when she did, she'd have material
for a paper, maybe even an entire book, the trade was
sure to call "seminal."

"Your sexual background . . ." McCann was saying.

"What *about* my sexual background?" she bristled,
coming out of her reverie.

"I was suggesting that the root of your problem may
be found in your sexual history. The adoption of a second identity is quite commonly the result of dissatisfac-
tion with the real one, often for reasons of sexual
inadequacy."

"Who the hell says I'm sexually inadequate?"

"Actually, quite a few inmates of this institution do. In
fact, every one whom I have interviewed—always ex-
cepting the deviants—attests to your inability to exhibit
thigmotaxic behavior."

She frowned. She had heard the term before, but
couldn't for the moment remember what it meant.

"Progress," Dr. Hartshorn smiled. "You see, if you

were *really* the clinical psychologist you claim to be, you'd know that thigmotaxic behavior—also called stereotaxis—is merely the movement of an organism in response to the stimulus of contact with a solid object— a paramecium prodded by a pin, for instance."

"Yes, yes—of course. Now I remember."

"And so do the inmates with whom you have come in contact. According to their nearly unanimous testimony, they have given you considerable stimulus and every opportunity to respond, and yet you have failed to do so. That argues a severe psychosexual dysfunction."

"It does nothing of the sort," Karine Collier replied indignantly. It was an outrageous falsehood, but she had to hand it to him: McCann-Hartshorn was quick on the uptake. To be effective, her interviews had to be conducted in privacy, so that the prisoners would be under no constraints to free and easy communication. Unfortunately, the sex-starved inmates frequently tried to take advantage of their isolation.

In such circumstances, unless things got really rough and she had to summon the gendarmes, she relied on her powers of dissuasion, and when they failed, a shot of disabling aerosol from a lipstick-sized dispenser on a silver chain around her neck.

After reading his dossier, especially those sections on his love life, Dr. Karine Collier had made sure of a full aerosol supply before her first interview with Keefe McCann. To her surprise, the man-of-a-hundred-women made no provocative moves. His knees stayed on his side of the table, his hands never sought hers, nor did a concupiscent glance steal from beneath his bushy black brows. He didn't even make any sexual allusions, the usual prelude to more direct action. At all times, he was the perfect gentleman, wrapped up in his role of the moment, completely indifferent to her physical charms.

Before the third interview—in the interests of science—she wore a V-necked sweater which exposed an interesting expanse of breast. Not once during the session did McCann's eyes linger upon it. Nor did he purposely avert his eyes.

For the fourth interview she wore a skirt with a slash up the side, revealing enough nylon-clad leg to cause a riot in a conclave of high-church bishops. McCann was unmoved.

For the fifth, she allowed her knee to stray—experimentally—in the direction of his. When they met, he responded with no answering pressure, but turned his chair slightly to one side and crossed his legs. She had never felt so humiliated in her life.

The man's indifference became a challenge. One way or another she was going to break him down, make him treat her like a woman. The fact that he was totally controlled, totally aloof, merely poured oil on the fire of her determination.

McCann's intimation that she was sexually inadequate was especially hard to bear, for there was some truth in it. As a woman of the new century, she prided herself on her emancipation. She had experimented with a succession of lovers. None had proved satisfying. Some were inept. Others were entirely intent on self-gratification. But most treated her with a slavish reverence and acolytic devotion to which she had to force herself to respond—and her response, under those circumstances, *had* been inadequate. Being on a pedestal gratified the ego, but a pedestal was a very uncomfortable place to make love. Less veneration, more venery, she wanted to scream at these so-called men, but what was the use if you had to tell them?

Judging by his dossier, dripping with details of numerous armours, McCann wasn't a man you'd have to tell anything. And yet he had proved immune to her obvious beauty and increasingly obvious insinuations. For some inexplicable reason his omnivorous carnal appetite stopped short of Karine Colliers.

She couldn't have him. Therefore she wanted him. It was a story as old as Adam and Eve. She didn't realize it yet, but she was falling in love.

5. HANDY
3 SEPTEMBER 2016

"AND JUST WHAT THE GODDAMNED HELL IS *THIS*?" growled Admiral Ricardo Rivera Handy, glaring at the stack of files his secretary had placed before him on the desk.

"Con men," said Mrs. Biggs.

"You're out of your mind, Biggs. What the hell would I want with con men?"

"Weren't you complaining yesterday that every time the Atomic Yields Estimates Service plants an officer in Moscow the KGB gets a make on him before he can even check into the Hotel Metropole?"

"Yesterday," the admiral said grumpily. "Also, the day before yesterday, *and* the day before that. What's that got to do with con men?"

"Well, our officers keep getting blown because the Russians discover their identity. The fact that we both know that the KGB has planted agents inside AYES doesn't solve the problem. So, go *outside* the Service. Get somebody whose *business* is fraud, who can change guises so fast that even the Russians won't be able to keep up. A con man."

Admiral Rivera looked at Mrs. Biggs with admiration. "You're a jewel, Biggs. You can take an hour for lunch today—no, no," he said, taking a file from the stack and opening it, "no demonstrations of gratitude. You know I hate scenes."

Con men. They might be the answer, at that. God knew there must be *some* answer to the problem which had been plaguing him for the last eleven years, ever since he had become chief of the Atomic Yields Estimates Service.

AYES was to the CIA what the New York Yankees were to Vassar's softball team. So far as the public knew, the sole function of the service was to maintain an up-to-date inventory of the nuclear stockpiles of Russia, China, Israel, India, Brazil, England, Pakistan, France, Libya, and the other twenty-odd other nuclear powers. But its real, undisclosed mission was to supply the president and Joint Chiefs of Staff with daily, highly detailed, and accurate intelligence estimates of all America's enemies, potential and actual, Russia in particular.

In recent years, those estimates were as often wrong as right. The trouble was that, in these days of relatively open borders, Russian moles had burrowed into Handy's shop with such zeal that nobody inside AYES could ever be sure whether they were dealing with an honest-to-God American or some Russian look-alike clone.

AYES's task had been sabotaged by the Russo-American Cultural Agreement of 1992. That agreement was hailed as the most imaginative step toward ending the Cold War that had been taken in seventy years but, as usual with Russo-American treaties, the Russians had walked away from the table with most of the goodies.

One of the agreement's clauses stipulated that, for "better understanding of mutual problems and to promote cultural interchange," both English and Russian would be taught in the two nation's schools beginning with the primary grades. Native-speaking language teachers would be exchanged and granted permanent residence status. And, as of the year 2010 in both the

United States and Russia, all news media reaching more than one million people would print, or broadcast, their entire output in both languages. By the mid-twenty-first century every citizen in both countries would be completely bilingual.

The language agreement did, indeed, promote mutual understanding. But another clause, calling for the exchange of 15,000 university students annually, was a Soviet Trojan Horse unsuspectingly drawn into the American camp. It had been the main source of Admiral Ricardo Rivera Handy's headaches during the past decade.

Under the student exchange program, the Americans were distributed by the Russians among a dozen provincial universities remote from population centers, there to be spied upon by relays of the KGB's Section K operatives. Courted by "dissidents" and supposed votaries of the American Way of Life, they were spoon-fed carefully calibrated doses of disinformation which a whole new Washington bureaucracy spent millions of man-hours separating the occasional grain of wheat from mountains of chaff. On the other hand, any American who proselytized or engaged in serious political discussion was summarily expelled for "interference in the internal affairs of the sovereign USSR."

Meanwhile, every year 15,000 young Russians of both sexes, steeped from infancy in American language and culture—and Marxism-Leninism-Stalinism—at special KGB schools, freely elected to study at American institutions of higher learning of their choice. The choice was generally the Washington, D. C. area or at colleges near defense industries. They did not proselytize or engage in political discussions. But they made a business of blackmailing homosexual government officials and seducing senior civil servants and military leaders or their wives. They systematically stole defense secrets, government documents, and classified military manuals. They actively recruited young campus dreamers to work for the emancipation of the workers of the world. And an alarming number of the Russian youngsters disappeared after a few years and, with impeccably crafted false identities, surfaced later to insinuate themselves into U.S. government service, where by sheer intellect and hard work they rose to positions of responsibility and trust, even in the super-secret AYES.

To be sure, it wouldn't have been all that difficult to root them out. The venerable polygraph would have picked up at least fifty percent of the Russian plants, and virtually all the others would have been unmasked by the various truth sera and other well-established means. But the American Civil Liberties Union, with a helping hand from various left-wing groups thoughtfully financed by the KGB, had steamrollered a bill through Congress prohibiting such "barbaric" (not to mention effective) methods of establishing a job-seeker's loyalty, on the grounds that they were intolerable invasions of the individual's privacy.

In fiscal 2015 alone, Admiral Handy's counterespionage section had unmasked six Russian agents, including one who had achieved super-grade civil service status. All had forthwith disappeared so quietly and completely that even the ACLU was not alerted, but that AYES was still infested with communist vermin, Admiral Handy had no doubt.

One AYES staffer of whose loyalty he was reasonably sure was his secretary, Mrs. Biggs. She had been investigated—and cleared—no fewer than eight times in as many years by various agencies. Her late husband had been Handy's long-time chief yeoman, and only after he died did his widow take his place. She was efficient, impersonal (Handy had to think hard to remember her given name—Lucinda), devoted, and ugly as sin. Mrs.

Biggs, ageless at fifty-odd years, was a tall, rectangular woman whom clothes apparently couldn't be made to fit and whose one concession to femininity was a neatly coiffed black wig which had the unfortunate tendency to slide down over her eyes when she took dictation. On the other hand, her secretarial skills were superlative, and she had the indispensable faculty of anticipating Handy's desires. When at mid-morning he felt the need for a third cup of coffee, it always seemed to materialize at his elbow. If he had made a rash commitment to attend a meeting devoted mainly to the recirculation of hot air, he would find that she had canceled it immediately thereafter, making vague mention of a sudden attack of logus of the bogus. And when a problem obviously had no solution, Biggs usually found one.

At the moment the most pressing problem was what to do about Stanley Pollock.

Dr. Stanley Pollock was that rarest of birds, a successful American agent nesting in one of the Soviet Union's highest and most secret branches, thanks to Russia's own aggressive recruiting methods.

A homosexual since his days at Choate, Pollock had formed a liaison with a handsome young classmate which endured through their days at the Massachusetts Institute of Technology. It continued through his pro forma marriage, during the early years of which he became father to three boys whose teenage antipathy he returned with disinterest. At forty-two, still married and still walking both sides of the street, he had been appointed chief of Chemical Warfare Research, an agency of the Department of Defense at Aberdeen, Maryland. There he worked with conspicuous success in the development of various nasty surprises for the Russians.

Stanley Pollock had a brilliant mind and the arrogant manner of the infallible scientific genius. Underneath the smug exterior, however, was the troubled soul of a man

who has never been tested in the crucible of life and is
convinced that when the chips are down, he will be unmasked as a fraud and coward. The test came in the
guise of a burly Russian in a seedy trench coat and a Sam
Spade hat who, one day while Pollock was walking in the
Maryland woods, appeared out of the mist and invited
him to view some interesting action pictures featuring
none other than his Choate classmate and Stanley Pollock himself.

Pollock feigned panic, but his heart was serene. The
poor native Russian seemed to believe that photographic
proof of his homosexuality, well-known to the security
section of the Nuclear, Chemical, and Biological Research Agency, would frighten Pollock into betraying his
country. Yet the Russian's overtures were apparently serious, for he proceeded in the usual way to demand
nothing in return for the photographs but the most recent
telephone directory of the NCBRA. He even promised a
$1,000 bonus—obviously the lever for really important
blackmail—if Pollock produced the delivery within a
week.

Pollock yielded, after some inspired playacting.
Pleased and rather surprised at his own coolness, he delivered the directory to the Russian, burned the incriminating photographs on the spot, and professed to
believe the Russian's solemn word that he didn't possess
copies. After asking about discreetly among his many
close personal friends in the upper strata of the State
Department, Pollock made a telephone call to Admiral
Ricardo Rivera Handy, who had in those circles recently
achieved a frightening reputation for sparing traitors the
inconvenience of serving three years of a life sentence
before parole: they simply disappeared. He was also
known to have run a few talented doubles as triples.
After a thorough but very quiet investigation, Handy
decided that Pollock would be an ideal candidate—if

he had the guts for this most hazardous and harrowing of covert assignments.

Handy established a Project Pollock section. The usual procedure would have been to concoct plausible disinformation, mostly based on dead-end, blind-alley research at NCBRA to sell the Russians when they came calling again. But Handy had a better idea. Pollock continued to report to NCBRA but was relieved of his duties and access to all classified material. Then the Project Pollock group turned the clock back five years. As far as Pollock and his research were concerned, the current year, 2005, became 2000.

The first installment of the "latest" research Pollock produced on Russian demand—some copies of the compromising prints had turned up after all, of course—was actually work that he and his group had produced in February 2000, with the dates altered to appear to be February 2005. From that day onward, Pollock was allowed periodically to deliver the "latest" documents to his Russians, who never did realize that the obviously authentic material they were receiving had been made obsolete by five years of ensuing research.

Admiral Handy knew that the honeymoon wouldn't last forever. Sooner or later the Russians would learn, either from a security leak or from the subversion of some other scientist at Aberdeen, that they were being played for suckers. They would forthwith jab Pollock in the ass with a ricin-tipped umbrella ferule, or squirt him in the kisser with cyanide aerosol, and *au revoir* a very useful agent.

But, unbeknownst to Handy, the Russians, too, had been thinking about Dr. Stanley Pollock's future.

One day nearly four years after the establishment of Operation Pollock, Handy met the scientist by prearrangement at a health club sauna in Baltimore.

"The Russians want me to defect," said Pollock without preamble.

"The hell you say!"

"It's true. I thought at first they were suspicious, and wanted to get me out of the country to kill me. Then I realized that they could kill me right here anytime they wished. Of course, I played dumb—and reluctant. Why should I leave the States when I have everything I could desire in this country?"

Not everything, his Russian control had pointed out. At Aberdeen, he was working on assigned projects, on limited budgets, with a staff of nine men. In the Soviet Union he would be chief of an independent research and development organization, free to pursue any line of chemical warfare investigation he desired, with unlimited funds and all necessary personnel. He would be provided with friendly, virile young men, a dacha, a three-room apartment in Moscow, the rank of Colonel in the Chemical Warfare Services, and the prospect of becoming a Hero of the Soviet Union for any breakthrough discoveries in chemical warfare.

"What did you tell them?" asked Admiral Handy.

"That I'd have to think it over."

Admiral Handy thought it over. "Tell them you've thought it over, and on the whole, you're interested. But then you've got to bargain with the bastards, and bargain hard, or they'll get suspicious. Tell them they've got to make you a brigadier general—they call it General-Major. Also, you want a bigger apartment; you know one of the Julius Rosenberg's agents got *six* rooms. Things like that. I leave the details to you. The main thing is, go!"

"You really *want* me to defect?"

"You bet your ass. They'll probably assign you the hottest research projects. Who could ask for anything more?"

Pollock wiped the sweat from his forehead with a soggy towel. "Oh, I see. You expect me to sabotage the research."

"Nothing of the sort. Give the Russians your best."

Pollock was puzzled. "I don't understand. Do you mean—oh, *now* I see. You think I'm over the hill intellectually, that my best will be disappointing."

"On the contrary. I was thinking about that Neutralization Hypothesis you've developed in the little private laboratory we've let you play around with. My boys tell me it's the cat's culottes. They said that if you could publish it, you'd be a cinch to win the Nobel for chemistry."

"Oh, well, I don't know about *that*," said Pollock, with nicely feigned modesty.

"Well, *they* know. They're the smartest money can buy. On the other hand, I'm just an old blue-water salt, and I don't understand such things, so maybe—"

"Actually," said Pollock, warmed by the unexpected praise, "the Neutralization Hypothesis is very simple."

The Admiral chuckled.

"But it *is*. You see, it's merely the Yang-Yin principle applied to chemistry. Take a poison—a postsynaptic neurotoxin such as cobra venom, for example. Nerve signals reaching the neuromuscular junction where a nerve meets muscle produce the neutrotransmitter acetylcholine, which crosses the synaptic crevice, reaches the acetylcholine receptor, and causes muscular contraction. Cobra venom kills because the neurotoxin blocks the receptor sites for the transmission of acetylcholine. The muscles controlling breathing are paralyzed, and the victim dies."

Admiral Handy looked at Pollock uneasily. "The victim dies from the cobra bite. That I get."

"Well, then, let's take a simpler example—the action of carbon monoxide. Normally, oxygen-depleted red-blood cells become regenerated in the lungs, which inhale fresh air. But when they encounter carbon monoxide, a particularly greedy molecule, the blood's hemoglobin combines with it instead of oxygen. This union kills the red-blood cell—not to mention the unfortunate breather of carbon monoxide. That's clear, I hope."

"Go on," said Handy tersely. At the Naval Academy, he had majored in weapons systems.

"Yes, well—my Neutralization Hypothesis argues that any substance, including but not limited to poisons, can be made chemically inert by combining that poison with a chemical *mirror-image* of that substance, closing up the molecular shell, so to speak, so that nothing else can react with it. How this is done is somewhat more complex. But basically, using my hypothesis, all we need is a sample of the substance from which a molecular model can be constructed. You see?"

Admiral Handy nodded, and leaned back against the dripping tiles. He was, as he professed, a blue-water sailor, and looked it. He was small and economically built, with just enough gray hair on his head to prove he hadn't been born bald, just enough firm jawbone to suggest he wasn't a man to trifle with, just enough icy blue in his eyes to freeze senators and other bunco artists into silence, for he was getting on in years, and had no time to waste on empty chatter.

"Yes, it's a great idea. And since my technical people have tried it on a variety of poisons and found it actually works, its our insurance against rude Russian surprises and makes your 'defection' one of this year's better ideas," Admiral Handy said. "Your being on the spot, in charge of advanced projects, will enable us to keep abreast their most promising research."

"How so? They certainly aren't going to allow me foreign contacts, or to publish anything substantive."

"True. But over the years we've succeeded in planting three agents in the Ministry of Chemical Pesticides, the rather transparent cover the Russkies use for chemical warfare R and D. You'll be contacted periodically by one of them."

"How would I know these men?"

"How *will* you know them? You won't, but they'll know you, all right. No fancy passwords. Just something to the effect that 'A mutual friend said you have a great recipe for borscht'—or beef strogonoff—or whatever. When you hear those words, you'll leave a specimen of your most recently developed chemical-warfare agent in a sealed vial, where he can see it. For insurance, each of the three will make a separate approach. When you've supplied each with the poison—or the poison's formula if you feel that's safer—then you can forget all about the whole thing."

"And go about my business of thinking about retirement in the Soviet Union?"

"Not at all. In a couple of years, if you tire of the game—no reason why you should though, since your work is your life—we'll engineer your kidnapping and forcible repatriation for trial. You're a traitor—remember? Of course, you'll retire to live in honored, opulent indolence. Meanwhile, they say Moscow is beautiful in springtime."

Unfortunately, Pollock never saw Moscow in the springtime. The Russians packed him off immediately upon arrival to a "secret" laboratory sunk beneath the Pripet Marshes in Byelorussia. Toward the end of 2015, he and his team perfected an agent which the Russians believed would be the ultimate CW weapon.

Anybody who possessed the brains to penetrate the Chemical Pesticides Directorate would have known about the development, yet as the day approached to deliver the finished weapon, Dr. Stanley Pollock was still waiting in vain for one of the American moles to surface, and remark upon his famous recipe for borscht. Both molecular blueprint on a microfiche imbedded in a Moscow subway ticket and needle-sized vial of the actual poison were ready, but nobody showed.

What Dr. Pollock never knew was that, two years before General Ignatiev returned to AES No. 23 from Moscow with murder in his heart, all three remaining agents had been gathered in by the KGB during a routine security sweep, and shot.

"Which leaves Pollock high and dry," Admiral Handy had said 14 months earlier, when reports of the disappearance of the AYES agents had been confirmed. Since then he had sent in three more, under various deep covers. One by one they broke contact, and were heard of no more. Unquestionably, AYES was penetrated. Unquestionably, any other operatives he sent would find a KGB reception committee waiting. But if AYES agents weren't the answer, what was?

As if in reply to his unvoiced question, Mr. Biggs had appeared with an armful of files on con men. By midnight, he had winnowed the stack to just three candidates—William Billings, Keefe McCann, and John/Joan Applegate, a transvestite. He pressed the buzzer.

Mrs. Biggs materialized, her wig askew, her lanky body swathed in a mauve, woolen bathrobe. The Admiral had a firm policy: she wasn't to leave the office until he did. Her policy was equally firm: she had to have her eight hours of sleep, even if it meant installing a cot in her office, as there were in the offices of all senior AYES officials. "Yes, sir?"

"Are Billings, McCann, and Applegate all available?"

"Yes, sir. They're all under lock and key."

"Billings would be ideal. He's a Marine veteran, married to a former firearms instructor, and he's imaginative and discreet."

"Yes, Billings would do just fine. But he's 55 years old. Perhaps this job calls for a more active man."

"Applegate's active enough," the Admiral reflected. "He's got to be, all the time changing clothes. And that could be a distinct advantage. You see, I've decided that this job calls for two people, preferably a man-and-wife team. The man does the work, and the woman covers his rear."

"An anatomical impossibility, if I may say so. But why Applegate?"

"We could insert him as a woman, giving him the opportunity to switch to a man's identity if things heated up."

Mrs. Biggs nodded. "Applegate would be fine, if it weren't for his predeliction for handsome young men. He's easily distracted."

The Admiral tossed Applegate's folder on top of the Billings file in the out box. As an afterthought, with a puckish smile, he reversed their order. "That leaves McCann. Trouble with McCann is, he likes the birdies too much. He just might decide to build a nest, furnish it with a couple of Muscovite nightingales, and forget why we sent him to Moscow."

"No chance of that. If you've read the report carefully, you'll have noticed that the dossier said—"

"Yes, I know—that prison life had left McCann completely impotent," said Admiral Handy with a snort. "Read back through the file, Biggs. I counted the women he left behind. A startling number, even allowing for the district attorney's exaggeration. The dossier must have been written by some sour old bitch who tried to get McCann to did—"

Mrs. Biggs had disappeared. She reappeared a moment later and laid a large glossy photograph on the desk. "That's Dr. Karine Collier, the author of McCann's dossier. She's a captain in the U. S. Army reserve. She provides psychological counseling to SAC pilots at MacDill. She has an active top-secret clearance. And she's—"

"—a bloody knockout. And she's right—Keefe McCann *must* have become impotent, or by now he'd have accumulated a couple more life sentences for attempted rape. Biggs, have my chopper ready for 0700 departure, and for Christ's sake get out of here and let a man get some sleep."

6. WATERSHED
4 SEPTEMBER 2016

"THEY SAY YOU'RE A PRETTY GOOD CON MAN, MCCANN. Okay, sell me something."

Keefe McCann examined the little man with the thinning gray crewcut and weathered face who spoke to him from across the table in the small room with whitewashed walls. The guard had told McCann only that he had a visitor.

One thing was certain: the old man wasn't another social worker, or prison psychologist, or reverend cleric sent to save Keefe McCann's soul from the fires of everlasting hell. His was an air of authority. He was a man whom people would obey without argument or opposition. He wasn't a lawyer, certainly—McCann detected no identifying fragrance of fraud, incompetence, or payoff. Captain of industry, major political figure, or army general was more likely. Since he had nothing better to do than push-ups back in his cell, McCann decided to investigate.

McCann leaned toward the little man in the baggy brown suit and said confidentially, "I have nothing to sell, but I know a fellow who's interested in buying."

The man in the brown suit just looked at him.

"A guy in my cell block wants to buy a piece of the great outdoors," McCann improvised. "Before he

52

checked in here at Hard Ass Hotel, he was chief engineer of Continental Aerospace, peddling bits and pieces to the competition on the side, which is how they nailed him. But that was only bread on the waters for the big stuff, the Mach-23 suborbital Moonrise bomber. While looking around for a buyer, he squirreled away a shoe box full of microfilm diagrams and specs of the key airframe and engine components. Now he's in here, he'll exchange them for a pair of running shoes."

If the guy had been a politician, the headlines would have leaped out at him: SENATOR BAFFLEGAB RECOVERS PRICELESS DEFENSE SECRETS. But no headlines were reflected in those hard little eyes.

"Alternatively," said the man with the five-digit number stenciled on his shirt pocket, without missing a beat, "he can raise two million dollars to finance a gubernatorial pardon, if that's the way it has to be."

Now, if the guy had been a businessman, the mere suggestion of exchanging the vital information on a project budgeted for $78 billion for a piddling $2 million would have given him apoplexy. But he didn't drop dead. He just sat there, staring at McCann with unblinking eyes.

"Yeah, I know," McCann went on, "two million sounds like a lot of money for a convicted engineer to throw around. But you see, some guy named Aleksei Karpinskiy has already offered *three* mil, not to mention political asylum in..."

The guy's jaw tensed.

Bingo! It was only for an instant, but it was enough.

Keefe McCann grinned. "What the hell are you here for, general?"

Admiral Handy regarded him somberly. He saw a man of medium height, good-looking but because of his broken nose hardly handsome, and guileless brown eyes which, Handy knew, had gulled a thousand suckers.

Nevertheless it was hard, looking at him, for the admiral to believe he was facing one of the great con artists of modern times.

"This year you'll be thirty, McCann," said the admiral. "It's a watershed year—on one side a life of theft, fraud, and deception since you were eleven years old, and on the other the prospect of the rest of your days in the cooler."

"Thank you for reviewing my life story, general, but shed no water—or tears. I'll be out of here in a week."

"How do you figure that?"

"Well, you didn't come here to commiserate with my plight; you could have written me a letter. Also, you appear to be too busy a man—you must be busy or you'd take time out to get that suit pressed, or better yet, go out and buy a new one—to come here to gloat, or plead for me to reform, or ask for information. You've come here because you want something from me. Okay—whatever it is, I'll give it to you. That's a promise."

"I'm happy to hear that. I . . ."

"In exchange for which I want *your* promise of springing me. I want out of here, and quick."

"*Everybody* wants out of here."

"Not as bad as I do. You see, the other inmates are individuals, with one life to live. With me, it's different. It's not just me that's locked up, it's a dozen different people, all locked up inside me trying to get out. And they can't get out while I'm in prison."

"How do you know I can obtain your release?"

"If you can't, we have nothing to talk about. But of course you can. You're the general. You have connections."

In spite of himself, Admiral R. R. Handy felt the stirrings of grudging respect for the crook sitting with folded arms opposite him. Fourteen months in a maximum security prison had obviously not dulled McCann's senses.

The speed with which he divined the "general's" intentions was evidence of a mental agility unimpaired by confinement. And he wanted out bad enough to write a blank check against his future.

"So you're not euphoric about the prospect of spending the rest of your life in this health resort?"

"No, general, I'm not."

"Were you serious about giving me anything I want?"

"Completely."

"How about *doing* anything I want?"

"You mean, *killing* somebody, I suppose?"

"I doubt that it will come to that—though it might."

Keefe McCann was pensive. He was playing a role that was not entirely familiar to him—himself—and he wasn't quite prepared for his reaction. To his surprise, he found himself saying, "There are a lot of guys in here who'll kill. Better try them—they like the work, and they've had experience."

The little man in the brown suit shook his head. "It's more likely that *you* will get yourself killed, although if you're as good at your various grafts as your record says, maybe not."

"Sacrificial lamb?"

"More like a Judas goat. But if you want security, stay in your cell."

"Any day now I bet you're going to tell me what you want me to do."

Admiral Handy put his folded arms on the table and leaned forward. "I want you to make a short trip to Russia. We'll put you in service uniform with authentic credentials, and you and a partner go in as members of the Mutual Inspection Team on the next rotation. I'll have you assigned as roving inspector, so you'll have the run of the place and can track down the man we're looking for. When you find him, you'll make a pickup."

"That's all?"

"That's it. You might have trouble getting to the guy, but that's the point: if just anybody could do it, why would I come to you?"

Keefe McCann thought it over. The assignment was bound to be dangerous—very dangerous—or the general wouldn't have come to him. On the other hand, going in as a member of a Mutual Inspection Team gave him the maximum mobility he had never enjoyed in his half-dozen previous trips to the Soviet Union. As a tourist, whole regions of the Soviet Union—more than four-fifths of the total area—had been out-of-bounds to him. As an MIT officer he would be tailed but his movement could in no way be restricted.

MIT agents from both blocs were busily wandering unhindered through one another's territory, sleuthing and snooping, and it was a measure of their vigilance that in the six years since unrestricted access had been instituted in both countries not a single violation of the agreement to cease production of nuclear weapons had been noted by either side. Nor had the presence of hordes of inspectors, some in uniform, others in mufti, caused undue friction with the local populations. The Mutual Inspection Treaty of 2009 had been an unparalleled success.

And that made it all the more curious that the general would come recruiting in the Pennsylvania State Prison, when he could have used any of hundreds of officers with vast experience in Russia. "Who are you, General?"

"'General' is close enough."

"And you work for . . . ?"

"Don't waste my time, young man."

McCann massaged his jaw. "How do you know I won't take off for parts unknown once I get through that gate? How do you know I won't disappear the minute I step off the plane in Moscow?"

"That's all taken care of."

McCann didn't like the sound of it. It was one thing to accept a nasty, difficult, even dangerous job in return for his freedom. It was quite another to volunteer for a suicide mission.

Admiral Handy observed McCann's indecision. "Well?"

The door opened and Dr. Karine Collier came in. She was wearing a high-necked dress of silk jersey that made the admiral's palms itch with remembrance of things past. McCann gave her a brief glance and returned to his contemplation of the general's offer. Admiral Handy felt like kicking him.

"Well?" said Karine Collier.

The admiral shook his head.

Karine was silent for a moment. Then, looking hard at him, she said to the admiral, "So, we'll have to fall back on my idea."

"I guess so," said Admiral Handy, wondering what the hell she was talking about but willing to play along.

"It's the obvious solution. Making the pickup will be easy so long as the approach is subtle. I'm a bona fide army officer, so as an MIT observer I'll blend with the scenery."

McCann laughed. "*You?* 'Blend with the scenery'? Honey, you'll *be* the scenery. Every gumshoe in Moscow will be on your case."

She ignored him. "Shall we go to my office to discuss the details?" she said to the admiral.

Admiral Handy rose and pushed his chair back. He walked across the room and opened the door for Dr. Collier.

"Hey! Wait a minute . . ." came McCann's voice, as Admiral Handy closed the door behind them. The admiral smiled. Dr. Karine Collier was a pretty good psychologist, at that.

7. THE BARKLEYS
12 SEPTEMBER 2016

"PLEASE ROLL UP YOUR SLEEVE," SAID DR. SEMM, A BE-spectacled man with tufts of dirty white hair growing out of his ears. He took the vial proferred by Admiral Handy and sponged the top with alcohol. "This won't hurt a bit—well, at least not very much."

"What's in the syringe?" said Keefe McCann, eyeing it nervously.

"A ball and chain," said Admiral Handy. "A little something to keep you from getting wanderlust. To be precise, the dissolved salts of various heavy metals which, unless you return here within ten days for chela-tion, will kill you as surely as cyanide—but slower, over a period of about a week, and with considerably more suffering."

Karine Collier stiffened.

"That's the way it's got to be, Dr. Collier," Handy said. "With a record like his, I had to strong-arm a lot of influential people to get him sprung. I can't afford to have him stroll off into the sunset."

"But what if I'm locked up or something, break my leg and get stuck in traction at some Russian hospital?" McCann protested. "What then?"

Admiral Handy shrugged. "Let me tell you how this works, McCann, so you don't leave here with the idiotic idea that you can go to some quack and get your blood changed and leave me holding the bag. That needle contains a cocktail of metal ions which, upon injection, will migrate to your organs—liver, kidneys, spleen, and so on. Now, if you knew the ions were lead, for instance, you could flush out your plumbing simply by using a chelating agent like ethylenediamine tetraacetate. But the gunk in that needle is a complex assortment of timed-release poisons, and if the wrong chelating agents are given—agents which have no metal ions to bond to —*they'll* kill you. Only when you return here before your ten days are up will the right chelating agents in the proper proportions be administered."

"And if I get the information you want, I go free— clean slate?"

"You have my word on it."

"How about something in writing?"

"Write it yourself, McCann—your document would probably look more authentic than mine . . . The needle, Dr. Watson."

The Washington-Moscow shuttle was fully booked but Commander Waldron Barkley, USN, and Mrs. Barkley had a compartment to themselves over the starboard wing, where the soft thrum of counter-rotating props lulled the passengers into restful slumber.

On the night table beside the double bed he placed what seemed to be an ordinary plastic pen, but its scrambler would electronically override the human voice within a ten-foot radius, so that hidden mikes recorded only undecipherable acoustic hash.

"Welcome to the bridal suite," said McCann cheerily. He had been in a buoyant mood now that they'd left Washington, confident that within a week he'd again be a free man.

Dr. Collier eyed him warily. Ever since they boarded

the plane, Keefe McCann had been Cdr. Waldron Barkley, USN, and nothing but Cdr. Waldron Barkley, USN, rambling on about his tour with the Joint Chiefs of Staff, ASW operations in the North Atlantic aboard the U.S.S. *Gwillam Forte*, running into an old Annapolis classmate in Georgetown, the lousy selection of jogging suits at the Pentagon PX, and his just-concluded stint at the MIT Officers' Training Course. Everything he said was a lie, of course, but an artful lie and wholly convincing. He even *looked* very much the modern Navy commander, with his ramrod military bearing, crew cut, and chest full of ribbons, badges, three black-braid stripes on his starched khakis, and the eight-pointed gold star of the MIT observer on his right jacket pocket. He could pass muster in any gathering of old salts.

As Mrs. Karine Barkley, Karine Collier was slightly less convincing. Looking at the Barkleys, men would wonder why a tall, slim, exceedingly shapely woman with long, black, wild-gypsy hair, and tumescent lips to match turgescent breasts would wed a mere commander when a woman like her could have admirals, millionaires, senators, or movie stars—whoever she wanted.

Karine Collier didn't wonder. Keefe McCann was the man she wanted. His rugged masculinity alone would suffice for most women. But added to that was the mystery of the man, his elusive nature, and the quicksilver quality that made him impossible to categorize or pin down. If he wasn't all things to all people, he came perilously close, and how he managed it was a source of constant fascination to her. He was unlike most men, whose narrow range of interest could be divined—and defined—in two or three meetings; the moment she could anticipate what a man was going to do or say, boredom set in. Whatever he was, Keefe McCann would never be a bore. But even those considerations were peripheral. The fire that McCann ignited most deeply within her was the fire of rejection. He had made her doubt her desirability.

What was behind his indifference, she didn't know and didn't much care. In prison, she had no choice but to suffer his unconcern. But now they were alone, together in a compartment scarcely larger than the double bed to which they would soon retire. Time was running out for Keefe McCann.

She had dressed to kill in a navy-blue suit with the skirt hem at mid-calf. The jacket had a high, flaring collar, and the narrow lapels were so cut that they outlined, rather than obscured, the breasts. French court circles a couple of centuries earlier had embraced the same style but left the breasts bare; today's fashion, with a sheer beige silk blouse under the jacket, was considerably more effective, especially on a woman with a bust like Karine Collier's. Her black hair, parted in the middle, cascaded over her shoulders. She wore black, spike-heeled pumps, and what leg she showed gave promise of even better things to come.

When bedtime came, Keefe McCann brushed his teeth in the tiny flip-up basin, stripped as usual to the buff, as indifferent to Karine Collier's presence as if she'd been a floor lamp, turned back the covers, and slipped between the sheets. He smiled. "Big day tomorrow."

"Big night *tonight*," she responded huskily, and began to undress. Removing one's clothes on stage before a thousand men is a profession; before one, an art. Karine Collier was an artist. She turned off the overhead light and dimmed the cove light over the door so that she was in silhouette. Languidly, she unbuttoned her jacket and let it slide with a *swish* of silk to the floor. She unzipped her skirt, unhurriedly. She had to tug it gently to clear her full hips, before it joined her jacket on the floor. Her sheer beige blouse went next, with agonizing slowness, as if reluctant to surrender the ripe bust it held in tight embrace.

Besides her high-heeled pumps, she wore black nylon stockings and lace garter belt, but neither slip nor brassiere. She stood, her back to the light, and began to brush her lustrous black hair with rhythmic strokes more erotic than any striptease. She didn't know whether the suspense was having its desired effect on Keefe McCann, for he lay there without making a sound, but it was certainly having an effect on her. Finally, able to contain herself no longer, she dropped the hairbrush and moved to his side of the bed. She pulled the covers back.

It took a moment to realize that what she intended to find there had failed to materialize. Her gaze drifted up across his muscular, hairy chest, and came to rest on his face. His eyes were closed. Keefe McCann was fast asleep.

They registered at the Novaya Rossiya, that most monumental and dismal of hotels in downtown Moscow. Commander Waldron Barkley asked for a room with twin beds and, when it was not forthcoming, slid his passport across the reception desk with the edge of a 100-ruble note peeking out. They were in luck: by the time the bellhop, a bent old man wearing a shoddy ersatz cossack costume, came to take them to the elevator, a vacant room with twin beds had miraculously materialized.

It was one of those boiling Moscow late summer days, nearly seventy in the shade. McCann ordered room service to bring up a tray of assorted soft drinks. While waiting, he shed his clothes and stepped into the shower. A tray of dusty bottles and smudged glasses was on the table when he stepped out. Ignoring Karine Collier, who sat stiffly at the dressing table pulling a brush through her hair, pretending not to be staring at his naked body in the mirror, he drank two bottles of the stuff before deciding it was supposed to be lemon-flavored. As for carbonation, there had been more in the clogged shower head.

He dressed in his khaki summer uniform, adjusted his cap squarely on his head, and picked up his red-white-and-blue flight bag. He stuck the scrambler-pen in his breast pocket and went to the door.

"Will half an hour be enough for you?" he asked.

"To do what?" said Karine Collier, turning to rivet him with a full frontal view of magnificent breasts, bare as the rest of her.

For a moment Keefe McCann just stared, a man in a trance. He had the semistoned look of one trying to dredge up some half-forgotten memory, and not quite succeeding. "Uh . . . what did you say?"

"I said, 'What would you *like* me to do?'" The way she said it, the word tinkled like a bell.

"Whatever women do in the shower, I suppose." He sighed, shook his head, and turned toward the door.

She glared at his back. "Half an hour will be ample," she said between her teeth.

"I'll be in the bar. We've discussed what you're to wear."

Nearly an hour later she made her entrance. Heads turned. One man choked on his drink and fell into a paroxysm of coughing. Another, mesmerized, walked into a waiter carrying a tray of glasses, which crashed to the floor. There were no other casualties, but if she had remained in the bar another minute or two, McCann would have feared for domestic tranquility. He took her by the elbow and steered her toward the entrance and out into the street.

"You're off to a good start, Collier," he said approvingly. "It looked for a minute there we'd have to call the fire and rescue squad."

She was wearing a blazing red skirt only marginally longer than a cummerbund, a matching red shirt, red open-toed high-heeled slippers, and big dark glasses with square red frames. Her black hair undulated in the breeze. On the street, traffic slowed, which was well, because pedestrians were walking into the paths of cars as they craned to get a better look at the leggy American.

"Where are we going?" she inquired.

"To the park. These streets are too crowded to see what kind of tail we—as opposed to you—have got."

They strolled along the bank of the Moskva River, pausing from time to time for Karine to toss pebbles in the water and give McCann a chance to spot their shadow. Since the KGB man made no attempt to dissimulate his surveillance, McCann made him without difficulty. He was a burly man of middle age, with short-cropped hair and a face with the grayish hue of a fresh corpse. McCann decided that his name must be Boris. Boris was probably alone. Only important Americans were accorded the honor of a two-man tail. Judging by his looks, Boris was a stupid, unimaginative clod, but in his various incarnations McCann had always found that underestimating the opposition is dangerous business. In the present situation, he counted on appearances being deceptive.

They wandered through the trees, passing an odiferous unpainted wooden structure labeled "Toilette," presumably for the French tourist trade, although any label would have been redundant. They walked by on the upwind side and arranged themselves on a bench overlooking the river some thirty yards beyond. The sun was blazing down, and the few Russians with leisure enough to be in a park during working hours had sought shade beneath the trees.

They sat for a few minutes on the bench while their

watcher idled forty yards or so away, pretending to examine some flowers growing beside the bicycle path.

McCann looked around casually. They faced a bund along the riverbank. Boris was stationed to his right. Over his right shoulder was the "Toilette." After they had been sitting for some minutes, talking idly, a middle-aged man of medium stature approached the little wooden structure. McCann rose. "This is where I leave you, my sweet," said McCann.

"Good luck."

He rose, slung his flight bag over his shoulder, and walked back the way he had come, fiddling with his belt buckle as if his business was urgent. As he passed Boris on the footpath, the Russian took a handkerchief from his pocket and made a show of noisily blowing his nose in what McCann supposed was a standard ploy to disarm the suspicions of stupid, unobservant Americans. McCann nodded pleasantly and entered the wooden shed.

In order to keep both Americans in sight, the Russian stared at the toilette for a few seconds, then swiveled his head to observe the woman, made sure she hadn't moved away, then returned his gaze to the little wooden shack. The third time his head turned in her direction, his eyes were held a moment longer: the American woman was stretching languorously in the sun, catlike, and her profile with her arms upthrust was something to behold, for she had unbuttoned the top two buttons of her shirt to get the full benefit of the sun. He tore his eyes away with regret.

The next time it was harder. She had unbuttoned the shirt even more and pulled it back, almost exposing her breasts. Totally relaxed, with her hands laced together behind her head, she had slid forward in the seat, hiking up her skirt nearly to her hips. At this distance, he couldn't tell whether she was wearing anything underneath. He took a tentative step in her direction, hoping she wasn't. He swallowed hard, glanced furtively around him, and moved closer.

As he did so, out of the corner of his eye he saw a figure slip out of the toilette and into the shadows, moving with deceptive speed. Cursing himself and the American's tricks, he trotted off in pursuit, thanking God that his training had saved him from making a complete fool of himself.

Taking a circuitous course through the trees, but headed in the direction of the park entrance and the underground station, the man in uniform never looked back. To the Russian, the American was serenely confident that his trick had worked and that even now his surveillant was gawking at the woman's exposed breasts. He reddened at the thought, and plunged ahead through the underbrush, taking a straight line to shorten the distance between them.

Now the American was no more than fifty yards away, and had broken out into the open sunlight. For the first time the Russian got a really good look at him. For some inexplicable reason, the American seemed to have shrunk: the man's sleeves extended down almost to his fingertips and his uniform cap down almost to his ears. *The man's uniform was three sizes too large for him.* Suddenly, the surveillant realized what had happened: the man who had entered the toilette just before the American got up from the bench was his confederate. The American had peeled off his jacket and cap, and the confederate had donned them and left as a decoy. And *he* had stupidly followed, leaving the American and his woman to make a getaway.

Well, he'd see about that. Though he appeared fat, he was in excellent condition. He set off at a dead run back through the woods the way he had come. Three minutes later he came to the toilette, glanced in, and found it empty. He looked toward the bench where the woman had been, and his eyes slid out of focus in shock: the woman was still there, sunning herself. But her skirt was now pulled down to mid-thigh, and her shirt was chastely buttoned. Of Commander Barkley, there was nothing to be seen.

The KGB man watched with growing anxiety until, half an hour later, the woman rose and, glancing neither to the right nor left, walked away quickly. For the next three hours she led her cursing surveillant on a tour of downtown Moscow. Not until the sun slanted down over the rooftops did she at last head back for the hotel, never having made the rendezvous with Commander Barkley that Boris had been expecting—*praying for*—all afternoon.

Meanwhile, the figure that the Russian had been following proceeded through the trees to the entrance of the park, down into the subway station, and aboard the first train, which came through two minutes later. He rode three stops, got off, and went into the men's room. In a booth he stripped off the oversize uniform jacket, rolled it up with his oversize uniform cap and stuffed them into the flight bag from which he had just taken those which he put there during his brief visit to the toilette. He now put them on and looked at himself in the mirror. A perfect fit. He waited until he was alone, then opened the waste can and shoved the flight bag to the bottom, covering it with wadded up copies of *Pravda*.

Adjusting his tie and setting his cap squarely on his head, Keefe McCann boarded the train which would take him to within one block of the Chemical Pesticides Directorate.

8. BOGOMOLOFF
13 SEPTEMBER 2016

THE MINISTRY OF AGRICULTURE'S CHEMICAL PESTI-
cides Directorate occupied one wing of an aged gray
concrete building off Moscow's Square of the Martyrs of
Smolensk. It was there that Keefe McCann directed his
steps after emerging from the subway station, having assured himself that he had evaded his surveillant.

The sentry at the doorway came to port arms, did a
smart about face, and escorted McCann directly to a
desk where a round little man with narrow Asian eyes
sat behind a sign identifying him as the sergeant of the
guard.

"I.D." snapped the sergeant.

Keefe McCann handed over the Mutual Inspection
Team card identifying him as Commander Waldron
Barkley.

"You Americans!" laughed the sergeant, his eyes dis-
appearing into the slits in his face. "So now you think
we're keeping bombs in the Ministry of Agriculture." He
stuck the plastic card into a slot in his computer and
tapped a key. An instant later full-face and profile images
of Keefe McCann flashed on the screen. Below were the
words. "Identification authenticated."

"Just doing my job, Sergeant. I don't pick the places I
inspect, you know. It's all done by computer, and I only

learn the location of the inspection sites myself an hour before I start out on my rounds. And by the way," McCann went on, steel entering his voice, "when American sergeants address a commander in the navy—American or Soviet—they customarily stand at attention and address that officer as 'sir.' Of course, it may be different in the Russian Army. Perhaps I should ask your commanding officer if this is the case."

The grin disappeared from the Russian's face. He scrambled to his feet, his heels clicking as he snapped to attention. He saluted smartly.

"Very sorry, sir. Misplaced sense of humor, sir. It won't happen again, sir."

"No, of course not," smiled McCann tolerantly. "Carry on, Sergeant, and kindly announce me to the occupants of...ah..." He took a slip of paper from his pocket and consulted it. "Rooms 107-D, 136-A, 291-F, 477-F and 701-C. I shall be coming along shortly and trust that while I'm on my way nothing will be moved."

"Yes, sir," the sergeant said, jotting down the room numbers. He reached for the telephone. "Will the Commander be requiring an escort?"

"No, thank you, Sergeant. Allow me to enjoy the thrill of discovery." McCann walked away down the long dim hall, lit only at intervals by seventy-five-watt fluorescent lights.

It must be a long time between thrills, you American bastard, said the sergeant between his teeth as he dialed the first number on his list. What a stupid arms agreement, he thought. Even unscheduled inspections like this one were a load of crap. The bombs the Soviet Union and the United States built in the frantic last two or three years before the agreement came into force were small and compact enough for a schoolgirl—a Russian schoolgirl, at least—to carry on her back. With as little as thirty seconds' warning, even if the weapons officers were unimaginative enough to hide them in their offices, they could be whisked away to some more secure location, just as the occupants of the five offices he had just called were doing with their secret files at that very moment. According to the agreement, unannounced inspections were limited to five distinct areas in any one structure, giving everybody plenty of time to hide whatever was necessary. Like most things thought up by politicians, this arrangement struck the sergeant as stupid.

He shrugged. But what did *he* know? He was just a sergeant. And after all, the Soviet-American Weapons Unlimited Inspection Agreement had been in force for nearly two decades, and there hadn't been a big shooting war since they signed it. He dialed the next office on the list.

Keefe McCann had ostentatiously laid the scrambler-pen on the desk of Comrade Dr. Valentin Bogomoloff, assistant chief of the Horticulture Pests Department, just as he had done in the three offices he had inspected earlier in the afternoon. It told Bogomoloff that the American naval officer was not a harmless inspector at all, but a dangerous *agent provocateur*. About one in every five so-called "inspectors" was, and Soviet officials had been warned to be on their guard against them—be polite, offer coffee and cigarettes, talk at length, and say nothing. It was difficult to learn if the Americans had any success at recruiting agents in their absurdly naive fashion. It was very unlikely, if only because the unlucky recipient of such inspections was scientifically interrogated immediately afterward to determine whether he had succumbed to American promises.

"Well, Commander," said Bogomoloff jovially, after they had introduced themselves, "any luck in the bomb department?" He was the new-breed Russian, bald and bearded but trim and elegant in a two-piece suit made to his measure in Paris. He placed a cup and saucer on McCann's side of the desk and raised his eyebrows interrogatively.

McCann nodded. "I'm not looking for bombs," he said. "I'm here to assassinate one of your people."

Bogomoloff recoiled, splashing tea across the desk. His eyes darted to the closed door and back to the American, suddenly grim. Was this 'American' a KGB provocateur? Was he really even an American? Had he inadvertantly said something incriminating? Bogomoloff's mind whirled. He blinked and swallowed. His head felt stuffed with cotton. "I'm afraid I don't understand," he said weakly.

"It's simple: I'm here to kill a man named Pollock. Know him?"

"No, of course not." Bogomoloff cursed himself. That wasn't the way to handle this man. In cases like this, when the provocateur could be either a real American or a member of the KGB masquerading as one, it was best to be noncommittal and vague. "That is, I did. What I mean to say is," he went on quickly, "I did perhaps *meet* a person of that name once. I can't be sure. In my work, I meet many people." He willed himself to relax, to slow down his wildly beating heart. "May I ask what is the meaning of this remarkable statement?"

Keefe McCann was wondering the same thing—the meaning of that remarkable statement, "I *did*..." Did McCann imagine the emphasis on the word "did"? He couldn't be sure, considering Bogomoloff's quick recovery, but if he had heard right, then what Bogomoloff had started to say was, "I *did*"—period. Meaning that Bogomoloff knew him once, but no more. And if no more, that meant that Stanley Pollock was dead. If Pollock was dead, that changed everything. But until he knew for sure one way or the other, he'd have to carry on as planned.

"Just what I said. I came here to kill Pollock. Look, Dr. Bogomoloff," he said, leaning forward, "I've got a problem, and I'm looking for your help in solving it."

"*Me?*" said Bogomoloff, recoiling. The man was obviously mad. And, as obviously, *not* KGB. Their approach would never be so stupidly direct. No doubt about it—the man was a dangerous provocateur. His hand edged toward the button on the underside of his desk.

"Don't," warned McCann. "If anybody comes through that door, I'll be forced to tell them about Felicia Stanford and those rainy Sunday afternoons back in the spring of 2009 and the sweet nothings about the directorate's chemical warfare research you whispered into her shell-like ears."

"Lies," said Bogomoloff, his ears ringing. "I told her nothing. What you say are lies, all lies."

"Sure."

They *were* lies. Bogomoloff had indeed shared the American Embassy secretary's bed, but he had not shared his confidences. Still, the damned Americans had somehow gotten videotapes and had used them to exact small favors from him from time to time. Not often, and never big ones. They were too smart to kill the goose.

And now this.

"I'd better fill you in on a little background so you'll know exactly where we stand, you and I, Comrade Bogomoloff," said Keefe McCann earnestly. "Just a week ago I was in Pennsylvania State Prison, serving a life term without parole for dusting off a couple of guys who thought they could muscle in on a protection business I was running in Philly. Somebody in the CIA got the bright idea that I might be willing to help them with a little problem they had. They promised me $500,000 and a free pardon if I'd do a quiet job on some guy named Sidney Pollock who..."

"*Stanley* Pollock," said Bogomoloff, and immediately regretted it.

The American did not seem to notice the slip. "Well, said I to myself, what do I have to lose? So the CIA fixed me up with this uniform and title, told me how to fake it as a member of the Mutual Inspection Team, and sent me to look you up. The deal is, when you tell me where I can find this Pollock guy, to stick him with *that*." He indicated the M1-J.

"An *electronic bug scrambler*?" blurted Bogomoloff, in spite of himself.

"It's been modified. I twist the top hard and a needle tipped with some kind of poison—they say it kills in four seconds—shoots out like a dart." He stood up, picked up the M1-J and aimed it at the memo pad on Bogomoloff's desk. He twisted the top, and a black-tipped needle shot out of the bottom of the device, penetrated the pad, and embedded itself in the green desk blotter. Bogomoloff sat transfixed as McCann, using his handkerchief, carefully extricated the needle and reinserted it in the M1-J. He leaned back in his chair.

"Well, Bogey, as I was saying, this guy offered me the paper and five hundred gees, and how could I turn down a deal like that? Especially with you here on the inside to hold my hand?" He smiled brightly.

Bogomoloff shook his head in wonder. "And you expect *me* to help you kill one of our most distinguished scientists, on the threat of telling my superiors about my ...ah...indiscretion with Felicia Stanford years ago?" His face hardened. "You mistake your man, Mr. Barkley, or whatever your name is."

"No I don't, Bogey. Just because I've been in stir doesn't mean my brains have turned to mush. That kind of 'indiscretion' gets you hung in this country. Hell, everybody knows that."

"I won't do it." The vein pulsating in Bogomoloff's forehead felt like a trip-hammer.

"Sure you will," said McCann soothingly. "You've got no choice. Neither do I. If I go back to the States without proof that old Pollock is dead, it's back in the slammer for me. If I fall, Comrade, so do you. Think it over."

Looking at the hard features of the convict sitting in his office in a naval officer's uniform, Bogomoloff believed him. This was a man who had killed. Another death, especially that of a Russian he had never met until this morning, would mean nothing to him. On the other hand, if he cooperated in any way with this murderer and was detected, his fate would be the same.

But what if he was *not* detected? After all, with the scrambler-pen activated, so far as anybody knew the visit was purely an official MIT inspection. Bogomoloff decided to see whether there was a safe path between the two alternatives of betraying his country or refusing to do so and being exposed as a leaker of secrets to a foreign agent—both of which were capital crimes. "What," he said, examining his fingernails, "if I helped you to solve your dilemma? Without..." he added quickly, "talking about such criminal nonsense as killing people? How would you be able to show your gratitude?"

"You mean in money?"

"Do you have to be so crass?"

McCann laughed. "Now you're talking, Bogey. The guys who contracted me said they're willing to offer—so long as you go the route—to fix up a phony conference to which you'll be invited to get you out of the country, asylum, a new identity, a job, and $500,000, just like me."

Bogomoloff was silent, thinking it over. During the past decade the Americans had been able to engineer such defections. Sometimes. But not always. The offer required reflection. If he went through with it—and it was beginning to look as though he had no other choice —he would want assurances, not to mention more money, considering what inflation had been doing to the dollar. "What you say is interesting," he said. "I'll have to give it some thought."

"Sure," McCann smiled. "Take as long as you want, so long as it isn't more than the time it takes to rewind this little gem." From the breast pocket of his jacket he took a packet of *121mm*, the current American brand of choice among cigarettes. He pressed his thumb against one side for a few seconds, then pressed it again.

The sound of Bogomoloff's voice issued from the packet.

"Well, Commander," he was saying, "any luck in the bomb department?"

"I'm not looking for bombs," came back the voice of Keefe McCann. "I'm here to assassinate one of your men."

McCann pressed the side of the package again, and the voices fell silent. "Nifty little gadget, isn't it?" he remarked to the stunned Dr. Valentin Bogomoloff. "CIA gadget. Overrides the M1-J—the scrambler-pen. Cute, isn't it?"

Bogomoloff's head was swimming. If the KGB didn't kill him for his association with Felicia Stanford, they surely would for what was on that tape. He calculated his chances of hitting the blackmailing bastard on the head with the desk lamp and destroying the tape but, looking at the lean and muscular American, decided that his chances were poor. He had talked too much. He'd run out of options. Except one.

His hand edged toward the M1-J on the edge of the desk. All he had to do was point it at the America's chest and twist the top. He could then destroy the tape and

think up some story about how the American tried to kill
him, and he managed . . .

"That black stuff on the needle is printer's ink,"
McCann drawled. "So forget about being clever and
make up your mind. Is it going to be me—or the KGB?"

Bogomoloff wilted. "Well?" he said, finally, his voice
a whisper.

"Like I said, I've got to get to Stanley Pollock."

"Impossible."

"Would you like me to whistle another stanza of Our
Song, Comrade?"

"What I mean is, you *can't* kill Dr. Stanley Pollock."

"I can—with your help."

Bogomoloff smiled thinly. "That would be crowning
testimony to American efficiency. You see, Dr. Pollock
is already dead."

"And why the hell should I believe *that*?"

"It's true. He was shot by Major-General Viktor
Aleksandrovich Ignatiev. As an American spy."

"Oh, sure. Now I remember—I read all about it in the
New York Times."

"If I can prove it, will you go away and leave me
alone?"

"One thing at a time, Bogey."

Bogomoloff rose and crossed the room to his file cabinets. All documents of secret classification had been
hurriedly removed when he was alerted that an American inspector was on his way, but his unclassified papers
were still here. There had been several references to Dr.
Pollock's death in the files—a collection taken up by
members of AES No. 23 for a floral wreath; the conference at which the question was raised as to whether his
body should be cremated as he had wished, or buried in
the Cemetery of Heroes of the Union of Soviet Socialist
Republics, which he rated as posthumous recipient of of
the Order of Lenin; whether to divide his extensive li-

brary among his coworkers or add it to the ministry's collection.

He extracted papers from half a dozen files and handed them to the young American. Each was marked in the upper left corner with the file name and serial number. "These ought to convince you. I'm sure you'll appreciate that I could scarcely have fabricated them in advance, since it wasn't until two hours ago I knew of your existence, and believed until you stepped into my office that you were a bona fide MIT inspector, not a dirty blackmailer."

Keefe McCann skimmed through the papers, folded them carefully and stuck them in an inside pocket. He rose, pocketed the M1-J, and walked to the door. "Hell, Bogey," he said, opening it, "even dirty blackmailers have to eat."

9. KONEV
14 SEPTEMBER 2016

LIAM O'SHAUGHNESSEY KONEV, ACTING DIRECTOR OF
KGB Section K, responsible for the surveillance and re-
cruitment of foreigners visiting the Soviet Union, was a
fervent believer in the virtues of the computer. It was a
matter of necessity, since at any one time upward of
110,000 foreigners were either traveling or resident in the
Soviet Union as students, businessmen, tourists or spies.
Thus, though on paper only acting section chief of a directorate, Konev was in fact commander of the largest
single labor bloc outside the armed forces, for an average
of five operatives were assigned to each foreigner for
round-the-clock surveillance.

The only way to keep track of the immense amount of
data that flowed into Section K every hour—reports of
meetings between foreigners and Soviet citizens, facsim-
iles of intercepted letters, tape recordings of conversa-
tions, telephone calls and lovers' confidences, logs of
arrivals and departures, and background information on
probable spies pouring in from KGB Section G operatives in other countries—was by computer, and Konev
manipulated it with the virtuosity of an Albert
Schweitzer playing Bach.

It was unwritten protocol that foreigners would make
things easy for themselves by making things easy for the

surveillants who invariably followed them; when they didn't, they were automatically promoted to Level-4 investigation, which involved routine analysis of their home-country file to detect possible connection with espionage agencies. Immediately upon accreditation to the Soviet Union, diplomats, members of sports delegations, visiting scholars, and members of the American, French, British, and Chinese mutual inspection teams were also subject to special investigation, Level-3, which involved in-depth analysis of home-country files and presumption of espionage activity. Level-2 investigation, of course, was carried out in the Soviet Union itself; it involved interrogation of all Russian contacts of known foreign spies to provide evidence of espionage acceptable to the ten-nation Mixed Commission on Unauthorized Intelligence Collection Practices, which then arranged for spy swaps.

Level-1 investigations concerned imminent threats to Russian national security, and were monitored by Liam O'Shaughnessey Konev personally.

The son of a Russian agent working as professor of Slavic literature at Trinity College, Dublin, and the Irish communist graduate student he married, Konev had teethed on codes, secret inks, burst transmission, deceit, indirection, and identity switches—which presented few difficulties despite his freckles and flaming red hair. Arriving in Moscow for the first time at the age of thirteen, he was sent to schools for the sons and daughters of the Soviet elite to train in the USSR's most prestigious profession—espionage. In due course he graduated from the Institute for International Relations, where he had become as fluent in Chinese, Spanish and Arabic as in his native Russian, English, and Gaelic.

Assigned to the United States as an illegal, he specialized in the theft of weapons and computer systems, and was never suspected, let alone detected, during his four

years on the job. On his return to Moscow, his rise to the
position of acting chief of Section K at the age of thirty-
seven was meteoric. Even more remarkable than his
speedy ascent was the absence of jealousy on the part of
his fellow workers, who recognized in him a man of
genius on a level far above mere talent.

By the time the red-tagged folder on Commander
Waldron Barkley reached Konev's desk the following
morning at 7:30, the investigation of the American officer was proceeding routinely through Levels 2 and 3.
Neither would be completed for at least a week. That the
already-weighty folder was on his desk so early was unusual. Something serious was afoot. He summoned his
chief of staff, Gorielskiy.

"Summary," he instructed, tapping the file.

"An American nuclear arms inspector, sir. The first
day in Moscow—yesterday—he deliberately loses his
surveillant in the rush hour crowds in the Metro. He
shows up an hour later at the Ministry of Agriculture for
five snap inspections—alone."

"On the *first* day?" Inspectors *never* started work the
first day. They underwent a two-week country briefing at
their embassy, and the first month on the job they were
always accompanied by an experienced man.

"Exactly. There's more, sir. All five visits were to offices in the Directorate of Chemical Pesticides."

Konev, in the act of reaching for a cigarette from the
box on his desk, froze. His hands came to rest on the
edge of the desk, his fingers drumming noiselessly on the
polished rosewood surface. His antenna had detected
danger signals.

The uncharacteristic burst of activity from a new inspector was in itself very suspicious. And, he deliberately gave his tail the slip. Finally, he inspected five
offices in the Ministry of Agriculture, of all places.

Konev pressed a button on his console and picked up the telephone.

"Aleksis Mikhailovich?" he said. "Konev here. We have a problem . . ." He went on to describe the disturbing series of events culminating in Commander Waldron Barkley's visit to the Ministry of Agriculture. As Minister of Agriculture, Aleksis Mikhailovich Miloslavskiy would be aware of the significance of American interest in one of his directorates.

"Yes," said Miloslavskiy, "I see. No, Barkley is not known to me, although of course I will check with my deputies. Which departments did he visit, by the way?"

Konev told him, and when Miloslavskiy didn't reply immediately, wondered if the connection had gone bad.

Then suddenly, in a tone of great urgency, Miloslavaskiy said: "Arrest him—Priority One. Your chief will confirm this order within two minutes."

Konev hung up the telephone and depressed a lever on his desk console. "This is Priority One. Fax full-face and profile pictures and description of Commander Waldron, Barkley, MIT, to all mobile patrols, taxi kiosks, hotel and cafe doormen, bus and train stations, and airports. Commander Barkley must be detained and brought here under heavy guard."

He flicked the lever up and turned to his chief of staff. "I want everybody he spoke with at the directorate brought in and sweated. Wring them dry. Meanwhile, put Bremelskiy on the files of the offices Barkley visited—check against the directorate log-books whether any papers have been abstracted. Then check photocopy records for the past month to be sure all copies are accounted for. Finally, every citizen Barkley has seen or spoken to since he arrived is to be put under Class One surveillance. If any act suspiciously, or are in contact with foreigners, instant interrogation of maximum rigor. Go."

The chief of staff went.

Liam O'Shaughnessey Konev rapidly scanned the dossier on Barkley. The large glossy KGB photograph taken at the airport showed a young man with bushy black eyebrows, crew cut and a pleasant half-smile on his lips. The accompanying record of schools, duty stations, transfers, recommendations, promotions, and other minutiae of military life seemed to be unremarkable. Level-3 investigation had missed very little. Barkley had graduated from the U.S. Naval Academy in 2006, had gone to sea as communications officer aboard a *Cragg*-class frigate, then been assigned as an aide to the deputy chief of the Joint Chiefs of Staff. As a lieutenant, he had served as engineering officer, then executive officer on attaining the rank of lieutenant-commander, on ASW duties aboard the U.S.S. *Gwillam Forte* in the North Atlantic. There had been other ships and schools, citations and commendations, and finally assignment to the Soviet Union as a member of the U.S. Mutual Inspection Team. Nothing suspicious there.

On a hunch, he turned to the computer at the side of his desk and called up the *Lucky Bag*—the Naval Academy yearbook—for 2006. In the index he found the name Waldron Barkley, number 233 in class standings. He turned to Barkley's biographical sketch and picture on page forty. He didn't have to read the three paragraphs of text: Waldron Barkley's picture showed a hatchet-faced man of grim aspect, with pale eyebrows and thin lips.

He stamped on the foot buzzer. Gorielskiy appeared in the doorway.

"Departing aircraft passenger manifests for the past fourteen hours," Konev snapped.

"Yes, sir."

Within the minute a list of passengers on Phoenix Air flight 118, which had departed for Boston, Philadelphia,

and Dallas the evening before at 1933, appeared on
Konev's screen. The name Waldron Barkley was not on
the list. An examination of the passenger manifests of
the other eighty-nine flights to foreign destinations which
had left Moscow's airports in the previous fourteen
hours showed that they were similarly devoid of men and
women named Barkley.

It took less than ten minutes to examine the manifests, but by then Liam O'Shaughnessy Konev had
thought of another, sickening possibility—sickening because, if it turned out to be true, this "Waldron Barkley"
was even more efficient and dangerous than he feared.

"Gorielskiy!" he bellowed.

Gorielskiy, who had been waiting for such a summons
just on the other side of the door, entered on the double.

"This port-of-entry photo of 'Waldron Barkley'—see
if it matches any of the airport departure photos during
the past fourteen hours."

Having worked for Konev for six years, Gorielskiy
was not only used to urgent demands but, by anticipating
them, was usually able to fulfill them efficiently and with
dispatch. He already had the best eight of his personal
staff collating every scrap of paper dealing with the passengers on those manifests, including surveillance reports for every hour the departing passengers had been
in the Soviet Union, records of their contacts, conversa-
tions, purchases, illnesses, and work or study habits. He
had a record of their foreign currency and customs decla-
rations. And he had at least two photographs of each of
them taken covertly, on entry into and departure from
the Soviet Union.

To these Gorielskiy and his men now gave their urgent
attention. Pinning the big glossies of "Commander Waldron Barkley" and his "wife" on the corkboard behind
his desk, he told his assistants to find matching pictures

from the departure photographs of the 19,334 passengers.

It took less than three minutes. Lars Neimi, his eyes almost invisible as a broad smile spread across his flat Lapp face, strode forward and placed two photographs on Gorielskiy's desk.

Gorielskiy hurried into Konev's office. "The names they used are Dr. and Mrs. Grant R. Delano. Dr. Delano arrived last month to give courses in experimental neurology at Moscow University. But the people who left using the Delano identity are Barkley and his wife, no question about it. Grace Airlines flight 101 left last night and is scheduled to arrive in Seattle, its first stop en route to San Francisco and Los Angeles, in approximately two-and-a-half hours."

Konev leaned back in his chair and heaved a sigh of relief. Time was on his side, for a change. He reached for the telephone.

"Matvei Feodorovich?" he said to the KGB chief who answered his ring, "Konev here. The Americans tried yesterday to penetrate the Directorate of Chemical Pesticides."

"Not again!" groaned Demidov.

Konev let that pass. He hadn't been informed of the earlier discovery and elimination of three American moles in that organization. It hadn't concerned his department.

"All I know is that an American documented as an MIT officer made contacts with five officials in the directorate. I have ordered immediate damage control measures and a thorough investigation, of course, but I require your authorization to intercept and interrogate the spurious officer."

"You don't need my authorization for that."

"Yes, sir, I do. He's evaded our surveillance and at the moment is bound for the United States by air."

"How the hell did he manage that?"

"I'll have a full report for you today, sir. But meanwhile I nead ..."

"The authorization? Very well. Take whatever measures you must, but for God's sake, be discreet. We can't afford to be seen to conduct active operations on U.S. soil. They might cut off our grain shipments again, and you know what that will do to the meat ration."

"Yes, sir. When can I have your written authorization, Comrade Matvei Feodorovich?"

"Don't you trust *anybody,* Konev?" Demidov sighed.

"No, sir. In our business, the word doesn't exist."

"Now, here's how we're going to handle this," said Konev to Gorielskiy when Demidov's written authorization arrived fifteen minutes later. Alert your best men and women in the Seattle, San Francisco, and Los Angeles operations sectors to meet that plane. Once Barkley and his wife have cleared immigration and customs, take them captive and remove them to one of our safe houses, where we can find out how much they've learned at the Directorate of Chemical Pesticides. It may, God willing, be nothing to worry about, but we must be sure.

"Four or five men should be sufficient to take Barkley and his woman. The remainder will be in reserve to deal with the delegation of government agents I would, if I were in Barkley's place, radio ahead to meet me."

"If that happens, things may get a little rough," Gorielskiy observed.

"Can't be helped. I am hoping he thinks he will be safe on American soil before we discover his business at the Directorate of Chemical Pesticides. But we can't count on that, so take all precautions. We want to talk with him, of course, but the main point is that he doesn't talk to anyone else. If Barkley and his wife are too heav-

ily protected to kidnap them, at least make sure they're
dead."

"But won't that . . ."

"Kill them both and whoever else gets in the way.
When the Americans protest, we'll say we thought them
GRU defectors or some such. Alert Disinformation Section to have a plausible excuse ready at hand. The Americans will squawk, but we'll allow some Jews to emigrate
to Israel and in a week the State Department will forget
all about it."

"Yes, sir," said Gorielskiy, turning to go.

"Just a minute, Misha," said Konev. "A man like
Barkley will have the captain of the aircraft radio ahead,
an hour or so before landing, to be met. Have our radio
technicians in the Seattle consulate try to jam that transmission until handoff to Seattle control. If they're successful, the plane will land before Barkley's people get
out to the airport."

"What if he laid on an arrival party before he left the
United States?"

Konev considered the possibility. "No," he said finally, "Barkley couldn't have counted on getting his information from the directorate so quickly, and couldn't
have hoped he would arrive and leave the very same day.
But we're dealing with a very astute agent, Misha, so
warn our men to expect anything. He might switch identities on the plane and leave in uniform with the crew. Or
he might wait until the service crew comes aboard, don
utility coveralls, and disappear in a caterer's truck. This
fellow is a professional. I want no slipups."

"There will be none, Comrade Konev."

At 0815, more than a hundred officers from Section K
rolled up to the Directorate of Chemical Pesticides in a
fleet of vans. They sealed off all entrances, allowing
workers to enter but none to leave. The day's work in

the directorate, only just begun, ceased entirely as the public address system summoned everyone who had seen the American naval officer the day before—or even *thought* they might have seen him—to report to the director's office. Meanwhile, five teams of nine men each repaired to the offices the bogus Barkley had visited. Three men from each team took the unlucky occupants of those offices to separate rooms for interrogation.

The interrogations were peremptory and efficient. The chief inquisitor first weakened his witness's will to resist with a five milliliter injection of Telmore. Then, while an apprentice interrogator clamped a telephone magneto on the rim of the desk and cranked it experimentally, the chief *sledovatel* invited the respondent to start talking, else he'd have to go with the flow of the current. While these discussions were in progress, the others of each team were meticulously going through the file cabinets in the five offices, comparing the documents and reports with the logs of all such files held in the central file office. The task was speeded by the Soviet system of stamping documents of each file serially, so that the absence of any document was quickly noted. Other investigators were doing the same in the heavily screened area on the second floor where all photocopies were made and logged.

The interrogators made the first breakthrough . . . after a fashion.

Dr. Valentin Bogomoloff had passed a miserable night, sick with fear of the possible consequences of his encounter with the American who had called himself Commander Waldron Barkley, the American who had deceived him with such humiliating ease, crowning his mortification by taking from his files papers which proved Stanley Pollock dead.

Bogomoloff knew very little about Pollock. He had seen him once or twice some years ago, knew he was a scientist who defected from the United States and that he had been engaged in some very secret and important work for the Soviet Union. He had never inquired further: curiosity was a dangerous faculty in Russia, and never more so than when it was rewarded with forbidden knowledge. The mere fact that the American had taken papers which indicated that Pollock was dead was, to Bogomoloff, of tremendous significance. If the man's death was so important to the Americans, how much more so must have been Pollock's activities when alive.

Bogomoloff hated pain much more than he feared death, and knew that in the hands of KGB inquisitors one was but a prelude to the other. Well, kill him they might, but torture—never. In his inspection trips to various horticultural laboratories and field stations he had been given demonstrations of the most powerful pesticides and had even taken samples away for "analysis at the directorate." The most powerful, an arsenical, he had formed into a pill the size of an aspirin tablet. He had held it in his hand all during the previous sleepless night, waiting for the knock on the door.

Miraculously, it didn't come. Maybe no one would ever suspect him, after all. Just the same, when he went to work the next day he put the pill in his jacket pocket. And, in the agonizing seconds while the KGB officers waited for the Telmore to take effect, he transferred the pill from pocket to mouth and very soon was beyond the KGB's reach forever.

"What else?" said Liam O'Shaughnessy, listening grim-faced to the news about Bogomoloff from Gorielskiy.

"Only the missing papers, sir. Nothing substantive, but all indicating that Pollock is dead. Of course, we don't know what Bogomoloff knew, what he might have overheard from other members of the directorate. The place is a hotbed of gossip, and . . ."

"And, if he had heard about . . . well, whatever it was at the directorate that Barkley went to discover, Bogomoloff might well have passed the information on to Barkley."

"If he did that," Gorielskiy pointed out, "Then why risk giving Barkley the papers?"

"You mean, because the information confirming Pollock's death is inconsequential compared to the information Bogomoloff might have given him with details about Pollock's secret research?"

"Exactly."

"No idea," Konev admitted. "When we've gone into Bogomoloff's affairs thoroughly maybe we'll know. Meanwhile, we can only be sure of a very few things: that Barkley knows that Pollock is dead, that he considers the information important enough to blow his carefully constructed cover by leaving Russia under another name, and that we've got to interrogate him and find out why."

"Yes, sir."

Konev looked at the clock. It was almost nine o'clock. Within twenty minutes Barkley's flight would be landing in Seattle. "Let's see where we stand." He pressed a button on the console beside his desk which would put him into voice contact, suitably scrambled, with Pushkin Control, the center in Seattle.

"Dzhigit, this is Kachalka."

"I am listening, Comrade General."

"What's the status of the flight?"

"Right on schedule, sir. In a few minutes Grace 101 will be contacting the tower for landing in . . . hold everything, Kachalka."

Konev stopped breathing, his sixth sense telling him that something had gone awry and that his plans to take

Barkley captive or kill him in the attempt were going to misfire.

"Sorry, sir. The captain just radioed ground control on the emergency frequency that a passenger has suffered a heart attack. He's requested an ambulance and that he be cleared immediately for an emergency landing."

Konev chuckled. Clever of Barkley, but it wasn't going to save him.

"The tower gave him clearance, of course?" said Konev.

"Yes, sir. The tower cleared him to land on runway 135. But it wasn't Seattle tower, sir—it was Vancouver."

10. THE TRANSCON EXPRESS 14 SEPTEMBER 2016

MCCANN CRACKED THE DOOR AND INSPECTED THE PAS-sageway outside Karine Collier's compartment. It was empty. Taking her bag in one hand and her elbow in the other, he guided her briskly down the corridor to his compartment. He ushered her in, locked the door behind them, and heaved her suitcase into the overhead luggage rack.

Outside, the rain was pelting down, smearing into a marine-green blur the Washington countryside through which the North Transcon Express was passing. Despite having slept on the plane from Moscow, they were both weary from a day on the run while looking over their shoulders for the Russian bloodhounds McCann feared might have already picked up their scent. First there had been the clangorous exit from Vancouver International Airport in the ambulance, and then the switch to the taxi as they entered the city. Then they paid off the cab at the Great Pacific Hotel, walked out a side entrance, took a second taxi to a car rental agency, and drove their rented car across the border down to Seattle and straight to the train station.

Such countermarches were second nature to Keefe

McCann, who had spent a lifetime laying down trails which led nowhere. He wasn't sure they were necessary in the relative security of North America, but he didn't believe in courting disaster when simple precaution could avoid it. The Soviets would have missed Commander and Mrs. Waldron Barkley by now. And the KGB's Section K would probably have learned of his visit to the Directorate of Chemical Pesticides. But, in view of the lapse of less than twenty-four hours since he made that visit, he doubted that they had yet discovered his interest in Dr. Stanley Pollock. Bogomoloff would have been very careful to conceal the fact that papers were missing from his files, but still . . .

The train compartment was more comfortable than the plane's cramped quarters. It had a queen-size bed, with the counterpane turned back, and two naugahide easy chairs with a table between them. On the table was a vase with synthetically scented artificial flowers, and on the wall opposite the bed a forty-five inch television panel brought the world to their bedside. Between the closet and the small bathroom was a fully stocked mini-bar. A large window afforded—weather permitting—a spectacular view of the countryside whizzing by at 220 miles per hour.

The amenities of the compartment did little to mollify Karine Collier's annoyance. It was moving, and she had had a bellyful of moving these past two days. First there was the flight to Moscow, then the playlet in the park on the Moscow River to distract their surveillant, the long and sweaty march back and forth through downtown Moscow to keep their KGB tail guessing and finally the pleasure of kicking off her shoes at the Novaya Rossiya and collapsing on her bed for a decent night's sleep.

But it was not to be. She had barely closed her eyes when McCann barged into their room and told her to get dressed and pack her bag. In the five minutes it took to do so McCann called to reserve a compartment on the night train for Leningrad. They paid their hotel bill and took a taxi to the railroad station. They bought tickets for Leningrad, entered their coach, walked swiftly to the front of the car, and rattled down the iron steps just as their tail was scrambling up the rear steps in their wake. They grabbed a cab to the airport. There, with passports identifying them as Dr. and Mrs. Grant R. Delano, they had taken the first flight out, which happened to be going to Seattle.

She was still sleeping the sleep of the drugged as the plane, flying a Great Circle course over the North Pole, crossed British Columbia. But McCann was on the flight deck, dropping the name of the Grace Airways CEO and suggesting to the captain the wisdom of requesting a weather check on UHF channel 332. The pilot did as asked. To his surprise, a terse message from the airline's operations chief came back, instructing him to put himself and his plane entirely at the disposal of Dr. Delano. The captain was relieved when Dr. Delano merely requested that the plane make an "emergency" landing at Vancouver International Airport.

There Dr. and Mrs. Delano quietly disembarked at the end of the runway, were picked up by a waiting ambulance, and disappeared from the captain's life as completely as from those of the platoon of Soviet agents awaiting them in Seattle.

Then there had been the switch from ambulance to taxi, the entrance and immediate smooth departure from the Great Pacific Hotel's side entrance, the rental car and the drive to Seattle. Even though it was obvious to Karine Collier that the KGB could not even have *guessed* where they were then, McCann, pointing out that any pursuers would be looking for a man and his wife, then insisted they book separate compartments, which they did under the names Omar Haffar and Carol

Uppendahl. All of which struck Karine Collier as an egregious waste of time and energy they could better expend in other, more intimate, enterprises, if only the big lug would come to life.

As McCann lodged her bag in the overhead rack of his compartment, it occurred to her that perhaps he would respond to subtle suggestion. "I would be pleased to know," she said frostily, "why you insisted on our taking two compartments and then forcing me to move in here with you. Is this some sort of crude attempt to put our relationship on a more personal, even sexual, basis?"

"Not me. The Russians," said Keefe McCann.

"I beg your pardon?"

"It's not me, but the *Russians* who are going to make crude attempts—on our lives. Having had twelve hours on the plane to think things over, I've decided that maybe I've made some grievous tactical blunders and that as a result of my miscalculations the Russians may come gunning for us before we can reach Washington."

Karine Collier removed her raincoat and hung it in the closet. She was wearing a high-necked knit-wool dress over smooth contours that would have started any ordinary man's pulse thumping. McCann knew, without counting, that his was steady at a solid sixty-five. Pity.

She opened the door of the minibar and filled two glasses with ice and scotch. "Dutch courage," she said, handing him one.

"You think I'm imagining things," he said.

"Of course you are."

"I gather you don't believe in instinct, premonition, or hunches."

"On the contrary, I am convinced that such phenomena exist, even in the higher animals. Of course, in your case . . ."

McCann sat back in his chair, sipping his drink. "Can't say I really blame you. But look at it this way: we still don't know exactly what my mission was, except that it was very important to the general—important enough to spring me from a life sentence and important enough for him to engineer your recall to active duty and that appointment to a professorship at Princeton. Point two: with Pollock dead, probably the rationale behind the mission no longer applies. Point three: if the rationale disappears, then Commander Waldron Barkley and his lovely wife present no menace to anybody."

"Exactly. So what's the worry?"

"The worry is, we're looking at the situation only from *our* point of view. But what are the Russians thinking? One: Waldron shakes his shadow. Two: why, they ask themselves, did he do that? Answer: to buy time to make contact with somebody at the Directorate of Chemical Pesticides, time enough to make a pickup and get the hell out of the country before that contact is investigated. Three: if that wasn't, in fact, what actually happened, then why the Waldrons' big rush to get out of Moscow that same night?"

Karine waved her hand dismissively. "Yes, I suppose that sooner or later they'll search Bogomoloff's files. And maybe they'll discover that something is missing, something that proves Pollock is dead. But if he's dead, what could he possibly pass to you?"

McCann sipped his scotch. He grimaced. "That's the point to which my stunning mental powers had brought me as we were crossing the North Pole, dear girl. I was feeling pretty satisfied with myself—a quick two-day job, and suddenly the prospect of freedom instead of life imprisonment. But then I crawled back into the identity of the Section K sleuth trying to figure out what, if anything, Commander Waldron Barkley had learned that could hurt the Soviet Union. It didn't take long for me to figure that one out.

"The American dusted out of Russia within hours of his visit to the directorate, the Section K sleuth would say. That means his mission, whatever it was, was accomplished—otherwise he'd still be here. What mission? Well, they'd run the five poor bastards I visited through the grinder, and before you could say 'Life at hard labor in Siberia' they'd learn that papers pertaining to Pollock's death were missing."

"Exactly."

"Not quite. Unlike me, the Russians know exactly what Pollock was up to. They'd know that he had information which, if transmitted to the Americans, could have spelled disaster for Russia. Under these circumstances, the Russians could only assume that, before he died, *Pollock had passed that information to Bogomoloff, and that Bogomoloff passed it on to me.*"

"But the papers . . ."

"Window dressing, they'd reason, something for Bogomoloff to fall back on in case of inquiry. Section K would expect him to alibi that, when pressured by me into arranging contact with Pollock, he produced papers showing Pollock dead. Ironically, that is exactly what happened. But of course Section K, consisting entirely of Russians, wouldn't believe him."

Karine was pensive. "What you're saying is, the Russians may think you've gotten away with some tremendous secret, when in reality you know nothing at all except that the secret died with Pollock."

"Change that 'may' to 'must' and you'll have it exactly right; they can't take the chance that it happened any other way. Once they've squeezed Bogomoloff and inspected his files—and we can only hope they haven't gotten around to him yet—they'll be baying after us like a pack of Siberian timber wolves."

"Yes," she said slowly, "I see what you mean." She brightened. "But still, I can't see anything to worry about. They don't know where we are, and in thirteen hours we'll be in New York."

"Thirteen hours is a long time," McCann pointed out. "You can fly from Moscow to New York in a lot less time than that—if they knew we were going there." He finished his drink and put down the glass. Outside, darkness had fallen—the same darkness that had overtaken them in Moscow the evening before—and the rain still drove against the window in horizontal streaks.

McCann picked up the telephone and dialed the number the general had given him.

A female voice answered on the first ring. "Hello?"

No "General Whosis' office." Just "hello."

"This is Dr. Julian R. Hartshorn," McCann said. "The general asked me to call."

"Of course, Doctor," the voice said without hesitation. "But he's probably in bed by now. It's nearly midnight, you know."

In Washington it would be, McCann realized suddenly. "It's important," he said without much hope. Short of invasion, secretaries do not disturb the repose of generals.

"I'll put you right through," she said.

A moment later the general's voice came on the line. "Where are you?"

"On the 7:40 North Transcon Express out of Seattle."

"All right. Now, say nothing except in reply to my questions—say nothing else. Got that?"

"Yes."

"Was your trip successful?"

"I did everything I possibly could."

"Fine. Did you bring home any souvenirs?"

"What I have, you'll want to see."

"Excellent. Now listen carefully. I want you to get off the train in Pittsburgh. You'll be met by one of my men —fellow named John Holmes. You'll recognize him by the red polka dot bow tie, green trench coat, and shock of black hair. He'll bring you in. Got that?"

"Yes, sir."

The line went dead.

"We get off in Pittsburgh," said McCann. "That'll be about nine in the morning. You'll be able to get all the sleep you want."

"Thank God," said Karine Collier, pushing the button that summoned room service.

A few minutes later came a knock on the door. Leaving the chain on, McCann opened the door. The white-toothed professional smile of an old, thin black man in a white jacket lit up the compartment. McCann removed the chain and bade him enter.

Karine ordered a shrimp cocktail, chateaubriand, baked potato, green beans, salad, apple pie, and ice cream. And a bottle of Remy Martin Napoleon cognac, with two snifters. McCann said that would be fine for him, too.

When he rolled in the table with their dinner, the old man asked whether they would like to order their breakfast now, so he could bring it when he made their wake-up call in the morning. Karine nodded and asked him to bring chilled fresh orange juice, ham and eggs over easy, whole wheat toast, a pot of coffee, and the *New York Times*.

"Make that two of everything," said McCann, seeing the waiter out the door and locking it after him.

Conversation during dinner was one-sided. McCann, for whom this was about the second nonprison meal in many months—aside from Russian food, which was even worse—downed each mouthful with visible pleas-

ure and left the talking to Karine Collier. She spoke of
her experiences in the prison and of the strange aberra-
tions she had encountered among the prisoners whose
psychological reformation had been in her charge—an
ax-murderer who specialized in probate lawyers, a
county road commissioner whose compulsive honesty so
alarmed local contractors that they got him imprisoned
on a trumped-up embezzling charge before they all went
broke, and a second-story man with a fetish for plastic
hair curlers. By the time they had finished dinner and
were working on one of the two bottles of cognac the
bemused white-jacket brought, she was into the story of
the traitor who stole a revolutionary microchip prototype
from Bell Labs and was showing it to prospective Russian purchasers, one of whom suddenly sneezed.

Keefe McCann sipped his cognac. "It disappeared?"

"Worse. The traitor, startled by the unexpected noise,
inhaled it, and by the time the FBI men who had been
following him intervened, the Russians were debating
the best way to carve him up to recover it."

McCann smiled sleepily. "It sounds as if you've had
some real beauties in your time."

"I have. But you, Keefe McCann, are the prize." She
rose from the chair opposite him, took his glass and set it
on the side table, and settled on his lap. She slipped her
arms around him and kissed him. It was like kissing a
cigar store Indian. Her lips parted and her tongue went
exploring. After some time it returned, her desire turned
to dust. She got up, glared down at him, and swung with
all her might.

The blow caught McCann on the cheekbone, and it
hurt. But he only smiled ruefully. "I guess I had that
coming."

"You certainly did, you cold-blooded bastard," she
hissed. "No man has ever humiliated me like that in my
life."

"That's because," sighed Keefe McCann, "they hadn't met Annabella Ames first."

And he told her the story of the girl from West Virginia and how, after their first lustful encounter, the charms of other women—even one so wonderfully endowed as Karine Collier—ceased to exist. He spoke of Annabella Ames with the reverential tones of an artist speaking of the luminosity of a Vermeer or the swirling subtleties of a Turner.

"So it isn't *me*," she said, her wounded pride somewhat salved by the only justification a woman can accept for a man's indifference. "You're in love."

McCann pondered. "Maybe that's the word. All I can tell you is that she burned me out like a scrap of paper under a blowtorch.

"Beautiful, you say?"

"Good-looking, in a West Virginia farm girl sort of way. Stacked. But not in your league by a country mile."

"Conversation?"

"I don't really know. We never talked about anything but the next roll in the hay."

"Spiritual qualities, then?"

McCann shook his head. "Spiritual qualities in Annabella Ames are about fifth priority, somewhere below conversation."

"Then what *is* her attraction, beyond the evident fact that she seems to be the best lay east—and west—of the Alleghanies?"

"What do you think I've been racking my brain about all these months in stir? Maybe she gave me a dose of the old mountain magic."

Maybe. Whatever it was, Karine Collier reflected, she didn't have it. The admission that she couldn't compete in love's lists with a barefoot, minimally attractive, probably illiterate hillbilly was a terrible blow to her self-

esteem and left her in a sour mood which kept her toss-
ing in bed until sleep, unlike McCann, finally came.

Karine Collier awakened, still depressed, the next
morning when a discreet knock on the door was followed by a voice announcing that breakfast had arrived
and that the train would be arriving in Pittsburgh in
just over an hour. Pulling the covers up about her,
she leaned over, unlocked the door, and removed the
chain.

The black steward of the night before rolled in the
table, covered with a starched white cloth and adorned
with a single red rose in a slender vase, and lifted the lid
of the chafing dish so that she could savor the aroma of
freshly cooked eggs and bacon. She put her finger to her
lips as a warning not to awaken her sleeping companion.
The steward smiled, nodded, and withdrew.

The three snifters of cognac she had drunk the night
before had left her furry-mouthed, and she finished off
both glasses of fresh orange juice and a cup of coffee
before McCann's nose began twitching. He rolled over
on his back and opened his eyes.

"Do I smell ham and eggs?" he said.

"You do, and if you want any, you'd better eat up.
We're due to pull in to Pittsburgh in approximately
thirty-five minutes."

Twenty minutes later, bathed and dressed, they were
sitting in the easy chairs watching the landscape stream
by.

"We'll be crossing the Ohio River soon," he commented. "When I was a kid, I rode a freight into Pittsburgh once. The cops were chasing me but a switchman
took pity on me and hid me in his shack under a pile of
coats."

Karine Collier said nothing. She stared unblinkingly
at the passing scenery.

"About last night," McCann said, looking at her from the corner of his eye. "I guess it must have been a shock to you, but it's nothing personal. I don't understand my reactions—my *lack* of reactions, I guess I should say—any more than you do."

She didn't move.

He turned to her, his eyes on hers. "Maybe if you bathed more often, brushed your teeth before going to bed, changed you skivvies every week or so . . ."

Not a tremor.

He shot out of his chair and kneeled before her. Her head sank slowly toward him as she seemed to try to bring him into focus. Her lips opened slightly, then closed again.

"Stand up!" McCann commanded.

It was a struggle, and she moved in exaggerated slow motion, as though she was neck-deep in molasses. But finally she was on her feet, unaided.

"Sit down!"

She slumped into the chair, her head a little to one side.

It wasn't a stroke; she wouldn't have been able to get out of the chair without assistance if it had been. But something had gone wrong with her central nervous system. She was sufficiently conscious to obey his commands, after a fashion, but she couldn't speak and couldn't focus her eyes.

Drugged.

It had to be the breakfast. And since he had eaten bacon and eggs, and toast and coffee, it had to be the juice, both glasses of which she had drunk. So that meant he was supposed to be drugged, too. For a moment he thought of seeking help, but ruled out the idea immediately. Whoever had attempted to drug him would be watching their door, just in case, as actually happened, he discovered something was amiss. They'd be armed. He wasn't.

The train was slowing down as it crossed the bridge over the Ohio River. Within two minutes they'd be in the station. Alone, he might smash out the window and make a run for it, but that would mean leaving Karine behind. On the other hand, Karine had been drugged, not killed. That suggested that whoever did it wanted them alive.

Alive for what? For questioning about what they had learned in the Soviet Union, obviously. They'd be taken to some remote and quiet spot where questions could be asked without any interference from nosy neighbors who might call the police if they heard screaming. That meant a reprieve, but only if he allowed his captors to believe that *both* he and Karine had been incapacitated.

The train slowed as it glided into the station. McCann heard voices in the corridor outside their compartment. He remained in his chair, his face expressionless, his eyes staring sightlessly out the big plate glass window. People came and went on the platform outside, their faces on a level with his. Then a man, walking slowly, stopped directly in front of him.

McCann kept his eyes straight ahead but could tell that the man wore a green trench coat, a red polka dot bow tie, and had a shock of black hair. That would be Holmes, the man the general said would be there to meet him. McCann was considering giving him a wink as a discreet sign of recognition when three other men eased up alongside him and joined him in scrutiny of the two passengers sitting motionless in their chairs.

And then they were gone.

Moments later McCann heard footsteps in the corridor. The door opened silently and the four men wedged inside.

"You two take the woman and their suitcases," a

voice said behind him, "and Tony and I'll handle Barkley."

Another voice came from the doorway: "Anything I can do?"

McCann recognized the voice as that of their steward. He was about to shout for him to call the police when the first voice replied: "Yes, take this damned wig and burn it."

Hands slid under his armpits and he felt himself being raised to his feet. As he was being maneuvered through the doorway, out of the corner of his eye he glimpsed the man in the red polka dot necktie. He was as bald as a politician's lie.

11. HARTSHORN
14 SEPTEMBER 2016

"Now, then, Dr. Hartshorn," a voice was saying to him, "we're going to walk down the corridor and off the train. By now your legs will feel as if they're encased in concrete, but don't worry . . . we'll help you."

That little speech gave Keefe McCann a great deal of information. They thought he was Dr. Hartshorn, which meant that his call to the general had been compromised. In any future contacts, if he managed to get out of this predicament, such knowledge might be useful. If they thought he was Dr. Hartshorn, that meant that they didn't have a clue as to his true identity or, by extension, that of Karine Collier. They wouldn't connect him with Keefe McCann, a man who changed identities the way other men changed socks.

He allowed himself to be steered through the doorway in the wake of the two men who held Karine Collier by each arm, along the passageway, and onto the platform, which was at the level of the train's vestibule. He was gently propelled along the platform, now nearly empty of passengers, toward the concourse. At the curb outside the station, he was sure, an ambulance or van and driver would be waiting. Once inside he would have no chance of escape against four armed men.

Armed? It stood to reason, though no weapons had

been displayed. If he was to get away he'd need a weapon, and he'd need it before he passed the last car of the train on the way into the terminal.

McCann, walking with the stiff-legged gait of a robot, stumbled, sagged, and went down in a heap. The men flanking him bent over to raise him. His arms flailed weakly, like those of a half-drowned man, but when they got him to his feet he took a quick step back. They heard the metallic *snick!* of a bolt being pulled back and released.

Too late the bald-headed man's hand shot to his armpit to find the shoulder holster empty.

"Everybody hold it right there," said McCann, the pistol's silencer peeping out beneath the raincoat draped over his arm.

Tableau.

The two men closest to McCann were within point-blank range. The others, with one hand carrying a suitcase, the other gripping Karine Collier's arm, were poorly positioned for a fast draw. None of the four, observing the steadiness of McCann's hand, considered this the time or place for a demonstration of valor.

"Here's what we're going to do," said McCann softly in Russian. "When I give the word, the two of you with Mrs. Hartshorn release her arms and put down the bags, keeping your hands down at your sides. Then you'll move toward the open door of that car. The other two will follow in lockstep. If anybody has visions of an Order of Lenin dancing before his eyes, Baldy here will get it first, right in the jollies. Anybody who hasn't understood what I'm saying can ask for a translation—when the gunsmoke clears. Now, in slow motion—*schlep!*"

The two Russians released Karine and set the bags

down carefully, as if they were loaded with rare crystal. They moved slowly toward the entrance of the car.

"Put your arms around each other's shoulders," McCann instructed. "Pretend you're friends." He calculated that four free hands could make only half the trouble of eight. They complied. He herded the four men into the car and through the open door of the first compartment they reached. Ordering them facedown on the floor, he lowered the venetian blinds over the tinted-glass window. He relieved them of their shoulder-holstered weapons, then made one of the Russians bind and gag the others with their belts and neckties before wrapping up the fourth man himself.

He glanced between the louvers of the lowered blinds. Karine was standing just as they'd left her. A man with a thin black mustache and an oily smile was talking earnestly to her, presumably offering to show her the thousand-and-one fascinating sights of Pittsburgh, but when she continued to favor him with her thousand-yard stare, he slunk off.

During the process of disarming and tying up the four men they had not uttered a sound. Nor did they appear at all dismayed. It was as if this were a minor deviation in their schedule which they would straighten out when they had tired of humoring their captor. It was unnerving, but not nearly so much as it had been for McCann when he had been *their* captive.

McCann stuffed the four automatics, Soviet-issue Tokarev 7.62mn nine-shots, into his overcoat pockets and picked up the telephone. He dialed the general's number.

The female voice he had heard before answered. "Hello?"

"This is Dr. Hartshorn."

"Oh, yes, Dr. Hartshorn. Did Mr. Holmes meet you as planned?"

"Not exactly. I was met by four Russians—the bald one wore a black wig and a red polka dot tie, by the way—who probably did something nasty to Mr. Holmes before the train pulled in."

"I see. And?"

"And they're taking ten."

"I see," said the woman. "So under the circumstances, I gather you do not need to speak with the general?"

"Correct." Whatever he had to say would be immediately relayed to the KGB resident at the Russian Embassy in Washington, as doubtless had been his earlier telephone call to the general.

"May I suggest that you move on without delay?" said the woman.

McCann nodded approvingly. "My thought exactly."

"As to future contact with the general, I shall place an ad in the personals column in the leading daily in the city where ... let me think ... ah, yes, in the city where you were engaged in water sports. The ad will be in your name, and list a telephone number. The general will answer. Now, I suggest you get the hell out of there—and good luck!" The phone went dead.

Closing the door behind him, McCann passed swiftly down the passageway and onto the platform where Karine Collier still stood, stiff as a store mannequin. Taking her by the arm, he hailed a passing redcap, instructing him to grab the bags and follow them. Walking as fast as Karine could move, he ignored the signs pointing to the taxi ranks and instead descended from the concourse to the subway. The Russians would probably have the surface exits covered, but it was unlikely that their precautions would extend to the underground.

"This is as far as I go, captain," said the redcap when they reached the turnstiles.

A $50 bill materialized in McCann's hand. The redcap allowed that in special circumstances he could make an exception to union rules.

They boarded the first train to rumble into the station. At the third stop McCann emerged from the train at the head of his entourage, ascended to street level, and helped Karine into a taxi. "What's the nearest private airport with an air taxi service?" he asked the driver.

The cabbie scratched his red-veined nose. "That would be the Irene Francis Day Airport. About thirty-five minutes from here."

"I have a hundred bucks says you can't make it in twenty-five."

The cabbie chuckled as he engaged gears and the taxi shot forward, slamming its passengers against the seat.

Half an hour later they were airborne. The plane was a four-place Piper 224, and they were following a flight plan which would bring them into Washington, D.C., in forty minutes. McCann occupied the copilot's seat.

They were six minutes out and climbing through thin cloud cover when McCann asked: "If your engines suddenly quit on you right now, what would you do?"

The pilot chuckled. "I wouldn't cream my jeans, if that's what you mean. This baby flies like a glider. Deadstick, I can slick it in on any reasonably hard surface where there's a couple of hundred feet clear for rollout. See that county road down there?"

McCann looked down and nodded.

"That's my emergency landing field."

"Good," said McCann, uncovering the pistol in his lap. "Because this is an emergency."

"Me and my big mouth." The pilot shook his head and cut back the twin throttles. He wasn't worried. The plane didn't belong to him and this guy didn't look particularly bloodthirsty. Besides, the yarn would be good for a week of free drinks when he got back to Pittsburgh.

"Write down your number," said McCann.

The pilot complied, and McCann folded the paper and shoved it in his pocket. "I'll see you're paid for the plane. If you take your time about reporting in—an hour or so will be ample—you could earn yourself a bonus."

As the pilot climbed out and slammed the door behind him, McCann gunned the engine and the plane roared down the dirt road and into the air.

At one thousand feet, McCann brought the Piper to a course of one hundred degrees, approximately the heading of Washington, D.C., and set the autopilot. He broke out the maps, computed his exact compass heading, checked his fuel reserve and engine settings, then shoved the plane's nose down and descended to tree-top level. There he'd disappear from FAA radar and probably be reported down. That would give them some breathing space. He then put the plane in a gentle turn, bringing the heading around to 176 degrees.

They were well across the Pennsylvania line when he heard a weak voice from the seats behind him: "Where are we going?"

"Ah, you are again among the living."

"I never lost consciousness. But until now my reflexes were haywire. It was in the food, wasn't it?"

"No—the orange juice."

"And those men—did you kill them?"

"Nah. I don't believe in blood sports."

"They'll come looking for us."

"Sure, but where I'm going it'll take a thousand years to find us."

"Where's that?"

"Volcano, West Virginia."

12. VOLCANO
14 SEPTEMBER 2016

AN HOUR OUT OF PITTSBURGH AND ON AUTOMATIC PILOT with the terrain avoidance gear set at 200 feet, the Piper 224 was skimming the hills and hollers of West Virginia, headed toward Volcano, 122 miles southeast of Clarksburg. The airways charts showed Volcano as having a concrete strip 3,600 feet long and a tower manned during daylight hours. At twelve miles out, according to the inertial navigation readout, McCann keyed in Volcano's tower-frequency VHF radio channel, identified himself, and requested landing instructions. Since no flight plan had been filed, he expected a query, to which he had the ready reply that he was on a routine cross-country flight and running low on gas. He was landing merely to refuel.

The tower did not reply.

He tried again, and a third time, but the tower remained mute. Its silence did not perturb McCann: in an era of very high fuel costs, many small-town airports had so little business that operations were virtually abandoned. All the better. The less fanfare, the less the risk of detection by people who might talk. For all practical purposes, Volcano, West Virginia, was as remote from Washington and international affairs as Launceston, Tasmania, but there was always a chance that even there the Russians had some free-lance taking his thirty rubles in return for information.

He was certain that Annabella Ames, whose mind was totally preoccupied with affairs south of the heart, would not be among them. That made her company all the more desirable, and he intended to partake of it copiously, as soon as he found a place to park the good Dr. Collier.

Three hundred meters out, the Piper cleared a low hill, banked smoothly to starboard, and settled down upon what must have been the runway, for it was the only level stretch of land in sight. Otherwise, it could have passed for rangeland, so lush were the grass and weeds growing out of innumerable cracks in the concrete. The plane slowed and eased forward on its nosewheel, the props making a banshee wail as they chewed twin paths through the underbrush. McCann cut back the throttles and taxied toward the tall latticework tower with the glassed-in booth on top.

The airport appeared deserted. McCann switched off the engines and helped Karine Collier down. He shouted a *hello!* which echoed back off the razorback hills surrounding the narrow valley. There was no answer. No sign of life came from the control tower and McCann was in no mood to climb the couple of dozen steps to confirm that it was empty. He took their two suitcases out of the baggage compartment and locked the aircraft's door. "Come on," he said to Karine Collier.

"Where to?"

McCann gestured with his chin to a weed-choked dirt road that undoubtedly led to Volcano. There he would register his traveling companion in the local hostelry and take off to spend a few relaxing hours with Annabella Ames while he decided what to do next.

Karine sighed, opened her bag, and replaced her high-heeled slippers with running shoes. According to the chart, Volcano was just under two miles from the airstrip. They started walking slowly down the dirt road winding through hills and valleys covered with stunted trees, waist-high brambles, sagging fences, and the musty odor of decaying undergrowth. A few birds chirping disconsolately in the bushes, and a mongrel dog which detoured around them and proceeded at a trot on an errand known only to himself, were the first indications that they were not the sole tenants of that bleak wilderness, but soon there were others.

They had gone only a quarter of a mile when they came upon an old woman squatting along the roadside. McCann had never seen a specimen of female humanity who more closely fit his conception of crone. She was right out of *Macbeth*— ancient, toothless, dressed in filthy rags, and with a predatory gleam in her rheumy eyes. She watched McCann and Karine Collier approach with a smile that somehow epitomized menace and evil, an impression in no way allayed by the sleek Dobermans sitting on either side of her, like statues hewn from obsidian. They were magnificent beasts, obviously worth more than the foul old female could make in a lifetime of rag-picking. What she was doing with such dogs they couldn't guess, for the creatures were as out of character as her jeweled headband and the leather briefcase of rich burgundy on which she rested her wrinkled arm, tattooed with dirt.

As they came abreast of her, she croaked: "Good-day to ya', Cap'n. And to you, Missy."

McCann and Karine returned her greeting civilly and asked if they were on the road to Volcano.

"'Deed you are, Cap'n. Can't miss it."

"Thank you."

"Name's Melanie."

"Thank you, Melanie."

"You're welcome, Cap'n," she said, and broke into raucous, unnerving laughter.

McCann and Karine hurried on without looking back.

Half a mile on, they were still shuddering as they thought of Melanie and her two watchdogs when they rounded a bend in the road and came upon her sister.

This one was fully as repulsive, emitted a disgusting aroma clearly discernible at ten paces, and had the same raucous voice, which volunteered that her name was Madeleine and that Volcano was just ahead. She, too, wore a jeweled headband, rested her arms on an expensive leather briefcase, and was flanked by dogs which followed their progress with unblinking eyes. Her dogs, however, were German shepherds, beautiful animals whose rigid immobility was testimony of training to stay —or slay.

"What kind of place *is* this? whispered Karine, when they were out of earshot.

McCann shook his head. He was as baffled and shaken by the appearance of the two old hags as she was.

Ten minutes later they came upon the first house. It had a swaybacked roof supporting a rusty satellite dish, unpainted siding shedding shingles, and a broken window replaced by a sheet of rain-warped cardboard. Surrounding the shack was a litter of abandoned artifacts—carcasses of automobiles, a broken-down refrigerator, a burned-out camper, a midden of tin cans, and other rubbish.

Rounding a curve in the road, they saw a depressing huddle of ramshackle buildings—a general store, an auto parts shop, a barbershop, a filling station, a feed store, and a funeral home. A mahogany casket in its gleaming glass showcase window alone gave evidence of human activity in Volcano, even if it was only dying. Strung out beyond, equally without sign of human life, was Volcano's residential section, two staggering lines of drab, dismal, decrepit houses glowering heavy-lidded at each other across the narrow dirt road. Though it was nearly noon, no sound could be heard except the sibilance of the dry wind hurrying to get out of town.

Karine Collier shivered. "What kind of place *is* this?" she asked again.

"Got me."

"But I thought you'd been here before. You said this Ames girl lives here."

"About four miles away. Here, I never got to come."

"Nothing left to spend, obviously."

McCann laughed, dryly. He turned toward the funeral home. "Let's see if anybody's alive in here."

He pushed open the door and entered. A dusty desk and blue-shaded lamp, a chair, a stack of boxes from a pharmaceutical company, and a few caskets on wooden sawhorses were the only furnishings, but light shone from the doorway to a room in the back. "Anybody home?" he called.

"*Two* of us, as a matter of fact," came a female voice from the back room. "Come on in."

McCann put down their bags and walked to the rear, followed by Karine Collier, who took one look and went right back the way she had come. The voice which had invited them in belonged to an elegant woman in her thirties with a long nose, lustrous dark eyes, and black hair done in a bun. Jodhpurs and polished leather riding boots showed beneath a blood-stained white plastic apron. She was putting the final stitches in the embalmed body of a man so emaciated he must have died of starvation.

"Well, *hello*," she said to Keefe McCann with a flashing smile that showed even white teeth. The big syringe she held in her rubber-gloved hand paused in midair. "Where in the world did you blow in from?"

"Landed at the airport."

"Engine trouble?"

"Yes, sort of."

"Well, that explains it. The weekly run isn't due back until after five o'clock."

"What run is that?"

The female mortician returned to her work. "Oh, supplies and things, you know. Volcano is very small, very out of the way. We have to send a truck out for the necessaries."

"My name's Kenneth L. Brent," said McCann, reviving the identity he had used as a sociology professor at the University of Chicago.

"Sylvia Crespi. I'm Volcano's mayor, undertaker, and liaison with the factory. You'll excuse me if I don't shake hands?"

"Of course."

"Tell me, Mr. Brent, didn't I see a woman come in with you?"

"My wife, Mrs. Brent. She has a weak stomach."

"She'll get used to it. After she's worked with me for a couple of weeks, it'll seem the most natural thing in the world. Besides, as my assistant, she'll get some very special privileges."

McCann laughed uneasily. "Very kind of you, but we're just passing through. We don't plan to stay long enough for Mrs. Brent to consider taking a job."

"Want to bet?" She stripped off her gloves and scrubbed her hands at a sink in the corner—which McCann was surprised to see was the same modern design as the sink used in the Midvale Sanitarium where he had practiced psychiatry. She dried her hands and hung up the apron on a nail. She walked to the back door and threw it open. "Look."

McCann looked, and what he saw made his knees turn to water. The broad grassy slope behind the mortu-

ary ran gently downhill for three hundred yards before
terminating on the banks of a meandering stream. The
whole area, the size of at least five football fields, was
filled with thousands of small white crosses laid out in
neat rows. Some fifty feet way, three crosses near the
building were planted at the head of mounds of fresh
earth.

"What the hell!" McCann gasped. A village the size of
Volcano couldn't produce that many bodies in a thousand years.

"More like heaven, you'd find, if you were able to
communicate with the men lying there." She smiled
wistfully.

"Men?"

"Mostly. Of course, women die, too, even in Volcano."

"You'll excuse me, Mrs. Crespi," stammered
McCann, panic seizing him by the throat, "but I just remembered that I have a spare set of manifold thermo-
couple baffles on the plane. Maybe while it's still light I
can . . ."

He stepped back, but instead of passing through the
open doorway, he felt something hard prodding him in
the right kidney.

"Hold it right there," a female voice behind him said.

"Oh, for God's sake, Marie," snorted Mrs. Crespi,
"stop dramatizing and put that shotgun down. Mr. Brent
isn't going anywhere, are you, Mr. Brent?"

McCann turned slowly. Facing him, the shotgun's
muzzle now pointed to the ground, was a woman in her
early fifties. Svelte and shapely, dressed in jeans, an
open shirt, and a scarf around her neck, her wind-blown
white hair arranged in a carefully casual fashion, Marie
was the woman every girl of twenty dreams of being if
she lives to be forty. Her worldly-wise violet eyes examined McCann. She smiled. It was the smile of a soft,

feminine, and happy woman. "Don't mind me, Mr. Brent," she said. "I used to do a little acting, and I guess I..."

"Marie Michaelson!" said McCann. He remembered her from the rerun of *The Countess of Monte Cristo.* She had been a stunning young actress in that film. A face as beautiful as hers was one he was not likely to forget.

"My dear," she said, putting out her hand and touching McCann's cheek gently, the gesture of a woman to a child who has just said something clever, "you don't know how gratifying it is to know that I am still remembered. And by such a handsome young man." She turned to Sylvia Crespi. "Can I have him, Sylvia...*please*?"

"You know the rules, Marie," said Mrs. Crespi sternly. "We'll have to examine the roster and see who has priority. You're fairly far down the list, I seem to recall, but if you really want him perhaps we can arrange it in exchange for a future draft choice. We'll take about it at dinner."

McCann grabbed the shotgun from Marie Michaelson's hands and snapped it shut. He didn't point it at either of the two women, but the menace was obvious. Except to them.

"You're not going to shoot anybody, Captain Haversham," said Sylvia Crespi.

"I hope not. I...hey! Where do you get this Haversham business? I told you my name is Brent. Kenneth L. Brent."

"It may well be, for all I know," she replied imperturbably. "But you called yourself Captain Martin T. Haversham and represented yourself to be an FAA check pilot the last time you landed in Volcano." She went to the desk in the room with the casket and took a file folder out of a drawer. She opened it and handed him several pictures of himself in the nude on a rumpled bed, fast asleep.

"Annabella Ames." McCann was possessed by a sudden feeling of dread. "Is she . . . ?"

"Dead?"

McCann's grip tightened around the stock of the shotgun.

"No," Sylvia Crespi laughed, "though it's not for want of trying. But it's only a matter of time. Every day she flirts with suicide—in her own fashion. She lives for and by the . . . ah . . . sword, and seems determined to *die* by the sword."

"What sword?"

"You—Captain T. Haversham, swordsman *sextraordinaire*— have to ask a question like that?"

13. F³
14 SEPTEMBER 2016

VIEWED FROM ANY PERSPECTIVE—DOWN ON THE MAIN street as he had first seen Volcano, or from the hills above —McCann decided it was nothing but a Potemkin village.

He recalled from his Russian studies that Grigoriy Aleksandrovich Potemkin, Prince of Tauris and lover of Catherine the Great, had constructed dozens of villages along the Dnieper, replete with gleaming facades and joyous, well-dressed peasants, to impress the Tsarina and her dipomat guests with the prosperity and happiness of her subjects as the royal party drifted down the river in a fleet of eighty-seven sumptuous barges. The villages were mostly fakes consisting of bare house- and shop-fronts, like props from a Hollywood Western. As for the "joyous" peasants, their clothing was stripped from them the moment the barges had glided past, then hurried overland to be donned by the serfs of the next village, in very temporary exchange for *their* rags. Potemkin's villages did their work well: Europe marveled at the wise and benevolent rule of Catherine the Great.

Volcano, too, was a Potemkin village, but with the opposite purpose in mind. At a dead end on a rutted township road, it was constructed to depress and repell any passerby who, lost on his way, happened upon the village. The gas pumps were empty, food at the "restaurant" nonexistent, store shelves innocent of goods, and houses bereft of people. No amenity survived to seduce the inadvertent visitor.

McCann, with the memory of all those fading wooden crosses in Volcano's cemetery fresh in mind, would have been glad to have gone back the way he had come, but Mayoress Sylvia Crespi counseled against any such rash move.

"Think back, Captain Haversham," she said, as the party of four saddled up their mounts in the stable behind the general store. "I'm sure you haven't forgotten your first trip to Volcano?"

Small chance. He'd remember those days and nights, filled with heat and passion, that had flown by in an erotic blur a little more than a year before, for all the days of his life. "In fact," he said, "if she hadn't forced me to leave before search-and-rescue found my plane and given me a bad case of coitus interruptus, I suspect my dying breath would have been drawn in Annabella Ames's arms."

"That was the idea—that you remain in Volcano until you drew your dying breath. With one important distinction: the last moments of men who die on the outside are almost invariably attended by sorrow. Yours would have been filled with ecstasy."

McCann threw the blanket over the back of the sorrel. "Would you mind backing up a little, Mrs. Crespi?"

"Dear Annabella," mused Mrs. Crespi as she fed her palomino a sugar cube. "You see, Captain, Annabella Ames is a rarity in today's Volcano—she was actually born and reared here. Most of our residents are from the outside—approximately 60 percent from beyond America's shores, in fact. Like the other denizens, she had no inkling of what actually went on at the plant on the other side of the hill. But when her father and mother died in an automobile accident three years ago, we decided to make her one of us, after a fashion.

"She agreed to make a pretense, at least, of continuing to farm her land. We would provide her with all the necessities—food, clothing, and any other amenities consistent with her situation as a young female rustic stuck in the hills of West Virginia. You see, her farm is on the perimeter of Volcano, on the only flat land except for our defunct airport, and we anticipated the possibility of a forced landing such as that which you made. Having Annabella there to deal with such situations made good sense."

"She agreed," said McCann, tightening the cinch under the sorrel's belly. "Agreed to what?"

"In return for continuing to occupy her farm, she was to have exclusive rights to any man—or men—who unwittingly wandered onto her property. And should none do so, we guaranteed her the services of a man from the Kama Pool five nights a week."

"Kama Pool—what's that?"

"It's for diving," said Marie Michaelson, laughing, "not swimming."

McCann looked at her blankly. "Anyway," he said, turning back to Sylvia Crespi, "what makes you so sure that 'any man' who wandered onto her farm would *want* to provide his services?"

"You did, didn't you?"

"Well, yes, but . . ."

"Is Annabella Ames beautiful?"

"Not exactly," admitted McCann.

"Does she come within a country mile of the beauty, grace, elegance, education, poise, and charm of your own wife, Captain Haversham?"

"She's goddamned sexy. Sexiest woman I guess I've ever run across."

"So sexy that you would willingly have stayed for-

ever. So sexy, in short, that since you bedded down with
her you have never since so much as laid a finger on
your lovely wife?"

"How the hell did you know that?" bristled Karine
Collier, who had been listening intently as she saddled
her horse.

"I know just about everything of the recent sexual life
of Captain Martin T. Haversham, Mrs. Haversham."
Sylvia Crespi mounted her palomino and led the way as
the four riders proceeded at a walk along a worn path
that switched back and forth up the side of the hill overlooking Volcano. Marie Michaelson brought up the rear.

Mrs. Crespi had already made perfectly clear to the
Havershams the futility of trying to escape. Melanie and
Madeleine were just two of the round-the-clock guards
who commanded all approaches to Volcano. Their appearance frightened off most unwanted visitors, and
their trained man-hunting dogs were capable of dealing
with the rest. The woman in the airport tower—who had
heard their radio call but did not acknowledge it—had
alerted Melanie and Madeleine and the other sentinels
via the two-way UHF set each carried in her leather
briefcase that visitors had arrived at the strip even before
the Piper's wheels had touched down. Once the visitors
were within the security cordon, there was no way out.

"You must often have wondered," said she to
McCann as their horses mounted the rocky path, "what
mysterious hold Annabella Ames has over you."

"You can say that again."

"It's simple: she F-cubed you."

"F-cube? What the hell's that?"

"The code name we use in Gland Junction for the Ful-
minating Fornication Pheromone, also rather irrever-
ently called the Frenzied Fucking Factor."

"Pheromones." said Keefe McCann thoughtfully.

"Pheromones. *Of course*! Why the hell didn't I think of that?"

"Because you were submerged beneath the waves of passion. After all, it seldom occurs to drowning men to speculate on the chemical composition of water, does it?"

Behind them Karine Collier said plaintively: "What the hell are you people talking about, anyway?"

"Would you care to enlighten your wife, Captain Haversham?" said Mrs. Crespi.

"I can try, although I don't know a hell of a lot. Pheromones are organic compounds, part of the reproductive apparatus of the lower orders, mainly insects, although there has been some suspicion that certain humans still retain vestiges of pheromonic activity."

"Really?"

"So the scientists claim. At some time in one's life, it happens to most everybody. You walk into a crowded room, a noisy cocktail party, say, and suddenly across the room your glance locks in on some woman, and at the same instant, almost as if you turned a switch, her eyes meet yours. You know, without a word passing between you, that you share the overwhelming desire to leap into bed together and pull down the curtain on the world for two weeks. Chemistry, we always called it. And that seems to be precisely what it is: pheromones, complex molecules wafting from the female to some receptive male on her wavelength, and then—bingo!"

"Very good," said Mrs. Crespi. "Very good, indeed, Captain. In our laboratory in Volcano, work on pheromones has been going on for the past quarter century. It started as a means of pest control. For instance, the gypsy moth, which once wiped out millions of acres of our forests annually, is controlled by a powerful pheromone excreted by the female. Called glypure, this pheromone is so potent that about one twenty-millionth of a billionth of a billionth of a gram—just a few hundred molecules—can cause the male to go into copulatory spasms. We used glypure to bait traps, and lo!—no more gypsy moth. The cockroach possesses a similarly powerful pheromone, which is why both the cockroach and the gypsy moth are on the endangered species list, since our laboratories licensed the synthetic analogues which went into production fifteen years ago."

Karine Collier sniffed. "Nonsense. The anatomy and physiology of cockroaches and gypsy moth have absolutely no relation to that of humans."

"True," said Mrs. Crespi, "but there is plenty of evidence that the phenomenon is shared by both plants and many higher animals. Certain trees attacked by insects release a pheromone which, carried downwind, causes other trees of the same species to manufacture an insect-specific repellant. The dog who marks his territory by lifting his leg at a fire hydrant does so with a pheromone. The rhinoceros, which has notoriously bad eyesight, would probably try to mate with an acacia tree or a cruising Range Rover if it wasn't for the pheromone in the female's dung and urine which attracts him to her. Male monkeys mate with the female exhibiting the highest degree of hormonal activity, as determined by density of pheromone release, thus producing offspring from the genetically hardiest specimens. And then there's the squirrel monkey, which displays an erect phallus in greeting, courtship, aggression, and other kinds of social interaction. But sever the glands governing pheromone release and no erections occur."

"Captain Haversham is not a squirrel monkey," Karine Collier pointed out stiffly.

"He's a prisoner of his glands all the same," Mrs. Crespi insisted. "During the past twenty-four years there have been revolutionary discoveries at the lab just beyond the hill we're now ascending. For example, we found that some women exude a pheromone, and that some men are capable of detecting it. After many attempts, our predecessors synthesized the pheromone. This pheromone is detected by the human male by means of the vomeronasal organ, a vestigial apparatus that runs from the nose to the brain. Man's vomeronasel organ is analogous to the tongue of a snake, which picks up molecules of a prey's scent by darting its tongue into the air and conveys the signal to the brain by electrical impulse, and is there identified."

"Yes, this is all interesting," said Karine. "But are you telling me that this Annabella Ames girl was given this human pheromone to snare my husband?"

"To snare *any* man who intruded on the precincts of Volcano, West Virginia. She was supplied with a few nanomilligrams of the nonspecific pheromone, which would bring a man running from half a mile around. Do you recall how she dabbed at your bloody nose with a square of gauze when you first landed your plane, Captain Haversham?"

McCann nodded.

"The gauze was impregnated with F-cubed."

"And the men?" queried Keefe McCann.

Sylvia Crespi smiled enigmatically.

Keefe McCann suddenly felt cold. He remembered all those crosses down in the valley behind the mortuary. If Annabella Ames had not insisted that he return the rented Cessna before a search party located it, he would eventually have died of simple exhaustion, as did the rest of those poor devils buried beneath that field of crosses. It was a subject he didn't want to think about. "But she let me go."

"Yes," said Mrs. Crespi sadly. "That was unauthorized procedure. With the pheromone we supply a neutralizing acid, to be used, when, for example, one of us leaves Volcano to scout new male talent. When we find

the man we want, we apply the pheromone, and the man
—men, usually—come along as fast as their little feet
will carry them. Annabella foolishly fell in love with you,
Captain Haversham. That disturbed her judgment, and
she allowed you to leave without authorization. She admitted that she diluted the neutralizing agent sufficiently
to leave your desire for her intact yet not so much that
you couldn't tear yourself away. You may recall that she
put a fresh Band-Aid on your injured nose. It had been
treated with the neutralizing agent and effaced the
strongest effects of the pheromone. Otherwise, you
would have been back before nightfall."

"Where is she now?"

"Just where you left her—in her cabin beyond the
airstrip."

"When can I . . . ah . . . see her?"

"We'll have to give that some thought, Captain. I'm
not sure that reuniting you with Annabella would be
wise."

So *that* was the way it was going to be. Well, they
didn't know Keefe McCann if they thought a pair of females was going to keep him from getting to Annabella
Ames.

McCann studied the odds. His lady's home companion of the future might be ordained by Mrs. Crespi, but
his present mount at least was four-legged. He could
snatch the shotgun from the scabbard hanging from the
pommel of Marie Michaelson's saddle. If the dogs came
after them, he could shoot two and probably club the
other two cross-eyed before they could do either him or
Karine Collier any harm.

Sylvia Crespi observed him glancing sideways at the
firearm. She smiled. "Please don't, Captain. The dogs
are the least of the problem. The spark plugs from your
plane have also been removed. Besides, you'd never
make it as far as your plane in any case."

"Why not?"

"Do you see this?" She held up a little round box, the size and shape of a woman's compact. "It's a transmitter. I have only to open it, or drop it, and a signal is emitted. The signal ruptures one of those rhinestones on the headbands of the delicious Melanie and Madeleine and the others. The most powerful pheromone we've developed saturates their skin. Any man within a twelve-mile radius will be drawn to the nearest of them like iron filings to a magnet. And . . ."

"And?" McCann's heart was racing.

"Finders keepers."

14. PITTSBURGH CENTRAL
14 SEPTEMBER 2016

THE SLEEPING CAR ATTENDANT WAS MAKING THE rounds of the compartments of passengers debarking at Pittsburgh in search of forgotten items which, like the retainer from the man whom he believed to be working for the CIA, kept him in comfortable circumstances. He earned a bonus for such chores as he performed before breakfast that morning. In this case it involved merely putting a powder in the orange juice of the couple in compartment B-9. They had been ticketed to New York but would be getting off, so his Chicago contact told him, in Pittsburgh.

In Pittsburgh he learned that a glitch in the signal system ahead would hold the train in the station for at least an hour. Accordingly, he took his time about tidying up the newly vacated compartments C-1 and C-8 before finally unlocking the door of C-10. It needed tidying up, too: two bound men lay facedown on the floor while a third was wrestling with the knots of the rope binding the fourth. This was a matter for the police. The old man started to back out, but the one man whose hands were free seized him by the neck and dragged him into the compartment, locking the door.

He gagged and bound the old man and resumed untying the others. "Should I strangle him?" he asked in Russian, as Artur Artusov rose to his feet, massaging his wrists.

Artusov shook his head and made a mental note to have Kamenetskiy transferred. He was obviously one of those agents who thought his job was to kill anyone who made a mistake, or got in his way, or wore a necktie he didn't like. To be sure, that had been the way of the KGB in years past. But times had changed. The leadership had come to realize that a human being was a precious commodity, that resources of the state—food, shelter, education, medical care, military training—were expended on every one of them. To wantonly kill such useful instruments of the state's will was sheer stupidity and the grossest waste. One didn't strangle cows or shoot Chevrolets or burn wheat fields. Kamenetskiy would have to learn this simple truth.

Leaving the car attendant, Artusov, a man whose bland, forgettable face was a major asset as resident head of the KGB's American operations, walked without haste off the train and through the station to the ambulance parked at the entrance. He climbed into the front seat next to the driver while his three assistants crowded into the back. "Pittsburgh Central," he commanded.

Artusov wasn't worried that he wouldn't find the pseudonymous Commander Waldron Barkley or Dr. Julius R. Hartshorn or whoever he was before the American spy could reach Washington. First, as a last-ditch defense, he would fashion a cordon around Washington. Within half an hour agents and MIT officers in mufti would be at every bus and train station and airport serving the nation's capital, with pictures in hand of Barkley and his wife which Artusov would fax the moment he reached Pittsburgh Central at 211 Mellon Plaza, where the KGB maintained two floors of offices under cover of the local Soviet MIT mission.

Artusov strode through the outer room of the KGB

offices devoted to ransacking current scientific literature and scavenging information which would be useful to Russia and down the carpeted hall to the offices of the administrator. He pressed his palm on the ID plate and entered.

"Comrade Artusov!" said a handsome, middle-aged man in elegant tailoring, rising behind his glass desk and extending his hand. It wasn't often that Levitskiy had the honor of welcoming the Soviet's KGB chief in the United States who, based in New York, was ostensibly director of Soviet MIT personnel.

Artusov shook hands, walked to the wall map of the eastern United States, and in short, incisive commands ordered the deployment of the dragnet to intercept Barkley and his wife before they could reach the mysterious "general."

Vladimir Levitskiy was shocked to discover that their quarry had escaped, but careful not to let it show. He was afraid to ask what had gone wrong, for fear the operation had been botched by one of his men, in which case the ax would fall on *his* neck. But Artusov soon put him at ease.

"It was all my fault," Artusov said, when orders had been passed down the line and, for a moment, they could consider the next step. "Either that, or we're dealing with a very clever man." He sat down on the couch opposite the administrator's desk, lit a cigarette, and sipped the tea his host had just poured from the pot atop a big silver samovar on his office bar.

"We must, of course, assume that he is clever," responded a very relieved Levitskiy. "But must we also assume that, knowing he is being pursued, he will again try to contact this "general," whoever he may be."

Artusov pulled his nose and looked out across the city toward the soaring bridges at the confluence of the Allegheny and Monongahela rivers. "That's question one, certainly. You have the transcript of the telephone call?"

"Right here," said Levitskiy, producing it.

They studied it together.

"What it tells us is little more than it tells the general," commented Artusov. "It doesn't actually say the mission was successful, only that Barkley did 'everything possible.' 'Did you bring home any souvenirs?' the general inquires. 'What I have, you'll want to see,' replies Barkley. All in all, a vague report, though encouraging in tone. It certainly won't reassure the general that the mission was a complete and unqualified success, and no one will realize that better than Barkley himself. Oh, yes, he'll try to get to Washington, all right." He paced the length of the room, his eyes on the carpet, deep in thought. "It would help a great deal if we knew the identity of this general. It would be much easier to isolate one man from Barkley than an entire city."

Levitskiy knew better than to alibi. Artusov was a just man, but he was satisfied with nothing less than results. He pressed a button. "Genadiy Yefimovich," he said into the intercom, "what's the story on the number Hartshorn called from the train?"

"We're getting close, sir," came the reply. "Half an hour after our intercept we learned that it was an accommodation number that Dr. Hartshorn called. But it was routed through half the telephone exchanges in the United States, and the last three numbers it automatically tripped in sequence are changed daily. We've tracked down two of them and . . . hold on, sir." They heard a whispered conversation, and then Genadiy's voice again: "That call was routed to a telephone somewhere in the Atomic Yields Estimates Service headquarters. It may take a while to determine just which one."

"Very well. Stay on it."

Artusov nodded. "I thought so. The general is Admiral Ricardo Rivera Handy."

"Are you sure?"

"As sure as I am that Barkley is not one of Handy's regulars. We've got so many plants growing in the hallways at AYES that the place looks like an Amazonian rain forest. Poor Handy is running out of agents. Every time he sends someone to Moscow I've been forewarned weeks in advance, and all I have to do is pull him in as soon as I discover who his local Russian contacts are."

"That simplifies our problem," Levitskiy observed. "We watch Handy. And if for any reason we fail to intercept Barkley before he makes contact, we can always kill him when they meet. Always providing that you will authorize a Class One disposition."

Artusov nodded.

Levitskiy burned to know what threat Barkley presented to Russia was of such magnitude that General Lieutenant Artur Artusov not only supervised the hunt personally but did not even vaguely intimate the area of Russian national security Barkley's information jeopardized. But such questions were not asked, at least not by men like Vladimir Levitskiy, whose zeal and diplomatic talents had led to his promotion to head KGB's Pittsburgh regional operations. All he knew was that Artusov had arrived in Pittsburgh several hours before in pursuit of one Dr. Julius R. Hartshorn, alias Commander Waldron Barkley, and his wife; that Hartshorn/Barkley possessed information that must not reach Admiral Handy; and that he, Vladimir Levitskiy, had better make no mistakes.

A light blinked on Administrator Levitskiy's console. "Yes?"

"We've had word from Andrei's team, sir. They located the redcap who carried the Barkley's bags when they took the underground to Graham station."

"Go on."

"The redcap said he returned to the station and didn't see where they went. But considering Barkley expected to be met at the station, it was very likely that he took a cab at Graham. Andrei's got men talking to the taxi dispatchers now."

"Very well."

Artusov and Levitskiy sat in silence. The machine was in motion. All they could do now was wait.

Five minutes later the light blinked again.

"Sir, we've traced them to the Irene Francis Day Airport, a satellite field outside Pittsburgh with an air taxi service. The Barkleys took off just now for Washington in a Piper twin-engined plane."

Levitskiy went to the map, measured off distances with calipers, and flipped on his intercom.

"Have our men at all airfields in the Washington area be on the lookout for the Piper, whose registration number you will relay to them. They are to use their MIT credentials aggressively if American officials try to interfere. They will be prepared to move instantly on word from us. When it is determined where the Barkleys intend to land, everyone will head for that airfield as backup to the team on the spot. The Barkleys are to be taken alive if at all possible, but if there is the slightest chance they may escape, they are to be killed at once. Discreetly, of course. All stations acknowledge."

Artusov said nothing. He went to the wall map and studied it. Washington would be half an hour to forty minutes away in a twin-engined plane. But there was always the possibility that Barkley might decide on a more prudent course than landing at Washington itself. A careful man like him would land some distance away and then drive into Washington. It would take longer, but the heavy traffic would provide protective coloration. He walked over to Levitskiy's desk. "Is the scrambler secure?"

"Yes, sir."

"Get the AmerOps deputy director's office in Moscow."

Levitskiy pressed two buttons. "Go ahead, sir."

"This is Artusov," he said to the deputy director's assistant in Moscow, who reported that the deputy director was at home sleeping. "We have learned that a twin-engine Piper with Barkley and wife has just taken off from Irene Frances Day Airport outside Pittsburgh. I'd appreciate satellite surveillance of the Piper, with frequent reports to Pittsburgh Central.

"At once, sir."

Artusov broke the transmission. "I'm going after them . . ." he told Levitskiy. "Lay on the Boeing STOVL at Pittsburgh International for Departure the moment I arrive. Have another sixteen of your best men meet me there at once. Relay all messages from Moscow to the plane. I'll be on the flight deck."

"Yes, sir."

Twenty-five minutes later Artusov and his twenty-three assistants were airborne. By then, word had come from Moscow via Pittsburgh Central that the Piper had altered course, from a southeasterly heading which would take them to Washington to a course south by west, toward the Allegheny Mountains of West Virginia. Artusov, in the cockpit's right seat, ordered the pilot to a course of south by west.

Twelve minutes later came word from Pittsburgh Central that the Piper 224 had landed near a hamlet called Volcano in the state of West Virginia.

The pilot turned to Artusov, his eyebrows raised in interrogation.

Artusov nodded.

15. GLAND JUNCTION
14 SEPTEMBER 2016

THE TRAIL BEHIND VOLCANO LED UPWARD ACROSS HILLS and valleys thick with stunted trees and scraggly undergrowth but apparently utterly devoid of human life. In that remote corner of Appalachia one could wander for days without encountering a fellow human being, which was precisely what made Volcano so appealing to the administrators of Gland Junction, as the hidden complex was known to its inhabitants.

Keefe McCann, having seen the dimensions of the graveyard, realized that Gland Junction must be a sizable establishment. That meant, among other things, a system of supply—roads, trucks, warehouses, and workers. He saw no sign of any such things.

"This research facility you say you have here," said Keefe McCann, "must be pretty small potatoes."

"What makes you think so?" replied Sylvia Crespi.

"Well, Volcano is barely large enough to rate a place on the map, according to my flight chart."

Sylvia Crespi shook her head. "Your flight chart is in error. Gland Junction's population runs into the hundreds."

"Then how do you supply all those people?" said McCann. "If this Gland Junction place is as big as you say, it must take tons of supplies every day to keep it

137

going. And all that stuff isn't going to be brought in on horseback over a mountain trail."

"True. Everything comes by truck. A helicopter would be too conspicuous. But the trucks turn off the I-21A exit on the other side of the mountain and unload at a warehouse. The supplies are then hauled in at night by surface-effect transporters."

"Can't wait to see the place," said McCann without enthusiasm. He couldn't get that graveyard off his mind.

"Then you're not looking. It's dead ahead."

McCann perceived nothing but the entrance to a cave —shrouded with vines, dripping with the runoff of a vagrant mountain spring, yawning and forbidding. But his horse followed the others into the darkened interior without urging, and suddenly it was dark no more. Behind them steel doors *woosh*ed shut across the entrance, overhead lights sprang on, and they looked down a concrete-lined corridor leading to the stables. There they dismounted. Two heavily muscled young men in green coveralls came to lead the horses away. They greeted the four arrivals perfunctorily and with what appeared to McCann an abstracted and somewhat anxious air. They slapped the rumps of the horses, urging them into their stalls, and fell to with currycombs as though competing to see who would finish first.

"What's their hurry?" asked McCann.

"They belong to Countess Soraya Peshtavi. Whoever finishes first gets the next crack." She laughed huskily.

"Are you telling me women here get *two* men?"

"No," replied Marie Michaelson, her eyes boring into his. "They get *six*. And in the case of women with exceptionally active libidos, more. Muslims believe that it is the duty of four wives to keep one man happy. They've got the principle right, but their proportions are a little mixed up."

"Or upside down," Sylvia Crespi broke in, "Gland

Junction began on the democratic one-man-on-one-woman principle but in practice it soon became apparent that such a ratio is contrary to nature. We doubled the ratio of men to women, then doubled it again. But not until we reached the figure of six men for each woman did we achieve a relative equilibrium, although, as Marie points out, some exceptional women—she happens to be among them, by the way—require more. Until we determined the proper ratio, attrition was very high."

"Yes," said McCann grimly. "I noticed all those crosses in the cemetery down there."

The women laughed.

"You poor dear!" said Sylvia Crespi, patting him on the arm. "You were worried that you'd be diddled to death and planted to fertilize the zucchini?"

"Something like that."

"No, no—we *conserve* our assets here. Men at Gland Junction are like prize cows—we feed them the most nutritious fare, see that they have the proper amount of exercise—generally in a horizontal position—and milk them only at carefully regulated intervals. With such care, we expect them to last for a long, long time."

"But those crosses . . ."

"Well, occasionally a man—sometimes even a woman—*does* succumb to the exertions of the moment, mostly by heart attack. But those crosses are mainly stage props. We put them there in full view of the road so that anyone passing through will immediately connect the immense graveyard with empty houses and keep right on going. We have too good a thing going for us here to want to share it with the world."

"I'm here," McCann pointed out.

"Correction—you've *returned*. Come on, let me show you around your new home."

As they walked down the carpeted corridors branching off like a maze from the entrance, Sylvia Crespi briefly described the history of Gland Junction since its foundation in 1998. As the Center for Macromolecular Research, its mission was to investigate pheromonic phenomena among plants and insects, to isolate pheromones from the various species, to elaborate strategies for the use of pheromones in combating insect pests, and to synthesize these pheromones for use as pesticides in commercial quantities.

A private company, it was situated far from cities for the best of reasons: the research had potential applications to national defense—if the stuff they manufactured could kill roaches and moths, it might be useful in chemical warfare, and the farther away it was from the Soviet spies that descended en masse after the Russo-American Cultural Agreement of 1992, the better. Also, if something went wrong and the powerful substances they would produce got into the atmosphere or groundwater, the damage would be minimized by the installation's isolation.

Pheromones were a risk whose potency was fully appreciated. An amount sufficient to fill a demitasse cup could destroy the ecosystem of an entire continent by disrupting natural cycles with unforeseen consequences. Every safeguard would have to be observed and every possible consequence explored before any pheromone, no matter how promising, was released in nature. Research facilities were designed with fail-safe vapor hoods, high-pressure autoclaves, automation, clean rooms, incinerators, and other devices to protect the workers and researchers.

A natural cavern in the hills of West Virginia best answered the CMR's rigid specifications. It was remote, yet near enough to Washington and New York for visits and consultation. The physical confinement offered by a natural cave gave the architects who designed the CMR assurance that access and egress, for air and waste materials as well as for people and supplies, could be tightly controlled.

"Of course," said Sylvia Crespi, as she led Karine Collier and Keefe McCann through the fluorescent-lit green hallways of the research center, "like most companies with a hot idea for molecular manipulation, CMR grew fast. In the first eighteen months it produced a pheromone that attracted the coyote, a most elusive predator, and within two years there wasn't a single coyote left to molest the sheep anywhere in the American West. In gratitude, the senators from Wyoming, Montana, and Nevada became godfathers to CMR, and thereafter financing basic research became no problem."

The modest laboratory, according to Sylvia Crespi, grew to become a whole complex of labs investigating not only the pheromones of insects, plants, and the lower animals, but those of higher animals as well, including, finally, the primates.

"Our three living levels encompass spacious, comfortable, individual apartments for the women, and the dormitory level, where fourteen men share quarters. Two men in each dormitory room are on light housekeeping duty and prepare fortifying dinners for their roommates. Those who really excel get to cook for the women."

"Wonderful," commented McCann wryly. He recalled his days as *chef de cuisine* at Le Perigot in New Orleans and wondered how the women would like his cajun cooking. But his mind kept wandering back to Annabella Ames and how he was going to get out of this male cathouse and back into her hot embrace. Then he remembered Madeleine and Melanie, and shuddered. As Sylvia Crespi had told him, the question of his getting back to her would require some thought.

Their tour had apparently brought them to the upper level, which had a spacious balcony overlooking a putting course. In the distance under the cavern's roof, lit like daylight by lamps suspended from the ceiling, two women were playing a languid game of tennis on one of the four courts. Sylvia Crespi waved Karine Collier and Keefe McCann to a table where they had a panoramic view of the recreational facilities. The underground complex had been designed by a skilled landscape architect, with smooth green lawns, running streams, and palm trees. Beyond the tennis courts a swimming pool was under construction, and to one side was a vegetable garden producing mostly wilted leaves, apparently because the denizens of Gland Junction had better ways to spend their time. But where were all the people?

When McCann asked, Sylvia Crespi shrugged. "I'm afraid most of the women here are television junkies. There's a 120-inch television screen in each woman's apartment, in the ceiling over her bed, and several strategically placed projectors. So a woman with an inert man at her side and a heart going pit-a-pat for New Ideas need only punch in the number of any other apartment on her bedside remote control and she gets to witness action in full color, sometimes with a cast of thousands. Coffee, tea, or something stronger?" Sylvia asked her guests, as they sat in comfortable bamboo chairs around a big glass table.

"Scotch for me, please," said Karine Collier, who had kept a thoughtful, diplomatic silence. She had no idea where she stood in the present scheme of things and thought it wise to be silent until she received some hint.

"The same, only double," said McCann, who knew only too well the fate in store for him.

"Only this once" said Sylvia tolerantly. "The usual for us," she told the bronzed young man who came out to take their order. His arms and shoulders bulged his starched white jacket and trousers like those of a decathlon champion, but he was destined to be restricted for the rest of his days to the pole vault and broad jump.

"I don't mean to pry," said McCann, "but there are a few things I don't understand."

"Pry as much as you like," Sylvia Crespi returned. "Why not? Men never leave here, and women depart only to bring back more men, so there's no danger of a security leak. What puzzles you, Captain Haversham?"

"First of all, this is an expensive installation. Who's picking up the check, and with what?"

"Dr. Josephine Caldwell is the managing director of Gland Junction, and, not at all incidentally, the scientist chiefly responsible for synthesizing the first human pheromone. We'll introduce you to her in a day or two. But of course the human pheromone is not marketed. Our cash flow—and it is considerable—comes from the licensing of just two pheromones. Have you heard of Roach-No-Mo?"

"Sure."

"The pheromone that it contains is manufactured here and shipped out at the rate of four gallons a month, sufficient to produce 1,500 tons of roach killer. And our rodenticide Rat-Gat has just about rid American cities of the brown rat, and we're making good progress on working on a similar lure for the black rat. We observe strict precautions in delivery of these substances so that the manufacturers never know their source; we send everything by air express, from a different city each time. And the payment is handled through a Swiss bank. Does that answer your question?"

"But where do your *people* come from? We've seen twenty or thirty women so far, and all but a couple are knockouts."

"And the men aren't exactly repulsive, either," sighed Karine Collier.

"Those who *aren't* knockouts—and we do have a few—" Sylvia Crespi admitted, "are all holdovers from the days before Dr. Caldwell discovered F³. Once the pleasant powers of the pheromone were revealed here in the CMR, everybody naturally wanted to test it—with predictable results. The ensuing decade saw a sharp attrition due to impurities in the early batches of pheromone. Those who were not originally in excellent physical condition are no longer with us. Since then the product has been refined and there are no longer any observable side effects.

"Dr. Caldwell, on her trips to the outside, began to recruit the most lovely young women she could find. The union of handsome with beautiful appealed to her esthetic sense. Finding strong, handsome men was even easier: new female members usually choose their own on later shopping expeditions. Today we have 188 beautiful, elegant, charming, rich, and well-bred—especially well-bred—women in their twenties and thirties from seventeen countries around the world, and, at latest count, about 1,140 men devoted to women's pleasures—wholly. Some 300 are on hold, awaiting assignment."

Karine Collier's eyes widened.

"Would you like to see them?" said Marie Michaelson, who realized she suddenly had the opportunity to relieve Mrs. Haversham of her husband.

"Why, I . . ."

"I'll be right back," said Miss Michaelson, rising.

She returned a minute later bearing two large looseleaf albums, and opened one on the table before Karine.

"These are the new arrivals awaiting assignment," she explained.

Each page bore full-face and profile color photographs of a naked man, along with a brief resume of his background, sexual preference, and endurance. Karine turned the pages slowly, her face flushed as she examined the photographs and read the text beneath.

Keefe McCann glanced at a couple of the pictures, smiled as he watched Karine Collier absorbed in their perusal, and shrugged. With all those new playthings staring her in the eye, she had ceased to be his problem. He could now devote his energies to Annabella Ames, and God knew he'd built up a powerful head of steam in the past fourteen months in prison that cried for relief. "Okay, what about Annabella Ames? When do I get to see her?"

"I'm afraid letting you go to Annabella would violate Gland Junctions's rules of engagement, Captain," said Sylvia. "You can freely move around within the complex until the fifteenth, the day after tomorrow, when we make the semi-monthly draft of new arrivals. The rule is that whatever woman is shorthanded gets first choice, just as they do in professional football. The lucky man is first administered a neutralizer which absolutely obliterates any previous emotional attachments, then the receptor pheromone which corresponds to the particular female pheromone transuded by the woman who chooses him. That binds him to her unless and until she wishes to share or trade him, when a neutralizer is applied."

Neutralizer, thought McCann. If I can somehow find where it's kept, I can make myself immune to any...

"The neutralizer, by the way, is in the sole possession of Dr. Caldwell," Sylvia went on. "She personally applies it, just before the man's new patroness administers her own individual pheromone. After that, even if you wanted to use the neutralizer, you wouldn't, Captain—remember your irresistible attraction to Annabella."

Keefe McCann bit his lip, pondering the possibility of direct action.

Sylvia Crespi shook her head. "Forget it, Captain. Dr. Caldwell lives in relative seclusion with seven young men who, I need not tell you, *adore* her. No man enters or leaves her suite without her permission. If you made the attempt, the faithful seven would tear you to bits."

Karine Collier emptied her drink and took a deep breath. "And what about me?" Her hand rested on the picture of a spectacularly handsome young man with wavy blonde hair and the body of a Greek god.

"You?" Sylvia smiled. "A woman of your beauty must cause many heads to turn on the outside. Here, you are one among many. Still, there are compensations."

"Such as?"

"Well, if you decide to join our merry throng—and I really cannot imagine a woman who would not—you are permitted first pick among the 300-odd waiting assignment, as the first of your quota of six."

"Any man?"

"Any man at all."

"I'll take him," she said, pointing.

Sylvia Crespi looked at Christine Collier in wonderment. What kind of woman was this? With a choice among 300 of the most handsome and virile men in America, she had picked her own husband.

16. RUE BLISS
14 SEPTEMBER 2016

"WELL, WELL, *WELL*," MELANIE CROAKED WITH DE-
light. "What a fine body of men."

Two dozen of them, at rough count, were headed her
way down the same path on which the handsome man
and the lovely woman had appeared less than an hour
before. She had been alerted to the arrival of both con-
tingents by the tower sentry, who had, in accordance
with instructions, given no indication that the tower was
womaned. The ears of the Dobermans came to attention
as the file of men, most of them thickish about the
shoulders, stern of mien, and all in business suits and
looking like unsuccessful door-to-door salesmen,
rounded the bend in the dirt road. She calmed the dogs
with gentle reproach.

The man in the lead spotted Melanie first and strode
up to where she crouched, but not so close that the fleas
which obviously infested her raddled body would desert
her for greener pastures. "Good afternoon, madam,"
said Artur Artusov civilly.

"And good afternoon to you, young man," she replied, showing a yard of blackened gum. "And where
might all you handsome young men be going?"

"Volcano, I hope. Are we on the right road?"

"Oh, yes. Around here, all roads lead to Volcano."
She cackled with insane laughter. "But none lead out."

Artusov let that lie. Old women always spoke in epi-
grams. "Fine looking dogs you have there."

"Alpha and Omega they're called."

Artusov nodded pleasantly and walked on. Alpha and
Omega. Beginning and end. Whose beginning and whose
end he did not inquire, although before the day was finished he began to wish he had.

Farther down the road the silent party encountered
Madeleine, where a similar colloquy took place. After
they passed on, Artusov took the small two-way radio
from his lapel pocket. The coincidence of two foul old
women along the road, each with a pair of pedigreed
dogs, disturbed him. Something about those two slat-
terns, and especially their dogs, on so dismal and remote
a country road struck him as suspicious, although he
could not define his foreboding. A call to Pittsburgh
Central for backup was obviously in order, but as his
finger touched the transmit button he remembered that,
just as the KGB monitored every radio transmission
in America, so did the NSA, and if American security forces had not already been alerted to Barkley/
Hartshorn's presence here, it would be foolish to announce his own. Anyway, the two squads of KGB men,
all of them well armed, would be sufficient for any
contingency in this backwater. He put the transmitter
back in his pocket.

Volcano, when they arrived, was even more deserted
than Karine and Keefe McCann had found it. One look
down the street, with its forlorn collection of gaping-
windowed tumbledown shacks, and Artusov pointed first
to his men, then to the buildings on each side. The men
deployed, one to a building, knocked on the doors, and,
when there was no answer, walked in and made a search

of the premises. In every case but one they found no sign of human occupation. The one exception was the funeral home, and there the occupant was dead, cold, and laid out on an embalming table.

The dirt road leading out of the village was innocent of any recent tire tracks or footprints. That meant their quarry was hiding or had taken to the woods. Further search uncovered the narrow trail up the hill behind the village. Detailing two men to cover the flanks, Artusov started up the trail on foot, followed by his men in single file. He had gone only a few hundred paces when he came upon evidence, still warm to the touch, that a horse had passed this way. Yet, incongruously, no hoof-prints were were evident in the soft loam of the trail. Dropping to his knee, Artusov inspected the leaves.

Plastic! And the branches that he had brushed aside —plastic. A plastic trail among thousands of square miles of natural forest and scrub. Something definitely was amiss. NSA or no, he needed backup. With any luck, they would be in and out with the Barkleys in their possession, or dead, before NSA or AYES could react. He plucked the transmitter from his pocket and pressed the button. "Aunty Rose—come in," he whispered. But only static was heard in reply. West Virginia hills blocked his signal. After three tries without a response from either Aunty Rose or the plane, Artusov pocketed the radio and unlimbered his pistol. Motioning for the others to do the same, he turned to Aleksei, his deputy for the operation. "From here on we proceed as a line of skirmishers," he said quietly. "I'll lead as point. The rest of you fan out on both sides of the trail at five-meter intervals. We'll move without haste, observing every-thing and maintaining visual contact. Every man will have his weapon handy, and no talking. Above all, no shooting unless fired upon. Pass the word."

* * *

"Who are they?" asked Sylvia Crespi. The four had come to her office, having been summoned from the terrace by word that intruders had just been sighted. On the wall-size television monitor facing her desk a line of sweat-soaked men struggled up the hill through a thicket of brambles and wild rose. "Do you know them?"

"Can't be sure," said Keefe McCann. "Can you focus on the guy on the trail?"

Sylvia put the cursor on the figure and adjusted the zoom knob.

"That's him—the guy who tried to kidnap us off the train this morning in Pittsburgh."

"Oh? What could an FAA check pilot have done, pray tell, that would incite a regiment of men with automatic pistols in their hands to come after him?"

It was pretty obvious to McCann that sex and its daily—perhaps hourly—practice was at the center of Sylvia Crespi's universe, as it was of every man and woman who inhabited Gland Junction, but you could never tell. What if, just to keep her hand in, she livened her off hours, so to speak, by keeping tabs on this part of West Virginia for the Russians? Her high cheekbones could have betrayed the slavic origin of one planted here between sheets under deep cover. It probably wasn't the case, but with so many Russian infiltrators infesting the countryside it was best to take no chances. If he guessed wrong, she'd put him on ice for them before he could figure out a strategy to get clear of Gland Junction, as he was determined to do before they converted him into some kind of male nymphomaniac.

"Diamonds," he said.

"Diamonds? What diamonds?"

"Before I joined the FAA as a check pilot," McCann said, "I was flying the New York-Dakar-Lagos-Johannesburg run for Pan-African Airways. In Lagos, I became acquainted with a female artist who specialized in voodoo masks and other wood carvings. We got along pretty well, and after a steamy weekend on the beach she made me the present of a fine ebony statuette. I was flattered, and took it back to my flat in New York, where it adorned the mantel over my fireplace.

"While I was on my next run, somebody broke into my apartment and made off with the statuette. I was sorry, of course, but not nearly so sorry as when a couple of days ago the woman from Lagos turned up in New York and asked to see the statuette. When I told her what happened she blew her top and accused me of stealing the $11 million in uncut diamonds she had concealed inside the statuette. She said I hadn't seen the last of her.

"She was speaking the truth. The next afternoon, I saw this guy and five others just like him on the screen of the monitor covering the downstairs lobby. They were with my erstwhile female friend and arguing with the concierge. I didn't linger, but dusted right out of there. They caught up with me in Pittsburgh, where my wife was visiting her sick mother, but I managed to rent an airplane and escape. They must have followed me all the way here."

"And now they're on Rue Bliss, headed this way," said Sylvia Crespi pensively, watching the men toil up the mountain trail.

"Rue Bliss?"

"The name we've given to the path that leads to that which all men desire—the warm, eternal embrace of the woman of their dreams. I think I'd better go make preparations to receive them. Excuse us for a few minutes, won't you? Come along, Marie—I'll need you."

"Oh, what a liar you are!" said Karine Collier when the door had closed behind the two women.

McCann shrugged. "What did you want me to tell

them, the truth? What if one of them is on the Russian payroll? Here we are, walking around with information vital to national security, and there *they* are, two women about whom we know nothing at all—except, of course, that they are toothsome, beautifully stacked, and infinitely desirable. Couldn't take the risk."

"Well, you can forget about them. You're promised to me."

"Promised, maybe, but not delivered. You're the most delicious female who's come down the pike in a long time, Karine, but unfortunately Annabella Ames is the only female who can get a rise out of me."

"My friends are going to change all that."

"Maybe, but I doubt it. Until it happens, the memory lingers on. Romeo, you'll remember, felt exactly the same way about Juliet, even after she had drowned in the Thames."

"You've got it backward. It was Romeo who..."

The door opened and Sylvia Crespi and Marie Michaelson entered. They smiled benignly at Keefe McCann.

"You don't know," said Marie Michaelson throatily, "what it does for our morale to be told that we're 'toothsome, beautifully stacked, and infinitely desirable'— *without* our having given you a whiff of F^3." She held up her little compact-sized communicator.

"So they're Russians," Sylvia Crespi said. "Why didn't you tell us straight out?"

"Because he's a pathological liar," Karine flared, still burning because McCann thought he was still in love with his hillbilly inamorata.

"You're not a bad liar yourself," Sylvia pointed out, "claiming to be his wife. Not that we'd have been fooled in any case."

"Why not?"

"What woman in her right mind would prefer her husband to the prospect of ..."

"Getting back to the issue at hand," McCann broke in, "what do you propose to do about that regiment of Russians advancing upon Gland Junction?"

Sylvia Crespi shrugged. "Invite them in, of course. They all appear to be the type of men we customarily recruit, anyway. They've just saved us a trip to the outside."

"Listen," warned Keefe McCann. "You don't know who you're dealing with if you think they'll come quietly."

'Quietly or otherwise," Marie laughed. "It's all the same to us. Actually, otherwise would be the rule rather than the exception. Shall we go?"

Considering the artillery mustered by the opposition now cautiously approaching the mouth of the cavern-entrance to Gland Junction, McCann thought machine guns would be most appropriate for defense. Sylvia Crespi had a better way. On the way back from her office down to the cavern entrance she had her guests stopped off at the scheduling office, where she consulted the member's roster.

"I counted twenty-five men," she mused, as she ticked off twenty-five names from the roster. She then turned on the public address system and picked up a hand mike. "Ladies, it gives me great pleasure to announce the unexpected arrival of a new contingent. The gentlemen seem to range in age between twenty-five and perhaps forty, are apparently in excellent physical condition, and will be upon us, in a manner of speaking, within ten minutes. The twenty-five women at the top of the roster know their relative positions, so I won't bother to recite their names. I should remind Sra. Estella de la Mar that last week she traded her next pick to Yono Marasuke San, who accordingly will have the third and twenty-first draws. Please drop whatever or whoever you're doing and assemble immediately at the steel doors. And don't forget to bring along your personal sensitizers." She switched off the mike and led the way down the passage.

They weren't the first arrivals on the observation deck overlooking the cavern. Already, six women were present, six women who appeared to Keefe McCann to have stepped right off of Rue Bliss, the avenue of male dreams. To say they were lovely was rank injustice. Each, in her own way, was the epitome of grace and feminine perfection. One, slim and sleek beneath an ankle-length red silk cheongsam with a slit up to the waist, had long straight black hair and dark almond eyes that regarded McCann with naked lust. Another, wearing a bikini the size of a poker chip, was a long-legged Nordic woman in her early twenties whose honey-color hair, draped over both shoulders, most inadequately served for a top. A third had the dark lustrous skin and regal carriage of an Amharic princess, with a Greek or Italian grandfather in her genealogy. And they kept coming . . .

At the cavern entrance, Artur Artusov motioned to the others to wait, then cautiously entered the murky interior. The cavern was high-ceilinged and deep and seemed to extend some distance inside the mountain. He walked ahead, signaling to his men to follow at intervals. The last had just cleared the entrance when, with a muted thud, steel doors suddenly closed behind him and overhead lights sprang on. The musty air was still and stagnant no longer. They felt a slight draft as fresh scented air was pumped into the cavern. Tense and fearful when the lights first blazed down upon them, unaccountably they now relaxed and broke into easy smiles. They couldn't figure out what was happening. Was it the air?

Now, in the wall ahead of them, above the passage-way blocked by steel doors, Artusov saw a twenty-meter rectangle of dark-tinted plate glass. He couldn't see through it but correctly surmised that he and his companions were under observation. Artusov wasn't a man who panicked, but he experienced a keen sense of doubt, that the enemy—including probably Dr. Hartshorn himself—was behind that glass looking down at him. Yet he was unafraid, even unconcerned. He had the deep conviction that whatever happened he was going to emerge unscathed, even though a past in which violence and deception were far from unknown told him that he was being a fool.

"Please remove your clothing," came a feminine voice from nowhere. "All of it."

The men looked at each other, then to Artusov, waiting for instructions.

"*Nyet!*" he growled. "Also, not on your life."

"If you will look around you," the voice continued, "you will see there is no way through those solid steel doors at each end of the cavern. Your guns will not avail you against solid rock. There are no food and water in the chamber. However, if you prefer, we'll go away and come back in a day or two."

Artusov shook his head. Bluff wasn't going to work. "Do as she says," he instructed his men, and proceeded to divest himself of his garments, folding them in a neat pile at his feet, with his two automatic pistols on top.

"Now, then," said the woman, when they were all stripped, "please form a single rank."

They did so.

A steel door ahead of them opened and a woman stepped forth, as naked as they themselves. She wore her beauty like a halo, and it brought a collective gasp from the throats of the twenty-five men. She walked down the line as they stood, transfixed. She looked into the eyes of each man in turn, then dropped her eyes in quest of other virtues. After she had completed her inspection she came back up the line again. She stopped before a strapping young man of twenty-three, with a massive chest tapering to a narrow waist and arms like the limbs of an oak.

"And what is *your* name?" she asked sweetly.

"Vassiliy, ma'am," he gulped. He tried hard not to look down. Neither moved, but he suddenly realized their bodies were touching.

The woman put her forefinger on the bridge of his nose and gently stroked its length to the tip. "Come along, Vassiliy," she said. "We have things to...ah... talk about."

He followed her like a sheep. Artusov wanted to scream to Vassiliy to come back, not to be an idiot, but the words stuck in his throat.

Then came another woman, as gorgeous as the first. The routine was repeated. Gradually the members of Artusov's team leaving the cavern swelled as the ranks dwindled. He himself was chosen by a statuesque female with rounded limbs—by her accent apparently of Latin American ancestry—on the ninth draw. The moment her finger touched the tip of his nose he felt himself drawn to her as he had never been attracted to any human being in his life. His mind emptied of all thoughts save intense desire. He felt the blood rushing through his veins until it seemed as though a red curtain was drawn across his eyes. He was adrift in a sea of concupiscence, his vision blurring, his cheeks burning, and his hormones churning.

Passing through the door he saw the man who called himself Dr. Hartshorn gazing at him, obviously wanting to speak.

Pulled along by the aura of the Latin woman, Artur Artusov could only gasp plaintively, "Later."

17. DR. CALDWELL
14 SEPTEMBER 2016

IF IT HAD TO BE ANYBODY BUT ANNABELLA AMES, Keefe McCann reflected, his first choice might well be Karine Collier. She was beautiful and brainy, walked like a zephyr in springtime, and had a lilting laugh on the rare occasions she dismounted from her high horse of relentless professionalism and behaved like a human being. She preached, of course, but then, didn't *all* women?

On the other hand, Keefe McCann had no overwhelming desire to be Karine Collier's joy toy and every other woman's eunuch. Although, if he exercised his imagination, he could envision the prospect of reasonable contentment as a one-woman man, provided the woman were of the caliber of Karine Collier, he saw no reason to hasten the day, not, at least, while so delectable an assortment lay at hand as was assembled at Gland Junction.

As yet, no one had made a move to supply Karine Collier with the tailored F^3 which would, once his pheromonic memory had been erased, make him her slave-for-life. Only the unexpected arrival of the Russians had, in fact, saved him. But now that the Slavs were comfortably bedded down, it would be his turn. After which it would be only a matter of his personal endurance before he went to join the legion staring up at crosses in Volcano's graveyard.

"Your turn," said Sylvia Crespi, smiling at McCann as the last of the naked Russians was hauled away to a welcome fate. She had already sent Karine Collier to the lab, where a blood sample would be drawn for matching with the pheromone with which she would mark Keefe McCann as her private property. The process took approximately ten minutes.

"Now wait just a minute," said McCann desperately.

"Oh dear," Sylvia said, shaking her head sadly. "I *do* hope you don't intend to make a pother. It won't do you any good, and if your protests make me nervous, I may get the pheromones marking Karine and Melanie mixed up."

"I, for one, quite understand his disaffection," Marie Michaelson volunteered. "There *is* something rather indecent for a man to be F-cubed to his own wife, for heaven's sake, even if she's only been *playacting* the wife. But that can be easily remedied, my dear," she went on, turning to address Karine Collier, who was walking back from the lab, a glass vial in her hand. "I'll take him off your hands and give you two draft choices in exchange."

"Not on your life," said Karine Collier heatedly.

"Three?"

McCann intervened. "Forget it, both of you. You can warm your cold feet on somebody else's back. I'm already spoken for."

"You mean Annabella Ames?" sniffed Karine Collier. "As far as you're concerned, she's dead."

McCann smiled wryly. "But Dr. Semm isn't, and unless I see him in exactly eight days, *I* will be."

Karine paled. "Good God, I'd completely forgotten about Dr. Semm."

"Well, I hadn't. The hairy-eared little bastard has

been on my mind every minute since he jabbed me with that needle full of poison two days ago."

"Will somebody please tell me what the hell you are talking about?" broke in Sylvia Crespi. "Who is this Dr. Semm?"

McCann decided that then was not the time to weave one of his fanciful embroideries of the imaginary. Sticking strictly to the facts, he started back at the federal penitentiary, and in lean, terse sentences brought his story up to the uneasy present.

Sylvia tugged a shell-shaped ear thoughtfully. "I think we'd better consult Dr. Caldwell."

They found her propped up on pillows in a bed the size of a wrestling mat, reading *Vanity Fair*, though McCann couldn't comprehend why she would be doing so, considering that the women they had encountered at Gland Junction so far wore few if any clothes. In keeping with local fashions, bedclothes covered her only to the waist. Her strong firm breasts were a pleasant revelation to McCann, whose experience had seldom extended beyond women of forty. Sylvia Crespi said Dr. Caldwell was pushing fifty, but she looked as though she had drained the fountain of youth—and in fact he now lay asleep by Dr. Caldwell's side, snoring gently.

She put the magazine down and removed her glasses. "Well, Sylvia, what have we here—a gift from the staff?"

"Not exactly. This is Keefe McCann, also known as Captain Hartshorn."

"Of course. I didn't recognize him with his clothes on. Annabella."

"Exactly."

"You came back for her?" she said, looking at McCann.

"Not exactly. I came back because some Russians

were looking for me, and this was the most isolated spot
I could think of to hide for a while."

"And?"

"And the Russians followed him all the same," added
Sylvia, "as the result of which we now have two dozen
new and welcome additions to the menu at Gland Junction."

"Not to mention Mr. McCann. How serendipitous!"

"Not exactly. Tell her, Mr. McCann."

McCann told her. Everything: his lifelong predilection
for imposture; his earning sentences enough to keep him
behind bars until he died; how an anonymous general
rescued him from prison and thrice weekly uplifting interviews by Dr. Karine Collier; how he had been injected
with a metallic poison; and how Russians came to be
sent after him.

"Which means that you have only eight days to live,"
said Dr. Caldwell thoughtfully. "Well, young man, I can
guarantee that they will be the happiest eight days
you've ever experienced. Just to make those days and
nights more interesting, Sylvia," she said to her assistant, "may I suggest an eclectic mixture?"

"A very good idea, Dr. Caldwell. You're in luck,"
Sylvia said to McCann. "We'll give you a whiff of pheromone mixture marking *your* personal choice of, say, a
hundred different women. That way you'll be able to
enjoy the embraces of a different woman each time, as
though she were the only woman you've ever loved."
She chuckled. "My goodness, you may not even *last*
eight days!"

McCann wasn't amused. "Look here, Dr. Caldwell,"
he said earnestly. "I don't think you quite got the picture. I have in my possession information the General
needs to assess the Russian threat to *all* America—and
that includes Gland Junction. Without my information,

which he isn't going to get unless he agrees to having Dr. Semm chelate my blood, the Russians will be able to—"

To what? Keefe McCann suddenly realized he had no more knowledge of the nature of the weapon than the Admiral himself. But McCann had never allowed mere ignorance to pollute his air of authority.

"—to deploy a chemical agent," he went on blandly, "which will wipe out the ozone layer over the western hemisphere, thus exposing the American population to slow and agonizing death by solar ultraviolet and actinic radiation. And there is precious little time to spare. The Russians know I have the vital piece of the puzzle. They're on my trail, and the seriousness of the threat that I represent is indicated by the size of the delegation they sent to reason with me. And now that their posse is bedded down here at Gland Junction, out of communication with Mother Russia, the boys in the Kremlin will figure they've lost me. On that assumption, they may launch their secret weapon before I can get to the General so he can orchestrate countermeasures.

"I sure appreciate your wanting to make my last eight days on earth happy ones, but what about after that—for the rest of our country, for the rest of you? How many days do you think *you'll* have?"

Dr. Caldwell folded her arms under her breasts, brows furrowed in thought. The young man by her side awoke with a start, sat up in bed and looked at them with sleep-swollen eyes, muttered something incomprehensible, and collapsed once more. Dr. Caldwell pulled the bedclothes over his head. "The younger generation has no stamina." She shook her head. "Well, Mr. McCann, if what you say is true . . ."

"It's true, all right," broke in Karine Collier, suddenly alarmed at the prospect of having to share him with ninety-nine other delectable females. "I've been with him every minute since the general came to arrange his release from the federal prison."

"Then we can't force you to stay, obviously. But neither can we leave you free to tell the world about our happy little family at Gland Junction. You seem to be an imaginative fellow. Perhaps you have some idea of how we can resolve this paradox?"

"Sure. Let me go, and I promise not to talk."

Dr. Caldwell shook her head. "Impossible. The story of Gland Junction is too novel and exciting to suppress. You'd tell it someday, to someone, and every woman in the world would descend upon us like ravening wolves, all wanting to take a sitz bath in F^3. We'd be finished. You may be sincere, but by your own admission you've made a lifework of deception. Here, we believe in exposure. Here, we believe in exposure to the maximum— but not to the outside world."

"Can *I* make a suggestion?" said Karine tentatively.

"Certainly, my dear."

"Well, Sylvia told me that as a new member of Gland Junction I could choose any man I wanted, and I chose Keefe. The lab has just issued me my personalized pheromone. Why don't you let me go ahead and dope Keefe with it? That way, I would guarantee that he returns. After all, he'd have no choice."

"An excellent suggestion, my dear. The fox will guard the grapes, but who will watch the fox?"

"What do you mean?"

"Simply that once you have Mr. McCann by the tail, you would have no incentive to return here."

"I would." She colored. "Sylvia told me I could have five other men as well."

Dr. Caldwell considered. That was a possible solution, but by no means foolproof. Gland Junction had experience with women who fell in love with the first of the men alloted to them, languished, and, in a few cases, pined away themselves after the prolonged and continuous exertion of their lovers had sapped their virility. That Karine Collier was in love with Keefe McCann was obvious. That she'd bring him back to Gland Junction, judging by the maidenly flush on her cheeks when she reminded them that each woman there had a quota of six, was less convincing. But the suggestion was not entirely without merit, given a subtle twist.

"In the decade since the pheromone was first developed in CMR," said Dr. Caldwell, "I have never ceased to develop new variations. Once the basic chemistry was worked out, rearranging an atom or two in the complex molecules produced analogues with quite different properties. Now we possess a whole gamut of pheromones though, I must admit, we seldom have recourse to them. The simple pheromone, which draws the sensitized man to the woman wearing it, does everything that we require.

"However, we have others in stock. In my laboratory I have a quantity of the levopheromone, which is the chemical mirror image of the dextropheromone which we use here. It has the same effect on women that the dextropheromone has on men. We have four subpheromones which work only on men with the corresponding O, A, B, or A-B blood types. One class of pheromone is age-specific, one arouses insane passion in a youth whose glandular development is still incomplete, and another sends into raptures old men whose equipment has practically withered away. Another pheromone works at only short range—beyond two hundred meters its effect is negligible. And then there are the combinations."

"What kind of combinations?" said McCann. He liked the drift of her discourse. It was beginning to look as though some compromise might be worked out.

"Just this: we are faced with certain conflicting concerns. You say it is a matter of national urgency for you to leave Gland Junction. I dare not allow you to go, for fear you will reveal our secret. You are still obsessed with Annabella Ames. Dr. Karine Collier wants your body and, for all I know, your soul. Well, I believe there's a way to reconcile the irreconcilable." She crooked her finger at Sylvia Crespi, who went to her bedside.

Whatever Dr. Caldwell whispered into her ear must have been hilarious, for Sylvia broke into peals of laughter. She hurried from the room, looking back over her shoulder at McCann and Karine. As she closed the door behind her she was laughing harder than ever.

In a few minutes she was back, bearing a tray covered with a white towel, on which rested what appeared to be three felt-tip pens—black, white, and green. She picked up the white, advanced on McCann, and drew a line down the middle of his nose. "Feel anything?"

"Well, it's damp."

"How do you feel about Annabella Ames?"

"Who?"

"Annabella Ames."

Now that she mentioned it, he wondered what the hell he had ever seen in the girl. He could still recall with startling clarity each heady moment he had spent with her, and the memory of it sent blood surging toward the usual places. And if she were there in the room at this moment, he had no doubt he would want to relive some of those delicious hours. But the obsession had faded, unaccountably. "Great kid," he said mechanically.

"Well, in a minute or two you'll wonder what you ever saw in her." She took the black pencil from the tray, ran the felt point lightly down Karine Collier's nose.

Then she handed Karine a cotton gauze square and pointed to the vial in Karine's hand.

Karine unscrewed the top of the vial and dampened the sponge. She walked toward Keefe McCann with a triumphant smile.

McCann backed away at her approach. "Hold it! You promised there'd be none of this stuff. I've got to get to the general."

"And so you shall," said Dr. Caldwell. "But I'd advise you not to make things hard for yourself by forcing us to use the green."

"What's the green?"

"Melanie-specific pheromone."

McCann stood still while Karine Collier lightly ran the dampened sponge from the bridge of his nose to the tip.

"Feel anything?" asked Sylvia Crespi again.

"Not a thing," said McCann truthfully, then realized that he had just told a lie. He felt something. At first it was only a mere tingling of the skin as he looked at Karine Collier. But as he went on looking he felt a power that he couldn't control, didn't *want* to control, pulling him toward her. His feet moved by themselves. His breathing deepened, his face flushed, and a shiver of fierce desire shook his frame. His arms went out to envelop her. From the edge of consciousness, amid the roar that filled his ears he heard Dr. Caldwell cry out.

"Don't let him make a mess of my rug!"

He folded a willing Karine Collier in his arms. Their eyes met, then their lips . . . and then he felt cold steel touch his throat as a basin was thrust between them, and he was very, very sick.

Five minutes later, sprawled on the carpet, utterly exhausted, he found Sylvia Crespi wiping his face with a wet towel. "You poor dear," she said. "We really should have warned you."

"What the hell happened?" he said woozily.

"Karine administered her individual-specific pheromone, and your reaction was predictably the same as it
was to Annabella Ames."

"Okay, I understand that. But what happened then—
my shooting my cookies like that?"

"The black pen with which we marked Karine contains an antirape pheromone CMR developed by Dr.
Caldwell and her associates. Called ARP, it works on the
same principle as Anabuse, the antialcohol drug. Any
woman doped with it is immune to rape. The moment
any would-be attacker comes into skin contact with any
female so doped, he becomes violently ill."

"That's great," said McCann. "Caldwell giveth, Caldwell taketh away."

"Fortunately, the ARP is reversible. As soon as you
conclude your business with the general, you may return
to Gland Junction and we shall neutralize the medication."

"And Karine and I can then live happily ever after—
until I collapse from dehydration. Is that it?"

"That depends entirely on your powers of recuperation, I'm afraid."

"Thanks a lot. Am I free to go now?"

"Entirely."

He looked at Karine, who seemed distressed as
McCann himself. It was the same old story: he couldn't
live with her, and he couldn't live without her. "Coming?"

"Is that some kind of sick joke?" she snarled.

"I'll rephrase the question: are you accompanying
me?"

"Of course I am."

"Just don't touch me," he warned.

"It won't be easy, but I'll try not to."

Keefe McCann and Karine Collier wished Dr. Caldwell a totally insincere good afternoon and went to the door. As they passed through, they heard her voice behind them:

"Wake up, you worthless layabout! All this thinking has made me ravenous." They heard the slap of hand on flesh. "Up, *Up*, UP! You've got work to do."

18. DR. SEMM
15 SEPTEMBER 2016

EVER SINCE HE HAD TALKED TO THE GENERAL'S SECRE-
tary by telephone the morning before from the compartment of the Transcontinental Express, McCann had
pondered the meaning of her cryptic statement to the
effect that "for future contact with the general, I'll put an
ad in the biggest paper in the city where you were engaged in water sports. The ad, in your name, will give
you a number where the general can be reached."

Considering that the Russians were tuned in, it was an
inspired improvisation. All the Russians knew about him
was that he called himself Commander Waldron Barkley,
a.k.a. Dr. Julian R. Hartshorn.

Water sports ... That, he finally decided, could only
refer to his stint in Denver as a fire fighter with Ladder
Company 73. At the station he went by the name of
Larry Peal. Therefore he could expect to find an adver-
tisement in the classified section of *The Denver Post*, the
Skyline City's leading daily, followed by a phone
number.

"So it's off to Denver we go, right after breakfast,"
said McCann to Karine Collier, when they arose the following morning from a refreshing sleep. McCann had insisted on separate rooms, fearing that he might walk in
his sleep during the night and not wishing to lose the

excellent dinner prepared by Emile, the handsome young man-in-waiting who had been assigned to serve them during their brief stay at Gland Junction.

"We really don't have to go all the way to Denver to pick up a morning newspaper," Karine reminded him, as she sat across from him at the breakfast table, a tantalizing arm's length away. She was wearing a sheer yellow-silk dress, which didn't do much to conceal charms which her clothing rather emphasized than diminished. "We can have it faxed right here to Sylvia's office."

McCann snapped his fingers. "Why didn't *I* think of that?" he said, with mock chagrin. "Sure," he went on, serious again, "we could do that, but we've got to get the hell out of Gland Junction. There's no reason to suspect that our Russian friends informed their headquarters they were coming to Volcano, but we can't count on it. Furthermore, if I called the general from here they'd have a fix on us in five minutes. So we'll go to Denver, buy a newspaper, and give the other side some practice looking for needles in haystacks."

They were accompanied across the hills and down to Volcano by Sylvia Crespi, three as yet unassigned male recruits, and a body. It was enveloped in canvas and cradled in a Stokes stretcher lashed to the side of a mule. The recruits would dig a grave for the late lamented and for the body which Sylvia had just finished embalming when Keefe and Karine made their appearance in Volcano.

That was two martyrs to Venus in two days, McCann observed. If that was representative of the attrition at Gland Junction—and Sylvia Crespi assured him that it was *not*—it was well he was on his way to other parts. He wondered how many of those crosses were *really* stage money, after all.

Sylvia bade them "au revoir, but not farewell" at Vol-

cano's only active business establishment and radioed
ahead to inform Melanie and Madeleine that Keefe
McCann and Dr. Karine Collier were cleared to leave
town. As they trudged with their suitcases down the dirt
road leading to the air strip, they passed Madeleine and
her two watchdogs. She wished them a merry good-day,
which McCann acknowledged by picking up the pace.
Melanie, a mile farther along, expressed the hope that
they'd "hurry back," which sentiment McCann favored
with a sickly smile.

The aircraft was just as they had left it, though it had
been joined by a larger twin-engine commuter aircraft.
For a moment, McCann considered taking the larger
plane, just to sow confusion in the enemy's ranks, then
decided the unfamiliar flight envelope would give him
more trouble than the theft would be worth.

Four-and-a-half hours later they landed the Piper 224
at Mountain View Airport, a private field a few miles out
of Denver. The last two hours had been flown in strained
silence as the result of McCann's having convinced himself earlier that morning that the ARP must be water sol-
uble and that a good half hour's scrubbing under a hot
shower would surely wash it off. Somewhere over Mis-
souri he put the plane on autopilot and his theory to the
test. He reached—and retched. His excellent breakfast
was now distributed unevenly over the instrument panel.
She made him clean it up, using freshly laundered shirts
from his suitcase for the purpose. But since the air con-
ditioning unit wasn't working properly, a chill rose between them to accompany the fragrance which lingered
on . . . and on . . . and on . . .

Larry Peal, read the ad in the personals column of
The Denver Post, *Your mother has had a relapse. Please
call hospital. 820–1409.*

Keefe McCann finished off his cup of hot chocolate
and went to the cafe's pay phone. The area code wasn't

listed, but it would have to be one of three in the Washington area, either 202, 703 or 301. It turned out to be 202, and the familiar voice of the efficient secretary answered the first ring.

"Is this Larry?" she said in greeting.

"Yep."

"My boss just stepped out of the office, Larry. But if you call 515-0579 in ten minutes, you'll catch him. 'Bye."

McCann pushed the stop button on his chronometer as he heard the click.

"Let's go!" he told Karine Collier.

They drove the rented car in the direction of Colorado Springs for exactly nine minutes and then stopped at a roadside telephone. Inserting three dollar bills in the slot, he dialed (202) 515-0579. On the first ring he heard the general's gruff voice.

"Meet me at the marina of the Marine Corps Base in Quantico, Virginia. There's a boat tied up there, the *Booker Cat*. I'll be there in six hours." He rang off before McCann could frame a reply.

The Piper 224 would be hot by then, McCann reasoned. After all, the Russians had somehow managed to follow it to Volcano, West Virginia, and it was only reasonable to suppose that it had been kept under some kind of surveillance ever since. The most logical supposition was that it had been picked up by Russian satellite, and his pursuers had been given a fix on it at Volcano, to which they flew with all haste. But his Russian pursuers were now on ice, out of communication with Moscow. Even if the Russians backing up the operation had tracked the Piper 224 to Denver, it was unlikely that they'd be able to react in time to catch him, especially since he had taken the precaution of filing an in-flight flight plan for Pueblo, Colorado, but veered north toward Denver on an amended flight plan just as he was about to enter Pueblo airspace. Still, with the Russians, it was better to take no chances.

"Where to?" asked Karine, as they sped back up the highway into town.

"Colorado Springs. Ent Air Force Base."

"You're going north," she pointed out. "Colorado Springs is south."

"I know. I like to do things the hard way."

Ten minutes later he pulled up at the curb before an undistinguished apartment building and carried their bags inside, followed by a thoughtful Karine Collier.

"You're not going to try to...ah..." she began, as they entered the elevator and he punched the button for the eleventh floor.

"Not a chance. This is business." He led the way down the hall to No. 1112, keyed in the code, and stood aside to let Karine enter. The apartment's furnishings were minimal—an unmade bed, a table and one chair, a floor lamp, and not so much as a coffee cup in the kitchen. In one corner was a stack of some kind of furniture covered with canvas. The place had the musty smell of disuse.

McCann opened the wall-length closet. In it were several dozen suits, neatly hangered and enveloped in plastic, drawers full of shirts, socks and underwear, a rack of neckties, a dozen pairs of shoes, two shelves of hats, half a dozen topcoats and rain coats, luggage of expensive leather, utilitarian canvas, and cheap vinyl, and an assortment of metal file boxes. "Tools of the trade," said McCann, dragging out a portable computer and setting it up on the kitchen table. He married telephone and computer and sat down at the keyboard. "It'll be mid-afternoon in Washington, so Henderson should be working at home." He punched in the address and waited.

"Would you mind explaining what this is all about?" said Karine.

"Sure. I'm creating an identity. Most people think you just buy a Bible, put on a black suit, and turn your collar around and you'll be taken for a preacher. Actually, it's a bit more complicated than that, if you want to do it right. Especially if you're impersonating someone in authority —an officer in the services, a government official, or a foreign diplomat. In that closet are the clothing of twenty-odd professions including, if memory serves, the uniform of a rear-admiral of the U. S. Navy, all suitably worn and, in the case of the priest's costume, frayed. I've got apartments like this in New York, Washington, St. Louis, San Francisco, Miami, and Houston, all on paid-up five-year leases and all supplied with similar accoutrements."

"It must cost a fortune!"

"It takes money, but I figure I can always take it from my taxes as a legitimate business expense—should I ever get around to paying taxes. Ah—here comes our boy."

The screen sprang alive, and for the next five minutes Keefe McCann busied himself in constructing the personality he would assume on leaving the apartment.

"Eli Henderson's got access to the data bases at the Pentagon, State Department, and several other agencies," McCann explained, as he switched off the machine and picked up the tablet on which he had jotted down the information provided by his Washington contact, who expected to receive his usual $1,000 check in the mail in due course.

McCann pulled the canvas off the pile in the corner to reveal a small printing press, a laminating machine, a Polaroid passport camera on a tripod, and various other pieces of useful equipment. He went quickly through his files and brought forth a handful of blank cards—Navy officer's identification, Chevy Chase Country Club membership, California driver's license, two credit cards, and automobile registration. He sorted through a cardboard box filled with rings, wings, rank insignia, dog tags, and lodge pins, and put on a Naval Academy class ring with ruby setting. From a file drawer of blanks, he selected that of a restaurant near the naval base in Rota, Spain, a dry cleaner's bill from McLean, Virginia, and a bill from the clothing department of the Pentagon's naval small stores.

For the next hour and a half he busied himself with fingerprints, mug shots, filling in the bills in appropriate calligraphic styles, printing identification cards, and forging holographic ID strips. He stuffed the finished papers in a scruffy black wallet from yet another cardboard box, along with some spurious family pictures, and put it in his inside breast pocket. He dressed in the rear admiral's uniform, with five rows of stripes surmounted by the dolphins of the submarine service, adjusted his cap with the scrambled eggs on the brim, and saluted Karine Collier smartly. "Rear Admiral Doro Hembekides, USN, at your service, ma'am."

And he was.

Karine Collier had watched as McCann manufactured the phony documents, providing artful smudges of dirt, folding and refolding the fake bills, fraying the edges of the identification cards with sandpaper and rubbing the plastic lamination with jeweler's rouge to give them the patina of age and hard use, putting some Spanish 100-peseta notes among the American currency in his billfold. He worked quickly, absorbed in his task, devoting careful attention to the most minute details, building layer upon layer of his new identity as the Greek-American admiral who at the moment was assigned to unspecified intelligence duties. When he had committed to memory his own personal history, he went over the salient facts about Major-General Curtis W. Early also provided by Eli Henderson.

There was something eerie about the transformation of Keefe McGann to Rear Admiral Doro Hembekides. As he worked, he talked to himself, memorizing the details of the background provided by Henderson—immigrant from Salonika, arrived in the United States at age seven, worked in his father's restaurant, helped put his three sisters through school, enlisted in the Navy at seventeen, got a fleet appointment to the Naval Academy, went to sea in frigates, tranferred to subs, commanded the missile boat U.S.S. *Grouper*, promoted to flag rank and seconded to the Office of Naval Intelligence in 2015. By the time he had completed his false documentation he was no longer Keefe McCann, paroled con man. By the time he had moved back his hairline several inches with an electric razor and applied shadows to his eyes and jowls, aging him a good ten years, he was Rear Admiral Doro Hembekides, complete with the faintest Greek accent.

It was just after three in the afternoon when McCann and Karine Collier pulled up at the Ent AFB's main gate. A sentry in white belt and gloves saluted smartly and requested the admiral's identification.

"Please direct me to the commanding general's office," said McCann, displaying his I.D. card.

"Yes, sir. See that flagpole in the distance? The CG's building is just behind it."

The female captain who guarded the commanding general's privacy shot to her feet when McCann ushered Karine Collier into the office.

McCann returned her salute, removed his cap and placed it under his arm, and asked in a civil tone edged with authority if the commanding general would be good enough to receive them.

"Yes, sir," she said, and disappeared through a door

decorated with two large red stars. A moment later she held the door open for McCann to enter.

He ushered Karine into the room and closed the door. From behind a wide, glass-topped desk rose an imposing, red-faced man, top-heavy with stars and lopsided with seven rows of peacetime ribbons, wings, and other colorful baubles. He extended a beefy hand and encompassed his visitor, rather young for two stars, but that was today's Navy for you, and the lovely woman with him, in a broad smile.

"Well, Admiral," he boomed, shaking hands and waving his guests to the leather chairs opposite his desk, "you're a long way from blue water. What brings you to Colorado?"

"Perhaps I should ask you the same, General Early," said Keefe McCann. "The last time your name came up at the daily intelligence briefing—must have been all of three months ago—you were in charge of getting the Nighthawk operational at Edwards. What happened? I find it hard to believe a man like you would willingly give up piloting the hottest new interceptor in the Air Force to fly a desk."

"It's a bummer, all right," said the flattered General Early. "Fact is, they said I did a pretty good job and gave me a gong and another star, and *then* they said I was carrying too much rank for the job. You know how it is."

"I certainly do. My taste of wormwood and gall— promotion to flag rank and transfer to ONI—came after the *Grouper*, which I had the honor to command, got in that shoving match with the *Kiev* off Murmansk."

"Sure. I remember that."

"I thought you would. If memory serves, you were commanding the Stealth wing covering our northern approaches at the time."

General Early beamed. He'd never liked Navy men much—too stiff and starchy—but this Hembekides fel-

low was different. It was gratifying that the sister service
had a few officers who recognized that the Air Force was
pulling its weight. And the lady with him had perked up
considerably when she learned that she was in the presence of the man who had flight-tested the famous Nighthawk. He went to the liquor cabinet and told his guests
to name their poison, that the sun was over the yardarm,
and that he couldn't think of more congenial company to
share the first glass of the day.

"But I'm forgetting my manners," General Early said
when, prodded by McCann over the course of two
drinks, he had told the inside story of his fight to get the
Nighthawk out of the hangar and into the violet skies at
200,000 feet. "I haven't even asked what brings the admiral and his gracious lady to Ent AFB."

"Actually," said McCann, "we've come to ask a
favor. Dr. and Mrs. Delano are expected in Washington
this afternoon with information from our embassy in
Moscow. Another officer and I were sent from Washington to bring them in. We decided to split up to render
KGB surveillance more difficult and make sure that at
least one of the Delanos arrives in Washington on schedule. We came from Stapleton in Denver, which is crawl-
ing with KGB, in the hopes that . . ."

"But of course!" General Early assured him. "I'll
have my personal plane put at your disposal." He rose
and walked to the door. "Just give me a few minutes to
make the arrangements." He went out, closing the door
behind him. If Admiral Hembekides had a schedule to
meet, there would be no time to run a full check, but he
hadn't made major-general by going out on limbs.

"Colonel Deeb," he said to his deputy, "I want my
plane gassed and ready for immediate takeoff. Then I
want you to check whether there's an Admiral Doro
Hembekides on intelligence duty, and where he is now, if
possible. He used to skipper the *Grouper*. And look,

Ziad, contact the American Embassy in Moscow, and determine whether a Dr. and Mrs. Delano have been on a mission for . . . No, that won't do. Simply find out if a Dr. and Mrs. Delano left Moscow in the last couple of days."

"Roger, General."

"When you've got the dope, buzz me."

"Yes, sir."

General Early and his guests were finishing their second scotch and water when his phone rang.

"Everything seems to be in order, sir," said Colonel Deeb. "ONI admits there's such an officer but won't divulge his whereabouts. As for the Delanos, they did leave Moscow two days ago, according to Ambassador Hathon's secretary in Moscow. Very hush-hush."

"Fine." He hung up and smiled at his guests. "My deputy says the plane is ready anytime you are . . ."

"Andrews AFB in Washington, sir?" said the jet AR-6's pilot, a lieutenant-colonel who introduced himself as John Deutsch.

"Fargo, North Dakota, Colonel."

"But I thought . . ."

"Yes, I know, but I've changed my mind. File for the Air Force facility in Fargo, and instruct the tower on behalf of General Early that there is to be a jet standing by at the end of the strip when we land. We'll transfer to that plane and proceed from there."

"Cat and mouse with Russian surveillance satellites, sir?"

"Exactly."

In the cabin of the executive jet, Karine Collier made herself comfortable as McCann shut the door to the flight deck and the plane climbed toward cruise altitude. "What a waste!" she said.

"What's a waste?" McCann asked.

"All your elaborate preparations. You didn't need to go through all that to get us on this plane. You could have just put on your uniform and run a bluff. Why, General Early was so bowled over by your flattery that it never even entered his head to check up on us."

"Maybe," conceded McCann. "But it might not have worked out that way. What if he *had*?"

It was dusk when, two planes and four hours later, on flights that cross-stitched the American midwest, McCann and Karine Collier landed in a four-place Cessna sport plane at Baker Field in Quantico, forty miles south of Washington, D. C. A waiting staff car took them to the marina, where they found Admiral Ricardo Rivera Handy, attired as usual in an ill-fitting, ill-pressed brown suit, chewing on a cigar and pacing up and down the flood-lit dock as if it were a ship's quarterdeck.

He greeted them perfunctorily, pointedly ignoring McCann's uniform, and led them up a gangway and aboard the *Booker Cat*. The lines were slipped immediately and the idling engines sprang to life. The cruiser backed down into the Potomac, the engines were reversed, and the *Booker Cat*'s stern settled in the water as the boat surged toward mainstream, a ghostly roostertail rearing in its wake.

Down in the elegant salon, Admiral Handy opened the liquor cabinet and poured glasses half full of Green Stripe Glenderry Reserve and passed them around. "This Scotch is thirty-two years old, so kindly omit the ice or ginger ale or whatever you're used to spoiling good Scotch with. Cheers!" He drank half the amber liquid and smacked his lips. "Good thing this is official business. I could never afford this stuff if I had to buy it myself." Pleasantries over, he pointed a blunt finger at McCann. "Talk."

McCann talked. He stripped his discourse to essentials—how he had shaken his tail so that the people in the Directorate of Chemical Pesticides had no advance warning of his visit, how he had used gentle suasion and a bit of arm-twisting to break down Dr. Valentin Bogomoloff's defenses, and how Bogomoloff had volunteered the papers which McCann now produced from an inside pocket and handed over to the admiral.

"I'm old-school," growled Handy. "I can't read a word of that Russian gibberish. Get to the point—what's the formula?"

"There's no formula."

"*What?* Then what the hell are those papers about?"

"They're proof that Stanley Pollock is dead—has been for some time."

Blood slowly drained from the admiral's face. He felt more shock than surprise. He had been mentally preparing himself for bad news ever since he learned that McCann and Collier had taken off from Moscow the same day they arrived. It didn't stand to reason that in such a short time they could have contacted Pollock and received the microdot or other communication which contained the formula for the murderous chemical weapon he had presumably developed. Still, he had hoped for the best, and now his hopes were betrayed. Worse were the implications of the news.

The Russians had cultivated defection by leading scientists from the West by guaranteeing them the best possible working conditions, dachas, mistresses, medals, flattery, and the opportunity to pursue their individual lines of research without the restrictions of budget or national policy under which so many savants labored in the United States. They no longer used up their scientists and then killed them, as had often happened back in the gory Stalin days: the news would have eventually leaked, and the font of foreign expertise would have instantly dried up. Yet Stanley Pollock was dead. That could mean only one thing: he had invented a chemical weapon so devastating that the Russians couldn't take the smallest chance that the secret would escape. And so they took the sensible precaution of killing the one man who, if by some chance he *was* a double agent, could inform the Americans of the threat.

And now the threat of total annihilation of human life in America by some macabre chemical weapon had become an imminent reality. What form would it take— poisoning of the water supply, perhaps? Half a century ago it had been computed that a mere six kilograms of botulism toxin, which any moderately intelligent graduate student could produce in his garage in six months, could, if distributed in the nation's water supply, render every drop lethal. The Russians could easily improve on botulism. Nerve gas, maybe? Nerve gas was a thief in the night, which struck silently and without warning so that unless atropine was immediately injected into the veins of the victim, death resulted in three minutes. Or perhaps a new hallucinogen, one which induced a homicidal psychosis, so that every American would be trying to kill his neighbor. Or a super-swift sleeping potion introduced into the jet stream that passed over the American continent. If every American could be put to sleep for three days, they might awake to find Russian soldiers walking post on every street corner. The possibilities were harrowing and practically unlimited.

"There can't be any mistake, I suppose," said Admiral Handy, keeping his voice firmly under control.

"None whatever, I'm afraid, sir," replied McCann. "They didn't know I was coming, the papers have been in Bogomoloff's files for quite some time, and I think your analysts will find the internal evidence convincing. I *could* be wrong, but I don't think so."

Admiral Handy searched McCann's face. He found

no trace of guile. There seemed, indeed, no reason for McCann to lie; his life depended on bringing back a message from Pollock. And now the "general" would be expected to carry through his part of the bargain. He sat down heavily in an easy chair. McCann started to speak, but the admiral held up his hand. He needed time to think.

The boat was halfway to Washington when Admiral Handy finally broke out of his reverie. He went forward and up a ladder to the bridge. There he made two calls on the radio-telephone. They made him feel better, but not much.

"We'll be met by an ambulance and a couple of plain-clothes police cars," he informed McCann. "The Russians are probably still gunning for you, but once they know you've made your report to me they'll desist. Won't be any further point in it. But we've got to get you to Dr. Semm first."

He spoke no more during the remaining minutes before the boat slowed and pulled into a slip at the Seventh Street wharves. A contingent of competent-looking men was waiting. They walked the real admiral, Karine Collier, and McCann, still in uniform, to an ambulance, which took off at once with its siren silenced, preceded and trailed by two sedans carrying their armed escort.

The procession pulled up in front of an office building in southwest Washington. The cars' lights blinked out. The armed men emerged from their cars and unobtrusively took up posts covering the ambulance and the entrance. Only then came a rap on the ambulance door signaling all clear. The admiral alighted first, followed by Karine Collier and Keefe McCann. They walked quickly into the building, down a flight of steps and along a long corridor, and finally came to a door at which the admiral punched the key combination. The door opened.

It was the lab where Keefe McCann had received his

injection of the mystery heavy-metal solution what seemed months ago, but was actually less than four days past. The admiral turned on the lights and turned to the two men who followed them into the lab: "Where's Dr. Semm?"

"Don't know, sir. We relayed your message to his apartment, telling him to come at once."

"Call him up."

"Yes, sir."

But Dr. Semm's phone didn't answer. A car was dispatched to bring him. The men who drove it returned to say that Dr. Semm was not there. His apartment gave signs of a hasty departure—papers burned in the grate, file cases emptied on the floor, and the wall safe agape. Neither money nor passport were found, but all his clothes and luggage seemed to be there. Of course, he may have been traveling light.

"Check airports first, and then the other usual conveyances that may have taken the good doctor out of town."

"Aye, aye, sir," said one of the men.

The admiral favored him with a hard look. "And go over his apartment again. And find out who saw him last."

"Yes, sir."

They settled down to wait. The admiral sent out for pizza, but McCann had lost his appetite. By ten o'clock reports began coming in. Dr. Semm had taken a taxi from his apartment to Dulles Airport twenty minutes after being summoned to the laboratory. At 9:20 he was seen taking a plane for New York City, traveling under the name Norman Hopkins. At 10:10 Norman Hopkins arrived at La Guardia Airport, took a cab, and disappeared.

Meanwhile, a thorough search of his apartment revealed a UHF transmitter—a burst transmitter of the type issued KGB agents—concealed in the base of a floor lamp, along with a supply of one-time pads.

"Son of a bitch!" the admiral exploded. "The bastards are everywhere!"

"Tough break, admiral," began McCann "but at least..."

"How the hell did you know I'm an admiral?"

McCann laughed. "Your man acknowledged your command with an 'aye, 'aye, sir!' That and your age led me to suspect you rank somewhere above seaman second-class."

"Okay, I'm an admiral. But rank won't solve your problem, McCann."

"Sure it will. Just order your men to break out the chelation solution, produce the needle, and get on with it."

"That won't be so easy. Dr. Semm concocted the mixture himself. He kept the antidote—the chelation formula—in his head. But don't worry, we'll find him."

One of the admiral's aides, who'd been talking on the phone, put it down carefully. "We've found him. It seems some New York cops read APBs, after all."

"So?"

"Cop saw a guy who looked like the APB photo about to board the night train for Montreal, and braced him."

"Was it Semm?"

"Must have been."

"What do you mean?"

"When the cop asked the same question, 'Are you Dr. Semm?', the guy answered, 'Yes, I am.' Then he pulled out a gun and shot at the cop. He missed—but the cop didn't."

19. NIGHTMARE
15 SEPTEMBER 2016

"OUR SOVIET BROTHERS IN CHRIST MUST HAVE DECIDED to assassinate you for learning the fate of Stanley Pollock," mused Admiral Ricardo Rivera Handy as he offered a consolatory drink to Keefe McCann at a sumptuous safe house in Georgetown. "They had the reports of Dr. Semm in hand, of course, and when they ran them through their computers they must have discovered that Dr. Julian R. Hartshorn and Dr. Grant R. Delano and Keefe McCann were all the same person. That suggested a simple revenge: when you returned to Washington for chelation, Dr. Semm would make sure that the chelation didn't work, and you'd die on the table. But if that happened, there'd be an investigation, questions Semm couldn't answer, the chance he'd break—and talk. So he had to disappear. And when he was on the verge of capture, he mistakenly tried to shoot his way out."

The admiral's explanation sounded logical to Keefe McCann, but it was less than reassuring. In addition to the Russian posse sent to kill him, apparently Dr. Semm had been commissioned for the job as well. More assassins could well be waiting in the wings. Not that their efforts would really be necessary: now that the formula had died with Dr. Semm, in six days—seven at the outside—he'd be dead, too. And even if the chelation formula *had* been available, it would only have meant a stay of execution until he expired of joyful debilitation in Karine Collier's arms.

The alternative death sentence was no less certain. But now, at least, he had two choices. He could continue in the condition he currently found himself—perpetually inflamed by the presence of Karine Collier. He could no more stay away from her than will himself to stop breathing, or the blood to stop flowing through his veins. Yet he had only so much as to touch her with his fingertip and he was thrown into a convulsion of vomiting. Torn between satyriasis and sickness, between passion and puking, his nervous system would eventually revolt. His readings in psychiatry reminded him that rage and frustration can kill as surely as noose and knife.

There was, of course, the other choice: to return to Gland Junction as Dr. Caldwell had programmed him to do; she would provide the antidote to the antirape pheromone. But that last resort would *really* be the last. Sexual congress with Karine Collier was a capital idea, big yoke!—but how long he could survive it was another story. All men are mortal, and all men expect to die one day, but the cruelest fate is to know *which* day that day will be. It was a question he had, therefore, been at pains not to pose.

He hadn't yet mentioned Gland Junction to the admiral. There had been no reason to do so. But now he was almost tempted to drag the old bastard down to the hills of West Virginia and arrange for him to get a whiff of F^3 from the hands of Melanie or Madeleine as just recompense for having put him in a death-or-death situation. It would serve the old man right, gambling with people's lives.

"Have another," said the admiral, who observed McCann's black mood. He didn't wait for an answer, but filled a glass with smooth and potent Glenderry Reserve and handed it to McCann. His conscience about the events of the day disturbed him, but he wasn't afraid he wouldn't be able to sleep that night. He was a warrior, and the United States was at war with the Soviet Union —a silent, savage, and secret war. Wars always exact casualties, and if Keefe McCann was fated to fall, the admiral reflected, that was unfortunate, but at least he would be in the company of the legion of heroes who had believed, in the words of Homer, that "it is not unseemly for a man to die fighting in defense of his country."

Besides, McCann hadn't fallen yet. McCann himself didn't realize it yet, but he had not yet begun to fight. His single-handed sally into Russia, to extract in a few hours information Handy's operatives had not been able to uncover in a matter of years, attested to the man's daring and imagination. And daring and imagination, not tanks and aircraft and atomic weapons, were going to win the next battle of the behemoths. McCann was worth an entire general staff.

The three were sitting in the drawing room of a gray town house at 3009 P Street, in a part of Georgetown that had experienced urban decay in the late 1990s but was now making a comeback toward its former splendor. The furnishings were opulent, having been chosen by the wife of a defecting Russian colonel-general who had pointedly declined to bring her proletarian tastes to the new world. The admiral had invited McCann and Karine Collier to use it "for as long as you want to stay," an offer that McCann found easy to resist. Wherever he died, it wasn't going to be in Georgetown.

"It really *is* a tough break," commiserated the admiral.

"Yeah."

"But isn't there *anything* you can do?" implored Karine Collier, whose solicitude was a combination of unrequited passion and love, in what proportions she didn't allow herself to guess.

"Sure," replied the admiral, sipping his scotch. "And I'm doing it. Right now there's a team of biochemists working on the blood sample we took from McCann down at the lab. This will give us a quick qualitative reading on the poisons Dr. Semm injected into him."

McCann looked up, suddenly hopeful. "Why the hell didn't you say so before?"

Admiral Handy put up a cautioning hand. "If it had been that easy you could have gone out to any good hospital the day after we injected you and had the analysis made. But since those metal ions are now bound with cells in your liver, lungs, pancreas, and other organs, we're going to have to subject your blood to electrophoresis to determine exactly *how much* there is in your body. Only then can the chancre mechanics—excuse me—the doctors determine the precise amount of antidote needed to soak up the bound ions without throwing your system into irreversible shock with an antidote overdose. If you follow me."

"How long?" said McCann grimly.

"Two weeks maximum."

"Minimum?"

"Ten days—nine, if everything clicks."

"And I've got six-and-a-half."

"Yes, I'm afraid that's all you've got."

The half was ebbing away as Keefe McCann lay in bed, watching the lights of cars passing down P Street skittering off the ceiling and down the wall. In the other twin bed Karine Collier pitched and tossed in restless sleep. But for McCann, sleep would not come.

Like all condemned men, McCann thought about his past. It wasn't one he viewed without occasional self-reproach, but on the whole he wasn't ashamed of it and would have willingly relived even his follies, which provided a healthy, humbling leavening to his occasional triumphs. But he didn't waste too many moments soaking away his sorrows in water under the bridge. It was the future that he was going to miss that concerned him. Here he lay, unlaid, a man in the prime of life, in robust health, having not one but half a dozen professions, with a gorgeous woman who wanted him fully as ardently as he desired her only an arm's length away—a man condemned never to possess her, condemned instead to embrace the angel of death in six short days. It was a terrible injustice.

And the more he thought about it, the more unjust it seemed. It was all the admiral's fault. Well, not entirely. To be absolutely fair, the admiral was only the instrument of his unpleasant fate. The admiral was a warrior. Hot war, cold war—it was all the same to him. He fought the enemy on any terms and with whatever weapons came to hand. It was merely Keefe McCann's misfortune to have been chosen as his sharp, sure blade. And he *had* inflicted a wound on the enemy, a wound deep enough to send a company of foot-soldiers after him and to force a mole like Dr. Seem to the surface, his further services lost to the Russians. But McCann had to admit that such a wound was, in the long run, only a scratch on the Russian bear's butt.

If only he could, before his six days on this earth were up, *really* stick it to the goddamned Russians! Though he might not die happy, he would at least die with vengeance satisfied and grim satisfaction in taking his enemy along with him. Foolish thought, he told himself. One man against 324 million Russians? Still, since he couldn't go to sleep, he could at least dream . . .

* * *

He sat up in bed with a start, wet with sweat. Without being aware of it, sleep had stolen up and sandbagged him. And he had had a dream. He was in a plane flying far into the stratosphere, flying at a dozen times the speed of sound. Below him was the vast expanse of Russia, unwinding like a patchwork quilt. His gloved hand reached toward the arming lever. He yanked it down. He extended his index finger toward the instrument panel, where the release button was protected by a red shield against inadvertent release. He flipped the shield up, took a deep breath, and pushed the button. Looking over the side through the cockpit cowling, he watched the land slip by. For a minute, while *it* was still falling, it remained unchanged. Then, suddenly, the countryside liquefied, and the crimson liquid was the lifeblood seeping out of Russia.

He wiped the sweat from his face and put his feet on the floor. He was breathing hard, but it wasn't from the nightmare. It was from the excitement of discovery: he had found the answer he was looking for. He took a quick shower, dressed, and looked at the bedside clock. It was 2:37. He bent over to shake Karine Collier awake, but stayed his hand just in time.

"Karine," he whispered.

She snored on. It came as a nasty shock to realize that someone so wholly desirable as Karine could snore.

"Karine!" he shouted.

She bounded out of bed, naked and wide-eyed, and stood shivering with her hands over her breasts, totally unaware of her surroundings.

McCann spoke soothingly, apologized for frightening her, and told her everything was all right but that they had to get moving—and fast.

"Where are we going?"

"First, to Gland Junction."

She licked her lips. Slowly, comprehension dawned. Gland Junction meant Dr. Caldwell would neutralize the ARP and they could finally make love. She thanked God for the small favor which, she acknowledged philosophically, would get smaller all the time. McCann might have only six days to live, but she'd make certain he'd remember those days for the rest of his life. She'd . . .

"What do you mean, *first*?"

"That's only the first stop. For me, that is."

Karine Collier crossed her arms under her breasts. It was a comfortable fit. "And where will you be going from there, pray tell?"

"Russia."

At 3:05 AM the phone jangled on Admiral Handy's bedside table. His light was on and he was buried deep in the soft loam of the hybrid-tomato section of Burpee's Spring Seed Catalog.

"Handy."

"Sir, you asked me to report any unusual activity at the P Street house."

"Well?"

"A taxi just pulled up at the door and the gentleman and the lady are climbing into it. Shall we follow?"

The admiral considered. His men hadn't covered themselves with glory up to now and—who could say? —maybe the very man who called him was *himself* working for the Russians. Better let McCann get on with it, whatever he had in mind to do. "No—go on home." He hung up. With a sigh of satisfaction, he switched off the light. Now, sleep would come.

20. HEAT
16 SEPTEMBER 2016

THE SUMMER WAS TOO FAR ALONG FOR A SNOW JOB. Instead, at the Falls Church Community Airport just outside Washington, to which he directed the cab that picked them up at the house on P Street, McCann simply told the yawning FBO manager that his wife's mother had suddenly taken ill and that he needed to charter a plane pronto for Roanoke, Virginia. Twenty minutes later they were in the air in a six-place Cessna.

"We should be landing in Roanoke in about twelve minutes," said the pilot. It was just half an hour after takeoff, and dawn, like a thief scaling a porch roof, had just extended its fingers over the eastern horizon. The rolling landscape below them alternated between pale highlights of wooded hills and the deep purple shadows of intervening valleys, but here and there could be seen a flat section of paved secondary road.

"Sooner than that," said Keefe, letting the muzzle of the Tokarev peep from beneath the folds of his raincoat.

"Christ, mister!" said the pilot. "You don't want me to land down *there*?"

"I do, indeed."

"But there isn't a house or telephone within miles."

"That's why I picked it."

The pilot shrugged. He was paid to fly the plane, not

to dispute its possession with a man who looked as if he might be careless with firearms. He put the Cessna down gently on the pavement and braked it to a gentle stop. Climbing out, he accepted the telephone number the hijacker gave him with the assurance that he would be well repaid for his plane and trouble. "Sure," the pilot said, without conviction. Stealing a plane was bad enough; why did the guy have to try to con him as well?

Twenty minutes later McCann landed the Cessna at the Roanoke Municipal Airport. While it was being filled with gas, he left Karine Collier to engage the attention of the ground crew while he sauntered over to the fire fighters' shack. There he found the three men on duty sacked out in the sleeping quarters. Closing the door quietly upon them, he inspected the equipment bay. Nozzles, wrenches, axes, extension poles, Halligan tools, dividing breeching, pry bars, and lengths of coiled hose were neatly arranged on shelves and wall racks. By the door hung six fire suits, with their bubble helmets on hooks above them, as though newly and bloodlessly decapitated.

McCann had spent hours at a time working in such suits while with Denver's Ladder Company 73, pausing in his fire fighting labors only when a soft female voice in his helmet intoned, "You have oxygen left only for ten minutes, sir. Please replenish supply."

McCann found three extra suits in their factory boxes in the firehouse storeroom. He packed two of them, with fresh air-conditioning batteries, in their own aluminum cases. He carried the two cases to the stolen aircraft. Karine Collier was feigning interest in the ground crew's labors so successfully that they paid no notice to McCann as he switched the contents of their luggage with those of the two aluminum cases. He climbed into the airplane while she thanked them warmly and signed the name Mrs. Julian R. Hartshorn to the bill. They watched wistfully as her long nylon-sheathed legs disappeared into the cabin and McCann cranked up the twin engines.

Fifteen minutes later McCann set the Cessna down on the strip at Volcano. The commuter craft was still there, untouched since they left Gland Junction only twenty-six hours before. The Russians were obviously in the clouds at Gland Junction, without need for wings to transport them there. Karine Collier changed into her running shoes for the walk into town and they set out with their bags down the road to Volcano.

They arrived in the empty village without having seen either Melanie or Madeleine, and McCann decided that Dr. Caldwell's system of surveillance wasn't quite as foolproof as she imagined, if they had got this far without detection. He changed his mind when they opened the stable doors. Facing the door were two huge German shepherds, sitting motionless but looking at them with unwavering gazes. A moment later Madeleine appeared leading two saddled horses. She grinned at them through black teeth, her stench overpowering the earthy stable smells. She passed the reins to McCann with a lascivious wink.

Of *course* they knew he was coming: the control tower watch would have radioed them the moment the plane touched down. As for the horses, that was logical, too. Where else would McCann and Karine Collier be going but to Gland Junction? Still, the smooth and unobtrusive way their return had been handled reinforced McCann's respect for Dr. Caldwell's foresight. He'd been the only man who hadn't left Gland Junction by mule-back in a plain canvas wrapper, and if he were to do it a second time he'd have to be very careful in dealing with the resourceful woman.

The cavern entrance was dim, but the moment their horses had passed through the entrance the steel doors sprang shut behind them and the overhead lights flashed on.

"We didn't expect you back so soon," Sylvia Crespi's voice said from the loudspeaker.

"Neither did we," said McCann.

"Welcome, all the same. I gather that your mission to the general was a success?"

McCann shook his head. "I'm afraid not."

"That's reassur . . . what do you mean, 'I'm afraid not'?"

McCann smiled inwardly. That got her off balance. And he'd have to keep her off balance long enough to get through those inner steel doors that guarded the inner city of Gland Junction. "What I had to tell the general didn't give him the complete picture of the enemy's intentions he anticipated, unfortunately. As a matter of fact, he received intelligence from another source that the Russians are due to launch their weapons—whatever the hell it is—within seventy-two hours. And we can't do a damned thing about it."

"You're sure about this?" said Sylvia Crespi.

"There's always room for error. Intelligence reports have been known to be wrong, but yes—the general's pretty sure."

"Yet you returned here. Why?"

McCann smiled crookedly and looked with wholly unfeigned yearning at Karine Collier.

"Of course. You want us to detoxify you, neutralize the ARP, so you can spend your last moments in your beloved's arms."

"That's it."

"Well, we'll have to see what Dr. Caldwell says before anything else."

The steel doors slid back and McCann, followed by Karine Collier, walked toward the carpeted corridor where Sylvia Crespi, looking very lovely in a white jer-

sey jumpsuit, was awaiting them. With her was a handsome, muscular young man whom she addressed as
Jules. "But I spell it J-e-w-e-l-s, and if I wasn't so pos-
sessive I'd show you why. Take Keefe's bags, Jules."

McCann's one hope for survival was in those bags. If
Sylvia Crespi decided to take a look at their contents,
he'd never have a chance. He had observed that she carried a green marker pen suspended from a gold chain
around her neck, and he didn't need to be reminded that
one dab of the green on his skin and he'd end the few
days he had left in the revolting embraces of Madeleine
or Melanie, perhaps both.

"Where do we stay?" said McCann, as they mounted
the steps to the woman's level.

Sylvia Crespi stopped at a door, opened it to a spacious apartment whose central feature was a huge bed
and wall and ceiling mirrors. "This is Karine's apartment. You'll be able to enjoy it whenever she requires
your services, Keefe. At other times you'll live in a dormitory with the other men. Leave the bags here, Jewels,
and we'll go along to Dr. Caldwell's suite."

McCann kicked the door shut, and pistols appeared in
both hands. "Please don't allow your hands to develop
wanderlust, Sylvia. Remember—six days isn't much,
but it's a lot better than six seconds, and you won't have
even that if you try to perfume me with *eau de Melanie*."

Sylvia Crespi regarded him with amusement. "You're
wasting your time, Keefe. Instead of the ecstasy of Karine's passion, you . . ."

"We'll get to the ecstasy in due time. Right now, face
down on the floor. Any deviations from the program and
Jewels gets it—just about where you'd expect."

Sylvia Crespi lay facedown on the carpet. Jewels lay
down beside her. He had listened to McCann's threats
uncomprehendingly. In his universe there was room for

only Sylvia Crespi, and she was only an arm's length away. His arm spanned the distance.

McCann, one hand holding a pistol, the other fumbling with the catch on the suitcase, heard the faint whirr of a zipper, a suppressed moan, and the sound of thrashing bodies in a happy duel in which both would achieve satisfaction. He took one look and threw the pistol on the bed. He wouldn't be needing it. He hurriedly stripped to the buff and pulled on the Mark VIII fire suit. Karine was transfixed, breathing hard, observing an interpersonal encounter for which graduate studies in psychology had never prepared her. McCann jolted her out of her reverie: "Suit up!" he said.

McCann didn't think he'd need them, but he carried a pistol in each gloved hand as he emerged from the apartment enveloped in his fire suit. Behind him came Karine Collier, taking one last soulful look behind her as she reluctantly closed the door. Though the hallways were deserted—it was still midmorning—sounds of activity were heard behind many of the doors they passed as they proceeded toward Dr. Caldwell's quarters adjacent to the research laboratories. She was at her workbench, but with a different assistant from the last they'd seen with her.

"Can't you see I'm busy?" came a strangled gasp from Dr. Caldwell as their shadows fell across the bed. "Come back later. Or better yet, not at all."

"No can do," McCann apologized. He wrapped the pistol barrel in a towel and slugged the beautiful young man behind the ear. He didn't even sigh as he rolled off the bed and slumped in a heap on the floor.

Only then did Dr. Caldwell turn over on her back and see who had interrupted her morning labors. "*You!* I thought you . . ."

"Yes, I know," said McCann, cutting her off. "I'd like

to linger and chat and get the name of your instructor in erotic aerobics and all that, but we're in a hurry."

"That suit . . ."

"Exactly. It's air-tight, water-tight, and heat resistant. Has its own oxygen supply, helmet mike, and, like Ivory soap, it floats. In about ten seconds, it's going to float down to your storage facility and then float out with some of your special all-purpose pheromone, male and female. About three gallons of each should be sufficient. Also, a vial of the neutralizing agent for your antirape pheromone. And, since it's on the house, one of those 'wide-spectrum' kits Sylvia told me about—the ones with limited response, attenuated, slow-acting, age-specific, and other specialty pheromones."

Dr. Caldwell yawned and stretched her remarkably well constructed and well preserved limbs, like a cat wallowing in a sun beam. "You'll do nothing of the sort. This room is equipped with an alarm, a secret alarm which, for all you know, I may have already activated. If I have, in about eight of your ten seconds a mob of angry, active, and exceedingly virile young men are going to boil through that door and smear you all over the walls, poor dear. You can't shoot them all." She smiled angelically.

"I won't shoot any of them," McCann promised. He transferred a pistol to his pocket. A green felt marker pen appeared in its place. He took off the pen's cap and approached the naked woman.

When she saw what it was, she screamed and shrank back against the headboard.

"That's right, Dr. Caldwell. *Eau de Melanie*, and if you don't behave you're going to undergo a sudden reversal in sexual preferences. But somehow I don't think your lust for Melanie is going to compensate for the loss of young Lothario there."

"What do you want, exactly?" said Dr. Caldwell, her voice suddenly businesslike.

"I've just told you."

"And what do you plan to do with these six gallons of nonspecific pheromone?"

"There's a war on, you know. It's called the Cold War. Well, my good Doctor, the Cold War's about to get the hots."

21. NIGHTFLIGHT
16 SEPTEMBER 2016

THE ADMIRAL'S SECRETARY ANSWERED, AS SHE ALWAYS did, on the first ring.

"This is Andre Desautels," said McCann, using the name he had adopted while investigative reporter for the *Kansas City Star*.

"Oh, yes, Mr. Desautels. My boss was expecting your call. He's out right now, but he can be reached at 445–0436 in exactly ten minutes."

McCann thanked her and hung up. "Let's grab a cup of coffee," he said to Karine Collier. He needed one. It was four in the afternoon, and they had spent more of the day aloft than on the ground, flying first from Washington to Volcano via Roanoke, and then from Volcano to Minot, North Dakota, home of Argus Wing—the AYES special project air arm. They left the phone booth and drove to a bar and grille across the small town. He had called on the admiral's personal line, so the Russian Embassy in Washington would be routinely running a number trace. And although it was unlikely that they would associate his present alias with those they already knew, there was no point in taking unnecessary chances. While Karine was ordering coffee, McCann went to a pay phone and called the Washington area number the admiral's secretary had given him.

"Where the hell are you?" said the admiral without preamble.

"Minot, North Dakota."

"What the hell are you doing there?"

"Going to take a plane ride."

"Where to?"

"You really don't want to know the details, Uncle. But I still need your help."

"Shoot."

"Call the base commander and clear me for anything I ask."

The admiral hesitated. The AYES air base and the high-flying Argus Wing had been established as an adjunct of the Mutual Inspection Teams for reconnaissance of the Soviet Union; there wasn't an atomic weapon within ten miles of the base. Besides, none of the planes at Minot had racks which could accommodate an atomic bomb. What did McCann propose to do—dive a plane into the Kremlin?

Somehow, the admiral thought not. Guiles and wiles were McCann's stock in trade, not brute force. Whatever he had in mind would be much more imaginative and ultimately more nasty than a kamikaze attack on the Kremlin. And of course, that was what the admiral had counted on all along. His only concern was that it succeed, and if he was kept ignorant of the details, so much the better when explanations to the president were due.

"I suppose I can handle your request," the admiral said, finally. "Anything else?"

"Did Dr. Semm leave any papers—any clue to what he injected me with?"

"No, son, I'm sorry—he didn't."

"See you in church." McCann hung up.

The ICBM silos at Minot AFB which had been in America's first line of defense in the closing years of the twentieth century were still intact, loaded, serviced daily, and ready to go. But there was now a difference: with each American missile team was a team of Russian officers round-the-clock. Their sole duty was to maintain pressure—presumably with the weight of the hand or foot—on a key which produced a steady radio signal picked up by monitors in Russia. Were this signal to be interrupted, Russian defenses would be placed on instant alert.

In practice, an easy familiarity between Russian and United States Air Force officers had developed over the years, and defenses had become shockingly slack on both sides. The American officers went through the motions of a launching drill on each watch, but as a matter of slavish routine rather than life-or-death exigency. Once finished, they pushed back their chairs and joined the Russian observer-of-the-watch in a game of poker or bridge—seldom chess, which the Russians always won. As for the Russian-manned radio key, it was in a state of permanent depression, being held down by a 4 ¼ pound copy of the *Sioux U-11 ICBM, U.S. Air Force Maintenance, Operating and Launch Procedures for.*

Flight operations from the AYES base were an altogether different matter. Every six hours a Mach-5.6 Dekko scramjet took to the air headed due north across the polar icecap for Russia. By the time it reached the island of Novaya Zemlya in the Barents Sea, the four-place Dekko would be cruising in near-vacuum at 188,000 feet. The hypersonic craft then swept south from Leningrad, made a looping turn over the Black Sea, returned north across the Caspian Sea and the Ural Mountains, and refueled from a supersonic tanker over the North Pole before heading south for another north-south-north run over the Soviet Union. Altogether, each flight made six passes over Russia and two refueling rendezvous, subjecting the entire six million square miles of continental Russia to searching inspection in a little over four hours.

The four-times-daily missions—Russia flew an equal number over Canada and the United States—were strictly for surveillance, an open-skies policy that had finally been adopted more than half a century after President Dwight D. Eisenhower first proposed it. Armed with cameras, infrared sensors, side-scan radar, Geiger counters, and other inspection gear, the Argus scramjets laid bare everything that went on inside Russia which could possibly indicate preparations for a sneak attack against the American continent. Heat emissions from communications satellite launches, train and truck movements, troop transfers down to company level, the opening of a new uranium mine in Siberia, mass political rallies in Red Square—all were noted and assessed for war potential. Since no larger-scale war can begin without extensive preparations and troop movements, a successful sneak attack was impossible and peace thus assured.

Base commander P. D. Dandy was waiting for them in his office. A tall, narrow-waisted, black-mustachioed, hard-muscled man immaculately attired in a lieutenant-general's uniform but incongruously wearing dirty and scuffed tennis shoes, he welcomed McCann and Karine Collier with a crunching handshake and a warm smile. "I'm P. D. Dandy, but you can call me 'Pig-Dog' like my troops do—behind my back—if you so prefer. I'm the man who's going to authorize your little adventure over the Soviet Union, provided you can persuade me it's sufficiently nasty."

"On the contrary, General," McCann assured him, "what I've got in mind for them they're going to love so much that they'll forget all about taking over the United States and the rest of the world. In two weeks you will be able to stroll across the border with a squad of Girl Scouts and take over the Kremlin."

"Sure I will," said the general amiably. He'd seen several dozen ultimate weapons come and go, and the Russians were still there, making ugly faces in all directions. Still, the woman with the dreamer was a knockout. "Both going on this flight?" he inquired casually.

"Just me," replied McCann.

"Well, you'll be wanting to get on with it." He rubbed his hands briskly and summoned his chief of operations, Colonel Bakersmith. "It will be my honor to entertain your lovely lady until you return, so if you break a leg or fall out of Dekko Delta at 150,000 feet, you can be assured she's in good hands."

"Well, sir," said Colonel Bakersmith as they walked down the passageway toward the operations room, "how can I help you?"

"I suppose your Dekkos are equipped with fuel-dump nozzles, in the event you have to jettison fuel during an emergency landing?"

"That's right—one on each wingtip."

"If I wanted to inject an aerosol into the slipstream in such a way as to cover the entire U.S.S.R., would there be any problem in rigging it up?"

"Rigging—no. But we're limited in cargo capacity: you'd have to have a couple of shiploads of aerosol to cover six million square miles with even a microscopic layer of liquid."

"This stuff is extremely powerful and extremely concentrated. All I'll need is a remote timed-release mechanism."

"Dr. van Pelt is your man."

McCann's man turned out to be a woman—of sorts. She was flat-chested and fifty and wore thick-lensed horn-rimmed glasses. Her uncombed gray hair was al-

most as short as her downy mustache. Her white lab
coat had last been laundered two weeks before and was
holed with cigarette burns, and her sensible brogues
were a depressing complement to a pair of stout, vari-
cose legs. But she had kind, intelligent eyes and a soft,
feminine voice that belied her stumpy, masculine appearance.

"Easy as pie," she informed McCann when he had
described his problem.

"How long will it take?"

"If I work straight through it should be ready by
sunrise. I'll have to locate proper pressure containers for
your mysterious liquid, pressurize it with neon as a
nonreactive propellant, rig up a remote release and shut-
off control, and have the containers installed in the
wings' outboard fuel cells. That'll give you time for eight
hours rest and the two-hour briefing, since you say you
want to push the button yourself. And don't forget to
make noo-noo: there ain't no gentleman's lavoratories
aboard the Dekko."

McCann was assigned a room at bachelor officers'
quarters and was asleep before the echoes of his shoes
thudding on the floor had faded away. He was exhausted. The day had been long and wearying, but that
was the way he wanted it. He didn't dare allow himself
to think about the dawn five days hence, about the last
dawn he would ever see. He resolutely put out of his
mind visions of the suffering the metallic ions in his body
would cause before the machine sputtered and fell silent.
Would he have the guts to shorten the process once it
began? He didn't want to think about it. He didn't want
to think about anything—about Karine Collier kicking
hell out of Minot, North Dakota, with General Dandy,
about the saturated-fat saturated dinner they'd consume
at the officers' club, or about the two gallons of nonspecific pheromone he had handed over to Dr. van Pelt with

the injunction that it had to be handled by remote control so that not a single deadly molecule could escape. He wanted only to sleep—and not, perchance, to dream.

He slept until 0500, when he was shaken awake by a comely female sergeant and told he was expected at the breakfast table in twenty minutes. In the mess hall, he had a glass of fresh orange juice and a couple of cups of coffee, and met his fellow crew members—the two pilots and the systems officer. He dozed through the long briefing that followed, until nudged awake to be fitted for his G-suit and helmet. After he was togged out, Dr. van Pelt, looking more haggard than ever, stopped by the ready room to report that the canisters were installed and that he'd be briefed on the release procedure by the systems officer. She wished him a smooth flight, reminded him again to make noo-noo and, if he could—doo-doo—and departed.

The Dekko Delta 127 was all space-age aircraft. The canards seemed about the size of playing cards, and the wings, about six feet long, were tucked back against the long needle-nosed fuselage like those of a hawk plunging down upon its prey. The canopy covering the flight deck was flush with the fuselage so that both takeoff and landing were on instruments. Indeed, at the speed and height they were flying, there was little to see but the black sky above, for when they reached Russia on the other side of the earth it would be night.

Strapped in his seat, Keefe McCann felt like a man in a straightjacket, levers, buttons, and other projections hedged him in on all sides. The two pilots started the engines, which were located well to the rear of the cockpit, and the plane rumbled out on the tarmac, bouncing on its nose strut like a genuflecting courtier to the end of the runway. The pilot lined up his craft by reference to the flight director, applied power, and McCann was shoved back to his seat as though the plane were being shot off a catapult.

The noise was awesome, but the speed was even more so. The airspeed indicator registered 235 knots by the time the plane cleared the end of the runway. The pilot hauled back on the miniature stick at the left of his seat. The Dekko's nose rotated through an 85 degree angle, and they left the earth behind. They were passing through Mach-2.8 when the pilot leveled off at 185,000 feet. He applied more throttle and the Mach indicator rose slowly to Mach-4.2, the speed at which they'd cruise during the entire trip except for turns and over-the-pole refueling. The cabin was absolutely silent. Sound doesn't travel well at those altitudes, and even if it did, they would have left the sound of their engines far behind them.

The pilot, a freckled young lieutenant-colonel, put the ship on autopilot and removed his helmet. "Damned nuisance," he observed. "Nobody would wear it if it wasn't for stupid regulations."

"Isn't it safer?" ventured McCann.

"Not really. The cabin's pressurized, but if anything happened at this altitude and speed we'd buy the farm anyway. You'll probably have noticed by now that parachutes are not provided. Either this mother lands nice and smooth or you'll have about two seconds to observe that it isn't going to. Either way, you're not kept long in suspense."

Over the Barents Sea, forty seconds from Murmansk and the northwest coast of Russia, McCann flipped up the dispersal switch and locked it into position. It stayed in this position for the remainder of the flight, except the refueling runs over the north pole and the return leg from arctic Russia to Minot AFB.

Since the plane hewed to its flight plan by automatic pilot except during the Mach-1.3 refueling operation, the

crew was on its own. The pilot read a paperback about a
Mustang fighter pilot in World War II, looking up from
time to time to check his instruments. The copilot slept
fitfully. The weapons office/navigator listened to classi-
cal music on his headphones. Keefe McCann morosely
counted the hours before he would be flying on other
wings in another world.

Strapped into his seat, he experienced a growing
claustrophobia. It was not only the harness; fate, too,
held him immobilized. Here he was helpless, more a
prisoner than he had been even in the Pennsylvania State
Prison, for he was imprisoned by his own morbid
thoughts. The worst of it was that he *felt* good, bursting
with vitality and the will to live. No suggestion of the ion
illness that would kill him had yet manifested itself. But
like all men who have been told by doctors that their
robust health is only illusory, that they are actually dying
from some disease which is yet to display its ravages,
McCann was constantly on the alert for the first signs of
decline. Each cough, each transient moment of faint-
ness, each shooting pain, was the signal for panic, which
only a firm effort of will was able to quell. And confinement in this tiny flight deck intensified the dread of fast-
approaching death.

Only when the plane dropped out of the sky toward
the landing strip at Mach-1.6, and the ground came rushing up at them, did McCann's mood change. He felt his
pulse rate climb with the excitement of imminent danger.
But he knew he could relax when the pilot, his hands
folded in his lap, yawned elaborately just as the wheels
touched down, the spoilers and drag chute deployed, and
the thrust reversers roared. Only when the plane came to
a standstill at the end of the strip did the pilot resume
control of his craft and taxi it in to the hanger where,
McCann observed, General Dandy was awaiting him.

With him was Karine Collier, her yellow dress whipping around her long smooth legs in the noonday breeze.

"Good flight?" asked the general, as McCann climbed down the long ladder.

"I've had more exciting rides on a commuter train," McCann confessed.

"And that's just the way we want it. Our most exciting rides these days aren't in airplanes."

Was there a certain note in the general's voice? Perhaps, for it seemed to McCann that Karine avoided his eyes. Well, what the hell. Life was too short to worry about whether she was cheating on him already, since she would in any case have unlimited opportunities to cheat on him five days hence.

One thing was certain: as soon as he got back to his quarters, things were going to change abruptly. With his mission to Moscow behind him, he was going to take a hot shower, douse himself liberally with the contents of the vial of antirape pheromone neutralizer he had taken from Gland Junction, summon Karine Collier, double-lock the door, and worry about tomorrow when tomorrow came—if it ever did.

"I'm going to the BOQ," he announced to Karine. "Be at my room in fifteen minutes."

He had just stepped out of the shower when the telephone rang.

"Tell her I'm in Room 141," he said into the receiver.

"I'll make a note of it," came Dr. van Pelt's voice, "but that isn't why I'm calling you."

"Oh, Dr. Van Pelt, it's you."

"None other. Do you have a minute?"

"That's exactly what I can give you—sixty seconds."

"It's about the mysterious liquid I filled those pressure canisters with. I got to thinking about the effect of heat on it."

"What heat? The stuff was released at a couple of hundred degrees below zero or whatever it is at that altitude."

"Of course. It *is* close to absolute zero at night at those altitudes. But I forgot the heat of the engines, you see. The wingtips are far forward of the engines, but the exhaust is a fireball—more than 8,600 degrees Fahrenheit. That heat creates an expanding vortex like a fiery cone a hundred miles behind the Dekko Delta, don't you see?"

"Do you mean, maybe the aerosol was consumed by the exhaust?"

"That would be my bet. All you volunteered to me about it was that it is an organic compound. Well, I can't think of any organic substance on earth whose chemical makeup wouldn't be modified by such extremes of temperature and pressure."

While talking, McCann's hand, almost as if it had a life of its own, had opened the compartment of his suitcase in which he had stowed the vial of anti-ARP. He withdrew his hand. If Dr. van Pelt was right, that meant that the pheromone with which he had liberally doused the Soviet Union had been altered in its fundamental chemistry. And any alteration, Dr. Caldwell had assured him, rendered the substance totally ineffective. Well, it was for such contingencies that he had taken the precaution of bringing three times the amount necessary to get the job done.

But it did require a revision of his plans. No anti-antirape pheromone just yet. No Karine Collier between cool sheets. Another method of making Mother Russia a raving nymphomaniac.

But hold everything. There was a chance that Dr. van Pelt's calculations were wrong. What if the flame *didn't* alter the chemical structure of the F^3?

"No," said Dr. van Pelt grimly, when he suggested

that maybe her thesis was incorrect. "Don't get your hopes up."

"What do you mean?"

"Well, I know I'm cutting my throat for telling you this, but look—I'm first and foremost a scientist. A physical chemist, actually. Your mysterious solution intrigued me, and I wasn't about to let it get away before I got some inkling of what kind of poison could be so powerful a couple of gallons of it could do things to 300 million Russians."

"You didn't . . ."

"I did. Under the most comprehensive safeguards, naturally. The analysis was done under a hood, with absolute atmospheric integrity, and with less than a milligram of the substance."

"What kind of analysis?" said McCann with foreboding.

"Paper chromatography. But I'm afraid it didn't tell me much. I determined it had no alkaloids or, indeed, any of the usual poisons, hallucinogens, and other nasty things. In fact, it turned out to be a mixture of nothing more than complex alcohols mixed with a few exotic esters and various analogues of androsterone I'd never before encountered. I must confess, I'm no closer to knowing what was in those canisters than I was before I started the analysis."

"Good. You're not supposed to know."

"Please—I'll keep it to myself, I promise!"

"No soap, lady. Better you don't know."

There was a long, aggrieved silence at the end of the line. Finally, she sighed.

"All right, I won't push it. But this is one mystery I won't carry happily to the grave. I guess I'll just frame the chromatogram to remind myself that . . ."

"Frame the paper? *You've still got the paper chromatogram?*"

"Sure—I'm holding it up to the light right now, not that I see anything particularly interesting. So far as I can tell, it's harmless, and it sure ain't going to kill any Russians, if that's what you had in mind. I have tested it twenty ways to Sunday and—hold on, there's somebody at the door."

McCann felt his legs turn to water. He sat down on the bed. He heard, as from a great distance, the voice of Dr. van Pelt.

"Oh, it's you, general. What brings you—why are you *looking* at me that way? General—stop! You're tearing my lab coat. Get off of me, you crazy bastard! Let me up—let me *up*, I tell you!"

Then her voice tapered off. McCann heard the rustle of clothing, a rich muted sigh, and then her husky whisper, "On second thought . . ."

22. ART ACHES
17 SEPTEMBER 2016

CARMELITA DE LOS ANGELES WAS HER NAME, AND TO Arthur Artusov she was the woman he had sought only in his fantasies, aware that such perfection did not exist in real life. She had all the fire and passion traditionally associated with Latins, yet a tenderness and sensitivity he had never enjoyed at the hands of any woman. She was completely foreign in his experience—beautiful, tempestuous, ravenous for love, full of laughter and light-hearted, yet filled with unfathomable desires. For her, the sexual act was one of infinite possibilities, serendipitous surprises, and contortional complexities whose very facet required the loving attention to detail of a Persian portraitist painting a miniature. In her hands, lovemaking was a supreme work of art.

Comparisons with his wife Irina were as unrewarding as comparing a surrealist's daubs to a Murillo. Irina was short and thick-legged, had sagging breasts, skin the color and texture of the cabbage she cooked so inexpertly, the flat nose and slit eyes of the Lapps from whom she was descended, and the voice of a foghorn on a Baltic garbage scow. With her Artusov had fathered two sons, both of them spoiled and obsessed with decadent Western clothes, deafening music, and counter-revolutionary ideas, tolerated in the Institute for

International Relations and the Young Communist
League only because of their father's position, and without an iota of affection for either parent. Irina drank too
much, dressed like a streetwalker on Saturday night, and
endured his infrequent embraces with stoicism. But she
was, of course, the daughter of the second-ranking
member of the Central Committee, and therefore divorce
was now as impossible as marriage twenty-one years
earlier, due to her father's position as first secretary of
the Kiev Soviet, had been desirable.

Carmelita might have belonged to a different species,
so profound were her differences from Irina. Artusov
knew the secret of his attraction toward her—she shared
without reserve the pheromonic secrets of Gland Junction while they relaxed with a cigarette after their first
galvanic sexual encounter—but decided that her marking him as her property with her personalized pheromone was unnecessary: one look at her smooth rounded
limbs, her waist-length raven hair, and her smoldering
dark eyes, and he was a man floundering in a vast sea of
desire. Once he had actually made love with her he sank
between the waves, content to drown in her soft concav-
ities.

Yet, with that small portion of his brain that had not
been engulfed by passion, he realized what was happening and what his fate was going to be. Though in that first
day he was but one in a relay of lovers summoned to
Carmelita de los Angeles's suite, he recognized that even
his oft-demonstrated powers of recuperation would
eventually be exhausted. Resting in his single bunk in the
men's dormitory—double bunks had been abandoned
when Dr. Caldwell found that for each man a time came
when he no longer had the strength to climb to the upper
—he speculated as to how long he could possibly last.
Despite his demonstrated linguistic ability, he had never
been called upon for three or four sexual conjunctions in

a single day—and still wanting more, unquestionably sexual stress would eventually wear him down. He'd lose weight, shrivel, dry up, and one day simply be blown away like a corn husk in an autumn wind. And yet, knowing that, he lay in his bunk aquiver, his heart thumping as he waited for the next summons to the suite of Carmelita de los Angeles.

Artusov levered himself up on his elbow and gazed down the line of recumbent men. A few sat on the edge of their bunks, quietly expounding the virtues and performances of the women who possessed them, and derisively discounting the exploits of others who insisted theirs were more passionate, more imaginative, or longer lasting. But the majority of the men were either immersed in sex-drugged slumber or stared blankly at the ceiling of a chamber as austere and devoid of decoration as a monastery cell. Awake or asleep, there was only one thing on their minds—exquisite anticipation of the next ride on the Valkyries who would bear them into the Valhalla of venery.

Artur Artusov pondered his future. No room there for the KGB, or the Kremlin, or even Mother Russia. The sexual impulse had crushed all thoughts of that once all-consuming existence into a very small recess of his brain. It was only by a major effort of will that he could concentrate for as long as half a minute on his responsibilities as senior KGB resident before the recollection of Carmelita de los Angeles's sinuous body moving with exquisite grace and control against his own eclipsed every other thought. He *wanted* to think about his duties as resident; it was the patriotic thing to do. But a sense of realism kept throwing such lofty thoughts out the window, leaving him with the realization that politics and power and progress and prosperity were all children's playthings, that all life could offer was summed up in one word: *pizda*—what the Americans called poontang.

He sighed, thanked his seldom-acknowledged Russian Orthodox god for having delivered him to Gland Junction, and fell into a deep, troubled sleep.

Dr. Josephine Caldwell could not sleep, either in company or alone. After Keefe McCann and Karine Collier had left, carrying six gallons of the precious and potent F^3, all of it the dangerous, nonspecific variety, she had been a troubled woman. Dispersal of those pheromones among a population would have disastrous effects. But perhaps the greatest potential disaster would be that the pheromones could be traced back to Volcano, West Virginia, and Gland Junction would suddenly cease to exist, obliterated by the stroke of some undersexed bureaucrat's pen.

Keefe McCann's demands had to be met—his threat to dope her with Melanie-specific pheromone was too frightful to contemplate. Moreover, his objectives seemed just and honorable. Though she now considered herself less an American than the doyenne of Gland Junction, she could appreciate the necessity of preempting Russia's strike, which as McCann pointed out would destroy Gland Junction along with the rest of America. But once he had countered that threat, as he seemed confident he would do, what then?

McCann would, of course, be a national hero. And that would cause complications. For even if only the powerful few in the government knew that he was the author of Russia's discomfiture, they would want to know details. What was his weapon, and how did he obtain it?

By now, twenty-four hours after the theft of the pheromone, he had presumably made his arrangements to disperse it throughout Soviet Russia. His next step was predictable: still under the overpowering urge to sleep with Karine Collier, he would seek a quiet place—a

motel or remote country house, more than likely—and
apply to his skin the antirape pheromone neutralizer he
had taken from her laboratory. A moment later, and for
quite a few moments thereafter, his limbs would be tied
in a Gordian knot with those of Karine Collier. In that
state of suspenseful animation, his superiors would certainly track him down, subject him to intense interrogation, and discover the secret of Gland Junction.

But that would take time. And if they could find him,
so could Artur Artusov.

Two stalwart young men on light duty brought Artusov to Dr. Caldwell's office. He didn't come peacefully.
He struggled with his captors, trying to break away from
their grip, using all the *sambo* tricks he had learned at
the KGB Academy, to no avail: one of the young men
had been a Force Reconn captain with the Marines, the
other a full-contact karate champion of the West Coast
for three years. Knowing Artusov's background, they
were not gentle.

They thrust him through the doorway to the office
where Dr. Josephine Caldwell sat, handsome in a
powder-blue linen skirt, high-heeled shoes, pendulous
ivory earrings, and nothing else, behind her desk. His
ear was swelling from an open-handed chop, a front
tooth was loose behind a thick lip, and his right eye was
turning a ripe sunset mauve. But his head was clear and
it contained but a single thought, which he expressed
with vigor.

"I don't care *who* the hell you are," he yelled, when
Dr. Caldwell identified herself as the administrator of
Gland Junction. "The bell just rang, and it's my turn with
Carmelita, and by God I'm going to take it."

"Keep a civil tongue in your Muscovite mouth. You
are a wretched Russian KGB spy, and an enemy of my
country," said Dr. Caldwell, "and as such I hope you fry

in hell. But not just yet, for I have need of your services."

Artusov smelled quiff pro quo. "If I do what you want, can I get to . . ."

"Carmelita? Yes, you may. But first I must have your answer to a few questions."

"Ask."

"First, a certain Keefe McCann—who also goes by the names of Delano, Barkley, and Haversham—yesterday held up and robbed Gland Junction. You and your men were in pursuit of this man when you arrived here, is that not correct?"

"That is correct." Artusov was in no danger of forgetting why he had come to the place, but against the prospect of sleeping with Carmelita the reason now seemed trivial.

"So if I allow you to leave Gland Junction, you'd go after him?"

"Only if I can I take Carmelita with me."

"That's impossible, but we will arrange for you to come back to her."

Through compressed lips Artusov said: "No. It's Carmelita or nothing."

"Have it your way. Gentlemen, he is to be confined to his quarters until I . . ."

"Very well," said Artusov hastily. "I agree."

"And when you catch up with McCann, what will you do?"

"Kill him, of course," growled Artusov, praying it was not the answer this elegant woman sought. She looked man-hungry, all right, but not bloodthirsty. If he had guessed right, she would pick somebody less inclined to violence to find McCann and allow him to get back to Carmelita de los Angeles. "I'll kill him without mercy."

"Yes, that is exactly what you must do," said Dr. Caldwell, nodding with satisfaction.

"But it might take me days to find him," protested Artusov. "Being away from Carmelita even for a single day will kill me."

"Try cold showers. Or exercise your will power."

"Where Carmelita is concerned, I have none. Then Artusov thought of a more persuasive argument. "Frankly, I'm so obsessed with her that every other thought is driven right out of my head. But were she with me, you see . . ."

"No. That would never work. You'd spend all your time churning up the bedclothes instead of looking for McCann." She studied her long, manicured fingernails. It went against her principles to allow men to leave Gland Junction alive, but this was an emergency. She had to neutralize McCann, and Artusov was the only available man capable of doing so. Besides, while McCann had contrived to make himself a free agent, there were ways of guaranteeing that Artusov would do the job and return.

"Now, then, Comrade Artusov, here's what we're going to do: I'm going to give you an injection which will temporarily suppress your desire for Carmelita. However, the injection is like aspirin in that its effect will gradually wear off. The longer it takes you to find and kill McCann—*and* the woman who masquerades as his wife, by the way—the stronger your desire to be back with Carmelita will become."

"I see. How long do I have before the effect of the injection completely dissipates?"

"Three days."

That would be more than enough, Artusov calculated. With his network of agents and information it should take him no more than twelve hours to locate McCann, and once located, two or three seconds to kill him. Then he could hurry back to his beloved Carmelita, never to leave her again. Luck had come to his rescue.

Artusov bared his arm.

Dr. Caldwell picked up the needle. "Drop your pyjamas."

Artusov complied.

Dr. Caldwell came from behind the desk and swabbed his buttock with a sponge. She liked men, but with this one she was willing to make an exception. And she didn't like what circumstances had forced her to make him do. But to survive is the first law of life, and it didn't impair her chances of doing so by inflicting a little pain on the KGB bastard. She jabbed the needle in to the hilt.

Artusov didn't react at all. He waited until she extracted the needle, calmly pulled up his pyjama bottoms, and tied the cord. Eaten up by a compulsive craving for Carmelita de los Angeles, his face had been flushed, his pulse racing, and his eyes a little mad. But now, within seconds, a great calm descended over him. His face resumed its normal boiled-potato pallor, his pulse slowed, and his eyes narrowed to slits. Thoughts of Carmelita swirled briefly through his mind and then were gone, washed away like a dancing dust devil deluged under a sudden summer shower. Visions of a dead McCann—poisoned, shot, strangled, eaten by piranha, fallen from a high place, crushed beneath the treads of a bulldozer—filled his mind.

Washington Central occupied an entire sixteen-story building at 17th and K streets, and it was there, less than two hours after having received the injection and flown to the nation's capital in the commuter plane he personally piloted, that Artur Artusov established his command post. With the strands of information that came in from his myriad sources that afternoon Artusov would weave the rope that would hang McCann.

But the task proved much simpler than he imagined. A Cessna aircraft, quickly identified as having been stolen by McCann, had been spotted in Roanoke. There McCann had evidently stolen two fire fighting uniforms. It required no great intuitive leap for Artusov to grasp that air-tight suits with their own oxygen supply would be indispensable equipment for stealing the F^3 pheromone from Gland Junction. And why the F^3? Because Dr. Caldwell had mentioned a robbery, and the only thing worth taking from Gland Junction would be the pheromone.

What McCann would do with the pheromone was less clear. He might nourish hopes of enslaving large urban centers as Artusov himself had been enslaved, to profit by their diverted energies to seize power and make himself a dictator, even of so large a country as the United States. That would take consummate organization, but the weapon to do the job was in his hands, and McCann had already shown himself to be daring and resourceful.

On the other hand, he might be simply an idealist and patriot, devoted to the national cause. If so, he would be even more dangerous. If he were somehow able to spread the substance throughout Russia, perhaps by impregnating rain clouds with it, the chaos which would follow in its train would be more devastating than ten thousand hydrogen bombs.

The first possibility could be dealt with at relative leisure. It would take much time and the service of many confederates to subvert the United States in such a way as to redound to McCann's benefit. But the second allowed no such time margin. The F^3 was so powerful that a few liters of pheromone could turn the 300 million Russians literally upside down, were it to be distributed over the nation's six million square miles.

Only two methods of delivery were feasible: satellite and aircraft.

Artusov immediately warned Moscow of the danger. He was gratified to learn an hour later that the leaders in the Kremlin had decided to demand that the United States suspend all commercial and Dekko overflights immediately "for technical reasons," and gave orders that any satellite launched from America during the past twenty-four hours, and passing over Russia, be shot down forthwith.

By nine o'clock that evening, Washington Central had tracked McCann's Cessna to Minot AFB in North Dakota, where he had landed more than twenty-four hours before. He would have had plenty of time to board a Dekko surveillance aircraft and impregnate all of Russia with his F^3 poison. But Moscow reported no unusual activity. That meant that McCann must have failed. He would soon know he failed. He would try again.

But this time Artur Artusov would be waiting for him.

23. BANKROLL
18 SEPTEMBER 2016

FOR THE FIRST TIME IN DECADES, ADMIRAL RICARDO RI-vera Handy felt comfortable with his years. When in his fifties and the prime of life, he was considered too old for seagoing command and had been relegated as commandant of the Thirteenth Naval District. In his sixties, the abdundant energy he possessed in his fifties would have been valuable in his job as head of the Atomic Yields Estimates Service, to which declining powers allowed him to spend no more than fourteen hours a day trying to crowbar secrets out of Russia. But now, in his seventies, he rejoiced: he wouldn't have much longer to live, and the less the better, considering that he was probably going to spend his remaining days in solitary confinement in a federal penitentiary.

There was a bitter irony in his fate: the man whom he arranged to have freed from the penitentiary was the same man who would be responsible for the admiral's taking his place there—Keefe McCann. But the admiral didn't blame McCann. The young man had done his best to carry out the admiral's orders. He'd done even better. He had declared a one-man war against the Soviet Union, holding that nation responsible for cutting short his life through the instrumentality of its late agent Dr. Semm, who alone possessed the formula of the chelating agent which could save him. Since McCann had gone all the way, the least Handy could do was back him to the hilt, even though it was going to cost his freedom.

Or maybe his life. That depended on whether there would be bloodshed in Denver. McCann assured him that he would try to avoid it, but when a company of determined men descended upon a Federal Reserve Bank of the United States with the intention of removing every last greenback from its vaults, a little precautionary gunfire could never be ruled out. And if it came to that, Admiral Ricardo Rivera Handy would surely hang.

"What's yours, Mac?"

"Soda," replied Keefe McCann.

"Whiskey and soda?"

"Soda," said McCann firmly. "No whiskey."

The bartender grimaced. Two-bit patrons who drank soda were usually good for a two-bit tip. On the other hand, he decided philosophically, patrons such as this one—heavy in the shoulders and thick of the neck—who drank whiskey so early in the afternoon sometimes wrecked the bar before sundown. He sighed and filled the glass with the bubbling liquid.

"Who's the beautiful side of beef, Rif?" asked a blonde, who had been a brunette and eighteen pounds lighter three or four years ago, from down the bar.

"Big spender from back east," said Rif, not concerned that his voice would carry.

"Think he'd buy a thirsty woman a drink?"

"Sure, if you drink sarsaparilla."

"Ask the lady what she would like," said McCann, looking into his glass.

"A double of the usual," said the born-again blonde.

"One double, coming up," said Rif the bartender, pouring two jiggers of weak tea from a bottle labeled

'Vale of Tralee Irish Whiskey—eighteen years old.' He placed its next to McCann's drink on the bar.

The blonde detached herself from her bar stool and took up residence on the one beside McCann, allowing her skirt to slide two thirds the way up a shapely thigh whose thumb-bruised flesh was camouflaged by sheer nylon. She picked up her drink and looked McCann in the eye from beneath hooded lids. "Cheers!"

"Prosit!"

"Just get into town?" The blonde took a slug of the tea.

"Just."

"Denver's a pretty dull town. I'll bet you could use a little entertainment."

"The thought had crossed my mind." McCann's eyes were on the blonde's legs, uncrossed.

She finished the glass and put it on the bar, to be filled by Rif the bartender as rapidly as the law of gravity would allow. "You sure came to the right place. I'm Marsha."

"And I am Erasmus P. Kloppenhoffer. But friends call me Ras."

Marsha let her fingers coyly tiptoe up McCann's thigh. "Well, Ras, I know a place nearby where we can be more comfortable than this—a lot more comfortable." She prodded him with a sharp elbow. "If you know what I mean."

"No, not exactly, but I'm thinking about it."

"Aren't you the one?" she laughed, showing at least two dozen tobacco-yellowed teeth. "Pay the man, Ras, and let's be off to the races."

McCann peeled a couple of bills off a large roll and dropped them on the bar. The bartender shot a swift glance at the girl, who nodded frantically as she slid off the bar stool and walked toward the door of the deserted lounge, displaying her charms balanced atop four-inch heels in the time-honored hip-swinging manner of her hallowed profession.

At the door a cab appeared miraculously. McCann helped her into it but interrupted when she instructed the driver to take them to the Denver Hilton. "Make that the Sheraton."

"That's not a good idea, sweetie," Marsha cooed. "It's farther. And besides, the Sheraton's manager knows me. He may send for the boys in blue."

McCann made comforting noises, assuring her that the manager was a friend of his and that his only mission in life was to make the stay of Erasmus P. Kloppenhoffer in Denver as pleasant as possible.

And, indeed, so it transpired. The manager himself came from behind the desk at their approach, shook Mr. Kloppenhoffer's hand warmly, bowed from the waist to his lady, and personally escorted them to the elevator.

"A few guests will be arriving shortly," McCann said as they entered the elevator. "Will you please see that they find their way to my suite?"

"It will be my pleasure, sir," the manager assured him, wondering, as the doors slid closed on his guest, who this man could be that the chairman of the board had called him personally with orders to do anything— *anything*, that is—that would make Mr. Kloppenhoffer's stay a happy one. If his guest's happiness, the manager mused, could be procured by the company of $100-a-night calls girls, then his mission would be a simple one: Denver swarmed with Marshas to whom such guests were daily bred.

Marsha was delighted with the Presidential Suite, and in her exuberance began to shed her clothing, before her client changed his mind. Alas! She had no sooner allowed her skirt to fall to the floor than it appeared he already had. He held up an admonitory finger. "You heard me say that other guests were expected, I believe?"

"Why, sure. But it will cost extra."

"Price is no object. Uncle is paying."

"Then bring 'em on!"

"You misunderstand. *You* are going to supply the guest list."

Marsha regarded him blankly. Then her face broke into a grin. "Oh, *I* get it—a *party!*"

"Like you've never seen before," McCann promised.

"How many ladies would you like—three or four? Asian, black, local housewives, that blonde movie starlet who's in town? I can get them all, and there's an especially luscious little round Peruvian girl I know named Gloria. She's a real artiste."

"Yes—all those. *And* all their sisters."

"Wait a minute," said Marsha, suddenly wary. "You're a cop. You want me to round up all my friends so you can make your big bust."

"Big busts *are* what I had in mind, as a matter of fact. But as to my being with the police, nothing could be further from the truth." McCann took the roll of bills from his pocket and tossed it to her. She caught it and flipped through the sheaf of banknotes with the practiced hand of a bank teller. "Eight hundred and fifty dollars. For how many?"

"For you alone, my sweet. The same for each young lovely you can get to this suite within ninety minutes. And for each of them, providing she is a pretty young professional like yourself, *you* will receive a bonus of $100."

"What'll they have to do?"

"Nothing they haven't had a lot of practice in, I assure you. I will make the introductions, and after that it's up to them. They can come—or go."

Marsha was already on her way to the white tele-

phone on the desk in the drawing room. While she leafed
through her telephone book, methodically dialing one
number after another and spreading the good tidings with
a minimum of verbiage, McCann had room service send
up an assortment of refreshments—which required
steady replenishment, as a stream of free-enterprising females poured into the suite, spilling into the bedrooms
and onto the balcony. When McCann estimated that the
recruits would soon peak at 120-odd, he called a halt to
enlistments and the assembled ladies of the afternoon to
attention.

"I thank you all for coming along at such short notice.
My instructions are simple if somewhat different than
usual. We will begin the afternoon with a tour—no, no,
not around the world, my sweet," he gently corrected
Marsha, who had broken in with that stock suggestion,
"—but a tour of the Federal Reserve Bank which, as you
all know, is just a block and a half from here. Conducted
tours begin every half-hour, and you will all kindly assemble in the lobby of the bank by 3:30, which is a little
less than half an hour from now, so as to be in time for
the tour beginning at that time. Is all that perfectly
clear?"

A confused murmur arose from the congregation.
"Yeah," said one, her voice rising about the rest but apparently encapsulating a common sentiment, "but who's
the John? Or should I say, who are the Johns?"

"Your grammar is impeccable, but your question must
remain moot. Frankly, I don't know. But I will assure
you of this: the golfers and tennis players among you
may practice your strokes to your heart's content, and
those who don't want to play may, if they see fit, abstain
altogether once the entertainment commences. More immediately important is your honorarium, which I now
have the pleasure to distribute."

McCann moved the Gauguin copy on the wall behind

his desk to one side, spun the combination of the safe, and removed two briefcases, which he opened on the desk. Marsha, acting as drill sergeant, prodded the women into line as Keefe McCann crossed the eager palm of each young—and some not so young—woman with a banded sheaf of ten $100 bills. When Marsha's sharp eye had eliminated those who had been paid only to then fall back in at the end of the line, some $28,000 still remained.

He took her aside. "This is for you, Marsha. Since you are the hostess of this congregation of *filles de joie*, I trust you will not be sparing with the snacks and refreshments, which the hotel is providing as a goodwill gesture to the women's movement, in which you are all expert. In return for the gratuity, I'm depending on you to get your friends to the church on time, each and every one under her own power. Agreed?"

"You can count on me, Ras" she said, stuffing the bills into her large bag, from which she had to remove various electrical and plastic appliances and a change of underclothing to accommodate the loot. She slung the bag over her shoulder and wrapped McCann in a fierce embrace. "Next time you're in town, honey," she whispered in his ear, "it's on the house."

At 3:05 that afternoon Keefe McCann pulled up to the service entrance of Denver's Federal Reserve Bank in a panel truck bearing the legend "Mallory Air-Conditioning Services." He was dressed in overalls only slightly more streaked with grease than his hands and a baseball cap he wore with the bill facing backwards. He displayed his pass and work order to the guard on duty.

"Clinton Diver," said the guard, comparing his face with the photograph. "New man, aren't you?"

McCann confessed that he was a new man with Mallory.

"Sorry, but I've got to frisk you," said the guard, running his hands over McCann's body and then inspecting the two tool boxes to see that they contained no weapons. "What's in there?" he said, pointing to an aluminum case.

McCann opened the case and displayed the anticontamination suit. "New regulations. If there's a gas or freon leak, we can trace it back and shut the line down without getting asphyxiated."

The guard nodded without interest. "Hey, lard ass," he said to an overweight young man in uniform reading a comic book in the guard room, "take Diver here to the main air-conditioning unit. You're to stay with him and make sure he doesn't stuff any gold bars in his jockstrap, got it?" He winked at McCann.

McCann followed the young man down the stairs to the second basement, which contained the steam plant and other utilities. "Work order says the power expenditure is 4 percent above average for this time of year," McCann observed. "That usually means some jerk has either set the thermostat too low or that there's a broken windowpane somewhere letting in warm air."

"Not in this building," said the fat man, shaking his head. "There aren't a hell of a lot of windows to begin with—security, you know, and they're checked every two hours. None of them's broken, and since they're the permanent kind, you'd have to break 'em to open 'em. Must be your thermostat."

"Probably. All kind of things have been going wrong in this heat wave."

McCann looked at the air-conditioning unit. It was considerably bigger than he expected, filling a large underground room. But its controls and gauges all occupied a single panel, and it was to this that, crescent wrench in hand, he turned his attention.

"Well, well," he said, squinting at a pressure gauge, "here's the trouble, right here."

The fat guard looked over his shoulder, saw nothing, put his face closer, and felt nothing as McCann aimed the crescent wrench at the man's occiput and swung with minimum force. The guard crumpled in a heap on the floor.

McCann looked at his watch. It was 3:22. By now the streetwalkers would be walking in off the street, assembling for the tour in the cavernous entrance hall. The tour guides might be somewhat taken aback to discover so many attractive if garish young females simultaneously interested in the workings of the Federal Reserve System, but certainly they wouldn't be alarmed. Metal detectors and patrols of dogs trained to sniff out explosives were only two of the defenses of this urban fortress, but they were more than enough to cope with any visitors with larceny on their minds.

McCann donned the fire suit and tested the oxygen supply. His tank was at maximum pressure, and he'd need every minute of the three hours' supply to do what he had to do in Denver. Suited up, he drilled a small hole in the air-conditioning conduit leading from the compressor to the main line and threaded it. Then he produced a three-inch steel vial with a threaded nozzle and screwed it into the conduit. He consulted his watch. It was 3:46. By now all his female contractors would be inside, touring the building. The 276 workers, approximately one third of them female, would be in their offices shuffling papers at the rate which would produce clean desktops at precisely five o'clock, and at that hour they would stream out the cathedral doors in the front of the building like lemmings rushing to the sea.

Not today, boys and girls, said McCann to himself as he twisted the handle which opened the valve on the small steel vial, sending a weak and attenuated breath of nonspecific F^3 -3M into the air-conditioning ducts. It was one of the special-purpose pheromones Dr. Caldwell had conveniently packaged in kit form. The 3M variant, she had explained, would lose its potency within forty-eight hours or, she laughed smugly, at about the same time the youngest of the men exposed to it were losing theirs.

Encumbered by his fire suit, McCann waddled slowly up the steps to the guard room. It was already empty. Just to assure himself that all was going to plan, he opened the door to the main corridor, took a long look down its length, and shut it again. Dr. Caldwell's little elixir was doing its work splendidly. Embracing couples, some undressed, some only partially so, were scattered up and down the corridor, on the steps leading to the second floor, and presumably in the offices where desks had been cleared for commingling more purposeful than mere paper shuffling.

He walked back the way he had come. At the rear service entrance, through which he had entered the building, the last of three tractor-trailers was just backing up to the loading dock in the courtyard connected by an alley to the street. McCann showed himself, gave a thumbs up, and the three trucks' backdoors swung open. Out of each truck clambered ten men, all clad in fire suits. They quickly filed inside and formed a circle around McCann.

"The admiral tells me you ex-SEALs are the best men he's got," said McCann, his voice metallic through the helmet speaker. "I hope so, because you've not only got to ignore what you see here today—and that won't be easy—but forget you were ever here once you leave. Now, you've all been briefed. Each of you knows what he's supposed to do. One last word: anybody who forgets why he's here and decides to join in the fun—you'll know what I mean when you see it—is going to be left behind. I can guarantee you, he's going to regret it. Okay, men—let's get at it."

He opened the door and led his men down the main corridor. He walked briskly, but noticed that the men following him lagged as they inspected at close hand the gyrating, vibrating, plunging, clinging, rotating, rubbing, driving, whirling couples struggling in the heat of passion which time had not yet had a chance to cool.

One AYES technician broke off from the procession to man the switchboard and assure callers that the Federal Reserve Bank was still operating as usual, even though whoever it was they wanted couldn't come to the phone. Another went to the front entrance, where he took up post to see that no one by accident—it certainly wouldn't be by design once they whiffed the F^3-3M—wandered back into the street. Here, overlooking the vast hall on the floor of which an orgy of Roman proportions was in progress, he would harvest memories which he was certain would keep him awake for the rest of the nights of his life, trying to duplicate the improvisations the F^3 inspired.

But the rest, with Keefe McCann in the lead, went downstairs to the main vaults, shifting thrashing couples out of the way as they went, and began loading into canvas bags the banded stacks of greenbacks of denominations ranging from ones through hundreds which lay in neat piles on long lines of metal shelving. They heaved the bulging bags onto handcarts and trundled the handcarts into the two freight elevators. Soon two continuous lines of men were moving in opposite directions, one pushing loaded carts to the rear of the building to stack the bags of currency into the three trucks, and one returning with empty carts for a new load. And when the currency on the shelves was finally exhausted they began loading the hundreds of small wooden crates which contained currency ready for delivery to banks in the Denver federal reserve district.

The whole operation took somewhat less than an hour, and despite the suit's ventilating apparatus, by the time they were finished every man was sweating as if he was working a four-alarm fire. Not until all three trucks were loaded, leaving only enough space for the admiral's men to crowd together in the back, did McCann give the signal to saddle up. By then, activity among Marsha's minions and the employees of the Federal Reserve Bank, who were finding that a government career can, after all, be exciting, had slackened somewhat. Partners were being exchanged, and here and there groans of fatigue were heard.

Still in the fire suits, in which they would have to remain until decontaminated, McCann and his men climbed in the trucks and closed the doors behind them. In the three tractors the drivers, similarly attired, started engines. They lumbered through the empty courtyard and down the alley to the street. They headed east, leaving behind the towering Rockies, on the peaks of which the sun was preparing to impale itself.

An hour later the trucks pulled up to an abandoned airfield twenty-five miles northeast of Denver. There the men loaded more than a billion dollars in U. S. currency into four black, brooding, cargo helicopters. It was dark when the helicopters took off. They flew northwest. If they had possessed enough range, on that course they could reach the Asian continent. But that was not their destination: they were headed for Midas, a silver-mining ghost town in northwest Wyoming.

24. GEORGIA CRACKERS
10 SEPTEMBER 2016

WHEN EMMALINE BUTTERFIELD APPLIED FOR ADMISSION to Georgia Tech in 2009, her application was approved without delay. According to her record, she was just the kind of student Tech was seeking to help reclaim the university's image in the wake of the most recent coin-operated football machine scandal. Born on a hardscrabble farm near Valdosta, Georgia, she had run a small cattle-feeding operation while attending high school, where she had a straight-A average, played on the girl's field hockey team, sang in the church choir, placed second in the state's annual history-of-science competition with an exhibit on Roman road-building techniques, and was one of only seven girls in the graduating class of twenty-three who had neither a baby nor a state-financed abortion.

Her university career was a continuation of her high school successes. Already a native speaker of Russian and Mandarin Chinese, like the rest of her class, she added Georgian as an elective. The course in the language of that Transcaucasian republic had been added to the curriculum when Tbilisi, the Georgian SSR's capital, became sister city of Atlanta, Georgia, but it seldom had more than half a dozen students at any one time. After all, the Georgian Soviet Socialist Republic was considered inaccessible, primitive, and a cultural desert; its only distinction was the legendary longevity of its inhabitants.

After graduating with honors in physics, Emmaline Butterfield had been recruited by the Potomac Corporation, a Defense Department contractor, for secret research about which she never spoke to her friends. Not that she had many. She was a bookish young woman, pretty, but shy and reclusive, preferring the solitude of the library stacks to the more active life of her contemporaries. Still, she must have felt a restlessness of which her associates were unaware, for one day she resigned to accept a second lieutenant's commission in the Air Force. There her studious nature, scientific background, and, above all, her knowledge of Georgian, led to promotion to first lieutenant within eighteen months and assignment to the Mutual Inspection Team operating in the Soviet Union.

Stuart Worthington Sage had very little in common with Emmaline Butterfield. He had been in and out of six universities—expelled for boozing, adultery with faculty wives, fistfights, and poor grades—before finally drying out and straightening up in his twenty-sixth year. He then obtained a degree in aerospace engineering at the University of Illinois and kicked around Europe and Asia for two years on his family's ample allowance before returning to the United States, where he entered the army. The military life was not his choice, but his father had given him an ultimatum: "Serve your country in uniform as all patriotic young men must, or be cut out of my will."

He was a popular but lazy officer. He dodged all real work by attending a succession of schools—tank commander's school, helicopter pilot's school, and language school, where, according to classmates, he took the fourteen-month course in Georgian solely because it was taught by a very pretty young blonde. The schools, while useful for promotion and the avoidance of the responsibilities of command, had the disadvantage of adding to his service obligations. The life was pleasant and relaxed, but one day, when he was a major with nine years service, he decided he had had enough. When he discharged his service obligations thirty-two months hence, he would get out, for his father was becoming very fragile and would soon make his son a very wealthy man.

Browsing among available billets, Major Sage discovered an opening on the Mutual Inspection Team for a field-grade officer speaking Georgian. The Georgian SSR was an area of little activity and thus suited to his easygoing approach to life. Duty would require periodic trips to the mountainous Caucasus for unscheduled inspections of possible nuclear tests or missile launches. But the remainder of his time would be spent in Moscow, a land of opportunity for serious drinking and bed-hopping among shapely young Muscovites who preferred the free-spending American Johns to their own dour, ruble-pinching Ivans. Sage signed up.

The first meeting between Commanding Officer Major Stuart Worthington Sage of the Mutual Inspection Team, Georgia, and his new deputy, Captain Emmaline Butterfield, was not a happy one. She had been on post as Acting CO for eight months when he arrived to fill the empty slot, and had become accustomed to running the forty-two-man section as her personal fief. When Major Sage immediately relaxed restrictions on the off-hours activities of the troops, cut the paperwork by two-thirds, and took to arriving at the office an hour or more late every morning, her displeasure was evident, and to none more so than the MIT's commander, Major General Jonathan Boyd.

General Boyd had been in overall charge of the Mutual Inspection Teams for more than seven years. From his own travels he knew the Soviet Union more inti-

mately than the vast majority of senior Russian officers.
He also knew the Russian character and its predilection
for secrecy, indirection, and conspiracy. In general, he
liked the Russians, but trusted them not. His distrust
was magnified when the Russians systematically tried to
subvert each newly arriving MIT observer with sex,
booze, or blackmail. He therefore encouraged feuds
among the staff, insuring that everyone kept a watchful
eye on everyone else and informed him of any slackness
in vigilance or any tendency to succumb to the Russians'
machinations. Thus the Sage-Butterfield confrontation
was a welcome development: they'd keep each other
honest.

At the July Fourth celebration that year, it seemed
that perhaps the feud might end: Major Sage and Captain
Butterfield, both of whom had apparently drunk more
than usual, had been maneuvering for position in a most
unmilitary manner behind the embassy's potted palms.
The entente had been broken off abruptly when one of
the Russian guests happened to blunder upon them, and
in embarrassment they had gone separate ways. The
next day, the wall of discord was firmly back in place.

On September 15, 2016, General Boyd called Major
Sage and Captain Butterfield to his office. Waving them
to the leather couch, he took a seat in the easy chair
opposite them. "I have a little job for you people. Sorry
it comes on the eve of the annual MIT Costume Ball, but
I'm afraid that can't be helped. There's a satellite launch
scheduled for the twelfth—day after tomorrow—at the
new range fourteen klicks north of Tbilisi, and I want
you to check it out."

"Of course, sir," said Major Sage. "I can handle Captain Butterfield's duties with ease during her absence."

"I want you both to go."

Sage groaned. He had been elected marshall of the
ball and had invested $425 in an ornate Othello costume,

confiding laughingly to his buddies that he hoped Captain Butterfield would come as Desdemona so he could have the excuse to strangle her. "The two ranking officers in MIT-Georgia for a mere satellite shot, General? If I may say so, sir, that seems to be a misallocation of personnel resources. Besides, who'll mind the store?"—

"Your adjutant, Captain Wellmore."

Emmaline Butterfield coughed discreetly. "I'm afraid that for once I must agree with Major Sage," she said. "I am quite capable of conducting the inspection alone."

The general frowned. "Let me explain something. I've kept a running record of missile sites that have been constructed in Russia during the past twenty years." He unrolled a map of Russia on the coffee table in front of him and put ashtrays on the corners. He pointed to a cluster of dots. "You'll observe that, while the manufacturing centers for satellites and missiles is in European Russia, the actual launch sites are concentrated in Siberia in the thousand-mile stretch between Novosibirsk and Lake Baikal. But just three years ago they began building this new site north of Tbilisi. Why? Tbilisi has miserable rail connections with European-Russian manufacturing centers, no pool of technical expertise, and is smack in the middle of sawtooth mountains. It doesn't make sense."

"I shared your skepticism about that particular project, too, General," said Captain Butterfield primly. "But in my discussions with the Russians they volunteered that the move was in response to economic pressures. They have been able to use smaller, fuel-efficient launchers in Georgia since it's about as close to the equator as they can get, thus taking advantage of the slingshot effect. Also, they claim that in case of launch failure, no big population center will be endangered by the falling debris."

The general snorted. "Damned lies. A Russian that

speaks the truth is yet to be born. It would take two thousand years for fuel economies to repay the cost of building the Tbilisi missile site. As for not endangering the population, we're talking about men in the Kremlin who march their own people through minefields to clear them for the army's advance. No—there's something fishy going on down there, and you two are going to find out what it is. This is their first launch from Tbilisi, so they probably won't try anything, knowing we'll be especially on the alert. But keep a sharp eye out, ask questions, and don't let them buffalo you."

"You can depend on me, sir," said Captain Butterfield.

Major Sage sighed. "Hate to miss the party, sir, but I guess the country's security is worth the sacrifice."

The director of the Heroes of Labor Satellite Launcher Site Number 11 north of Tbilisi, Comrade Pyotr Petrovich Plotkin, apologized to the Mutual Inspection Team for not welcoming them in Georgian. "I realize," he said in Russian, "that you have gone to a great deal of trouble to learn the local language, but I myself have only a smattering of the tongue."

"Apologies are unnecessary, Comrade Director," said Major Sage. "Our Russian is also far superior to our Georgian."

"Shall we then—in the mother tongue—" said Plotkin, producing a bottle of excellent vodka from the glass cabinet in his office, "drink to the success of this mission?" He handed water glasses filled to the brim with vodka to his guests, smiled, and drank his down in a single draught.

"Old Russian trick, I believe," chuckled Sage. "You ate a pound of butter—doubtless surplus Danish butter, at that—before we arrived, and you expect us to keep pace, drink for drink, until we couldn't find our asses with four hands. Whereupon we return to Moscow too embarrassed to report that you put one over on us. I am getting warm?"

Plotkin beamed. "That would, I suppose, be one way to handle it. Perhaps you have other ideas?"

"I do, indeed," replied Major Sage, sipping from his glass. "Why don't we first inspect the launch site, then the missile and the satellite, and *then* get falling down drunk? That way we satisfy both official curiosity and our personal desire to inspect at close hand about two liters of this excellent vodka."

"Done!" Director Plotkin put his empty glass on his desk. "Come along!"

Though Site No. 11 was small as such installations go, it took the American observers two hours to make a complete tour. They visited the launchpad, blast-deflection chambers, service tower, rocket transporter, central control, fuel storage plant, and even the workers' dormitories. They filled page after page of standard inspection forms with meticulous, detailed notes which would later be analyzed by MIT for anomalies which would point to purposes inconsistent with the declared launch mission: to put into low orbit a satellite containing a revolutionary catalyst to test the feasibility of breaking down atmospheric CO_2 and NOx.

"The concept is important," Plotkin explained, "for both chemicals are 'greenhouse gases' responsible for the increase in the Earth's surface temperature. The atmosphere, more opaque to long-wave terrestrial infrared radiation than to incoming shortwave solar radiation, becomes even more of a blanket to terrestrial radiation as it is increasingly saturated with CO_2 and NOx, products of the burning of fossil fuels. The results are well-known: the progressive melting of the arctic ice cap, consequent raising of ocean levels, and with it threats of inundation of coastal cities such as New York, Hong Kong, Singa-

pore, and Los Angeles. Well, what we are trying to do
with this experiment is to break up these gases into their
harmless constituents, using a catalyst which, energized
by the sun's rays, separates the gases into molecular carbon, nitrogen, and oxygen. In elemental form, they will
offer less resistance to the passage of terrestrial radiation."

"A laudable objective," said Captain Butterfield.
"When are we going to see this mysterious catalyst?"

"Right now, if you like." Director Plotkin led the way
to the laboratory, where preparations were under way to
receive the American inspectors, after which the capsule
was to be sealed and attached to the rocket assembly for
launch that same afternoon.

In the clean room, Major Sage and Captain Butterfield donned seamless helmets and suits, then walked
through two air locks to the chamber where the glisten-
ing, cigar-shaped catalyst capsule was supported on
cushioned steel supports. They photographed and measured the container and jotted down its dimensions to the
nearest millimeter. With the aid of a big portable X ray
machine and from behind a leaded shield, they made a
series of shots of the entire stainless steel receptacle; the
actual X ray plates would form an addendum to their
report. They examined the two rows of spray nozzles
that would deploy the fine catalytic mist. They called for
the diagrams of the radio-controlled release mechanism,
which would dispense the aerosol in calibrated quantities
in response to ground command. And they inspected the
telemetered sensors which would radio to the ground the
relative proportions of carbon dioxide and nitrous oxide
after each pass over the Earth's surface. According to
the Russians' calculations each pass would, if the catalyst worked as designed, convert a detectable amount of
the two gases into their constituent elements.

"Looks good so far," commented Sage. He had studied the plans of the capsule filed by the Russians with MIT in Moscow, and could not discern any discrepancies.

"Why should there be?" said Captain Butterfield acidly. "A capsule is a capsule. It's what's in it that counts."

"All in good time. Let's get out of these stupid suits and into a bottle of that good vodka. The catalyst can wait."

"Excuse me, sir, but it cannot. The catalyst is the reason we're here. We've examined the capsule by X-ray, and can attest that it has no compartments. Therefore we must now breach at random one of the six inspection ports, remove a sample, and take it back to Moscow for analysis. The procedure detailed in the regulations is explicit."

"Yes, I suppose you're right," said Major Sage grudgingly. "You're the physicist—how big a sample do we need?"

"Ten milliliters should be sufficient; we'll take thirty."

Major Sage went to the pass-through panel behind which would be the instruments needed to extract a liquid sample. Watching them both from a glassed booth was Comrade Plotkin, expressionless. By agreement between the Americans and Russians, at this stage of the inspection there could be no interaction between the two parties. But the Russian was allowed to observe, and file either protest or exception to any procedure he felt violated the inspection protocols.

Major Sage opened the panel. Over the gloves of his clean suit he donned the surgical rubber gloves he found inside and carried the tray of instruments over to the table next to the capsule where Captain Butterfield was waiting.

Each scribbled a number on a paper concealed from the other, part of the general's elaborate precautions against collusion of one of his inspectors with the Russians.

"Subtract, add, divide, or multiply?" asked Sage.

"Subtract. Yours first, or mine?"

"Ladies first."

Her number was twenty-three, his was six. They subtracted six from twenty-three, yielding seventeen. That meant that they would number the inspection ports in rotation until number seventeen came up—which made it the fifth port. Using a special wrench, Captain Butterfield carefully, slowly, unscrewed number five port on the top of the capsule. She lifted out the plug.

Major Sage picked up a hypodermic syringe from the tray and inserted it into the capsule. He drew thirty milliliters of the pink fluid into the syringe. Moving with deliberation, he transferred the contents of the syringe to a small steel vial. He handed the syringe to Captain Butterfield, who deposited it in the receptacle labeled "For destruction." He then checked to see that the rubber gasket was properly sealed and screwed on the top of the steel vial.

"That's that," he said with relief. "Let's get the hell out of here." He led the way to the decontamination room, where they bathed in successive acid sprays and mists, finally rinsing off in distilled water. During the ten minute process, Major Sage kept a tight grip on the steel vial. After all, as Captain Butterfield had pointed out, it was the reason they were here.

Back in the office of Comrade Plotkin, the director once again broke out the office bottle. Major Sage accepted his glass, putting the steel vial on the director's desk where he could keep his eye on it as he drank.

"Well," said Plotkin, "did we pass?"

"It's rather too early to say, isn't it?" Captain Butterfield replied. "After all, your mysterious catalyst must be analyzed. But of course, knowing that, you people would never try to launch something that might imperil the good relations that exist between our two countries. As for the possibility that you might switch liquids, that would be detected by a comparison of traces between our sample liquid and that picked up by our space-based spectrometers. So I feel confident that we will give your launch a clean bill of health. In fact, I think," she said with a smile, "I can guarantee it." She raised her glass to the director. "Long live the greatest nation in the history of the world!"

"I'll drink to that," said Sage.

"And I," said Plotkin.

They drank. But only one glass. Both Sage and Butterfield were aware that their reports, both verbal and written, would be subjected to meticulous scrutiny on their return to Moscow. Any evidence of sloppy investigation or carelessness would meet with the strongest of reprimands from General Boyd. Any suggestion that they might have drunk more than civility demanded would be severely censured. Any deviation, however slight, from the strict investigative methods laid down by General Boyd would set fire to a powder train of interrogations that would blow up any story concocted to cover up collusion with the Russians.

There came a sound of marching feet in the cobbled courtyard outside the window. The footsteps stopped. There was a long silence, then a sharp command. A metallic ripple as six rifle bolts snicked back. Another command, and a crash of musketry.

Sage and Butterfield leapt to their feet and stood transfixed at the window. Below them they saw a crumpled, bloodied body on the ground, six soldiers, and an officer marching off.

Plotkin seemed to be expecting the sounds. As soon as the Americans' backs were turned, he swiftly grabbed the vial from the desk and dropped it in his right jacket pocket, at the same time removing an identical vial from his left pocket and putting it in its place. The whole movement occupied less than a second.

Sage and Butterfield turned to Plotkin, who sat unmoved.

"What the hell was *that*?" demanded Major Sage.

"Oh, nothing to be alarmed about, Major," said Plotkin negligently. "A public execution instills more fear in miscreants than the usual shot in the dark. Sorry to have exposed your sensibilities to the spectacle. Should have warned them to wait until you were off the base... Another vodka?"

"No, thanks," said Sage stiffly. "Perhaps you'd be good enough to show us to our quarters. I think we'd like to rest for a while before the launch." He picked up the steel vial from the desk.

"By all means!" Plotkin conducted his guests to the staff officers' quarters, where their bags had been put in adjoining rooms, with a shared bathroom between. He said he would return for them within two hours.

Captain Butterfield had taken a hot shower and was lying on her bed in her dressing gown, smoking a cigarette, when she heard the sound of the shower in the bathroom. She had just stubbed out the cigarette when the door opened and Major Sage walked in, clad in a terry cloth bathrobe and toweling his head dry.

"How did it go?" she asked.

"Very well, I thought."

"Me, too. And I don't think there's any doubt that General Boyd will put his seal of approval on our report."

"Not to mention that 'sample.'" Major Sage laughed. "It's probably Kool Aid."

"Probably. What do you think is actually in that capsule?"

"Beats me. It's not our headache. But we've still got to put our seals on the bottle."

"That's right." She rose and produced a small, tightly woven cloth bag from her suitcase, containing a metal ribbon and the MIT embossing device. She took the steel vial from Major Sage, dropped it into the bag, threaded the metal strip through the metal eyelets, and affixed her seal. She handed it to Sage, who added his own device.

She was wearing high heels and lipstick for the first time since Sage had met her months earlier. Her tight bun had been loosened, and her hair fell in soft folds around her shoulders. She lay down on the bed again. He sat beside her.

Captain Sage smiled a crooked smile. "I guess we can stop pretending to be enemies now?"

"Yes," said Emmaline Butterfield, her pulse quickening as she looked into the eyes of the ruggedly handsome Sage.

He lay down beside her, his elbow on the pillow and his head cradled in his hand. He gently pulled her bathrobe sash and separated the two halves of her robe. He looked down at her naked body. "My, my!" he said. "What a pleasant surprise."

She thrust him back against the pillows and tore his bathrobe away from his body. She said nothing. This was the moment for music, not words.

25. WINDBAG
19 SEPTEMBER 2016

In the 1890s, when silver fever ran high, Midas, Wyoming, built an opera house. It was still by far the biggest structure in the ghost town, its plush seats rotted with age and thickly layered with dust and its red velvet curtain hanging in shreds, an echo of the past that had not heard the lilt of a soprano voice for more than a century, until Karine Collier arrived with her crew of AYES technicians to despoil the concert hall of the few remaining relics of past glory. It was there that Keefe McCann found her shortly after midnight, following a three-hour helicopter flight from the abandoned airfield at Arco, Colorado.

"You're not finished yet?" said McCann, out of his suit and into the fresh night air for the first time in eight hours, after having been decontaminated in a makeshift shower unit flown in from Texas.

"Barely started," said Karine. Dozens of workmen were busily tearing out the rows of seats, pulling down the remnants of the curtain, and nailing sheets of plastic over the windows and holes in the walls. The stench of smoldering arc lights permeated the air, and shadows cast by the workers loomed like giants against the boxes and three balconies.

"Well, we've got to get moving. We take to the air by noon. That gives us just nine hours."

"What's the hurry?" asked Karine, who was clad in a tight Lestrex siren suite, which corruscated in the bright light like a toreodor's *traije de luces*.

"Because on the way here I stopped at a highway telephone to talk with the admiral. He says that somehow our old buddy Artur Artusov has managed to escape Gland Junction and has assembled a task force to track us down. Right now, he and his forty thieves are looking for us in the vicinity of Minot Air Force Base. They're under surveillance, but it won't be so tight that Artusov won't find out what happened there and that we're gone. He'll pick up our trail to Denver and follow it to Midas. I've calculated that he'll be boiling up over the horizon somewhere around early afternoon. We've got to get the show on the road before he arrives."

"Yes, I suppose so. But it all seems so complicated. If they're already under surveillance, why doesn't the admiral simply round them up before they can do any harm?" McCann shook his head. "Have you forgotten that Artusov and his merry men are all accredited MIT observers with the right to go anywhere and ask any questions they want. They have to be far from the public eye before we can deal with them properly. But we're shackled by another constraint as well. Artusov is keeping those comedians in the Kremlin apprised of his team's progress with radioed reports every fifteen minutes. We take them, we cut the transmissions, and then the comrades will awaken and inform a whole new network of sleepers. Before we can get a line on them they could blow our whole operation."

"Yes, but how do you know the Russians won't do that anyway—use sleepers as backup?"

"Sure, that's possible," McCann admitted. "But we can't guard against every contingency, can we? We'll just have to go on as planned and hope for the best. How much longer do you need here?"

"Come back in an hour."

When he returned to the opera house forty-five minutes later McCann found it bare, and the crew was sweeping and vacuuming up the dust. "We don't have time for that," he said to Karine Collier. "Have them knock off and get to work laying down the plastic sheeting. Have you tested the fans?"

"Exhaustively," said Karine, glancing at the balcony and box seats extending like a horseshoe around three sides of the great chamber. At intervals huge fans had been clamped to the balcony railing, their blades angled downward. Hooked up to a generator already pulsating outside the opera house, they would produce a veritable hurricane inside once they were turned on.

"Good. When you're finished up with the flooring, take your men to the dressing station and suit up."

Drawn up outside the opera house were the three trailers, surrounded by men clad in fire suits and air packs, waiting for orders to go ahead. Coming toward them from the far end of the street was a suited-up warden in an ATV making sure that no man was without protection against contamination by the F^3s. "That goes for you, too, sir," he said, as McCann strode out of the opera house.

"I'm on my way to the dressing station now," said McCann. "After the opera house crew is suited-up, make a final check for stragglers before you give the all-clear."

"Don't worry, Mr. McCann—everything's under control."

Twenty minutes later the wail of a siren warned all hands that they had five minutes to get to the dressing station. Seven minutes after that the siren sounded again, and the outside crew began stripping the trailers of the plastic tape which had kept the trucks and their cargo of bagged and boxed currency airtight. They opened the doors and began to lug the bags and boxes inside the opera house, where they emptied the contents onto the floor. Spaced around the perimeter of the room were fire fighters armed with chemical extinguishers to insure that no vagrant spark sent the growing pile of bills, soon waist deep across the entire opera house floor and stage, up in flames.

When the trucks were emptied, an AYES chemist carried two of the remaining steel containers of nonspecific F^3s into the opera house and attached them to cylinders of pressured xenon gas equipped with automatic timers. He left through the front door and sealed it after him with plastic tape.

Two minutes later the timer activated the release valve and the xenon gas combined with the F^3s to produce an aerosol which filled the empty chamber with a fine mist. The blades of the fans began to rotate, circulating the aerosol throughout the huge hall. Within a minute the movement of air had accelerated from a summer's breeze to a stiff wind to a howling tornado, and the millions upon millions of bills on the floor were seized in a whirlwind which made the whole interior of the opera house a solid green blur, had anybody been there to witness it. In the tempest, the mixture of money and pheromone was so complete that not a single square millimeter of any of the myriad bills churning through the air escaped being saturated by the F^3. Just to make sure that none escaped, and that even the new bills would look as though they had been long in circulation, McCann ordered the fans to run for the next thirty minutes.

That gave him just time enough to truck a dozen men some five miles down a prairie dirt road to rendezvous with a small caravan of tractors and their trailers that awaited them there. They had come from all over the

western United States. Each had been crammed full of
cargo and driven to this barren spot where, having left
their trucks with the keys in the ignition, the drivers
were bussed away. McCann's men now took the drivers'
places in the trucks, and soon a plume of dust could be
seen from Midas, growing ever larger as the cavalcade
approached the ghost town.

One of the trucks that pulled up in the main street was
filled with crates of white plastic bags, similar to those
used by housewifes for garbage disposal, but larger. A
few others were loaded with tall slender bottles of helium
gas. But ten trucks were crammed with balloons—six
thousand of them—and the miniature weather station
and radio transmitters which the balloons were designed
to carry into the upper atmosphere. Normally, a balloon
was released, the course and speed of its radiosonde was
plotted by radio triangulation and processed by computer, providing continuous record of wind speed and
direction at various altitudes. Balloon altitudes could be
preset by means of a radio-altimeter which governed the
release of water ballast to elevate, or of helium to lower,
the gas bag.

Encumbered by their suits, the men went about their
tasks slowly but methodically. The fans were turned off
and the doors to the opera house unsealed. One crew
entered the chamber and began stuffing the bills into the
white plastic bags. Another crew fastened the mouths of
the bags with a trick sailor knot which would automatically release should the supporting helium envelope be
ruptured.

Outside, a third crew was filling gas bags with helium,
tethering each to a truck until its cargo, crammed into a
white plastic bag, was suspended below. A technician at
the keyboard of a computer calculated the volume of helium with which each bag had to be inflated, and the
weight of its cargo, for the balloon to cruise at a given

altitude, which information was then scrawled on each bag with a marker pen.

The last item to be attached was the radio receiver and explosive device. On receipt of a coded shortwave signal from AYES in Washington, they would cause the explosive to ignite, blowing up the gas envelope and automatically releasing the contents of the white bag it was carrying.

The only trouble was, the explosive devices had not yet arrived.

The combined lifting forces of the tethered balloons were threatening to carry the dozen trucks away into the stratosphere when McCann called a halt. "Where the hell is that helicopter, Floyd?" he barked at the radioman manning the communications console.

"Five miles out and closing fast."

McCann strained his eyes toward the southwest, for the copters would be coming in from Salt Lake City, where the ordnance depot was located. He heard the distant buzz of a mosquito, then a mote danced on the horizon, methamorphosed into an ominous black bird with spinning wings, and swooped down to hover above them. Motionless in the air, it eased toward the ground the big cargo net slung beneath its belly. McCann's ground crew, bracing themselves against the prop wash, unhooked the sling and the helicopter wheeled and fled the way it had come.

The admiral had come through with the goods, just as McCann had ordered. The contents of the slings were pencil-thin explosive cartridges, with a wire from each end which needed only to be attached to the radio transceiver to complete the remote-controlled destructive device. McCann proposed to set each receiver to pick up one of some 6000 wavelengths.

Up to now, McCann had been moving so fast that he had devised no formal plan of action. And he didn't think he would need one now. He calculated that, after the balloons' release, at the rate of about a thousand an hour over the next six hours, they would quickly ascend to various preset altitudes between 28,000 and 46,000 feet. At that altitude the balloons would be captured by the jet stream blowing from the west, a fierce, unceasing wind that circles the world at mid-latitudes at speeds of from 80 to 250 miles an hour. It was precisely because the jet stream this season was so powerful over Midas that the admiral's meteorologists suggested this remote ghost town as the launch site. It was the same jet stream that made flying from America to Europe faster than the return trip by up to two hours. It was the jet stream which would carry McCann's six thousand balloons and their cargo of nearly a billion authentic U.S. dollars to Russia. There his radio signal would dump them so as to cover every city, town, and village in the Red empire.

"Yes, I understand your idea in principle," said Karine Collier, to whom he was explaining his plan as his men began to insert the cigarette-pack-size destruction device into the mouth of each balloon before tying it off with the nylon lines holding the bags of money. "But do you think it will work that way in practice?"

McCann smiled indulgently. "Your specialty is psychiatric social work, beautiful. I suggest you stick to it and leave the big think to the men."

"Oh, I *will*," she replied with deceptive sweetness. "I was just speculalting on how it will work. After all, there are so many things to think about—six thousand balloons, and all of those darling little bombs going off, and thousands and thousands of miles for those balloons to travel halfway around the world—I guess I can't understand how you're going to avoid being *overwhelmed* by so many variables."

"Let me give you a short course in radiosonde sabotage," said McCann, smiling smugly, "an instrument of war which, I may say with all humility, I have personally invented. The balloons are launched from Midas. They are carried to various levels of the upper atmosphere. By triangulation, thanks to the radio signal propagated by each balloon, we will track them as they transit the Western Hemisphere, the ocean, and Western Europe. They will arrive over western Russia like a great aerial wave breaking on a beach. The wave will take six hours to cross Russia's border, because it will take just that long for us to launch them all.

"Now then, as the leading edge of that wave passes over Russian territory, each balloon's transponder will advise us of its position. We will transmit a coded signal to detonate, say, three hundred of the balloons during the first twenty minutes our balloons appear over Russia. That will spread bills far and wide over thousands of square miles of the western USSR. We will continue, at intervals, to detonate more balloons as they approach targeted territory. In such wise, we shall cover the entire north Asian continent. Every single Russian will be running after those bills, grasping them in his or her grubby paws, as the case may be, with predictable consequences."

"How perfectly clever." She hesitated. "It's just that . . ."

"Yes?"

"Well, you said the signal AYES will send is to be coded?"

"Of course. Has to be, or the Russians could get on to it. Each transceiver receives and transmits on its own individual frequency, that is, six thousand different frequencies."

"And how long will it take for the balloons to drift across Russia, did you say?"

"Depends on the winds, of course, but our meteorologists tell me that in this season we can figure the jet stream will average 140 miles an hour at this latitude. It's about six thousand miles from western Russia to the Pacific coast. You can figure it out."

"I have already," said Karine Collier briskly. "Forty-two hours. Nearly two days and nights. The Russians are not stupid. Russian radio surveillance will pick up the balloons' transponder signals before they even clear Eastern European airspace. They'll realize, from their knowledge of the jet stream, that the balloons are targeted for Russia. They will turn on their jammers to blanket the balloons' beacons and transponders so that AYES receivers will pick up what sounds like a huge swarm of bees. Worse, the same jammers will prevent your coded signals from detonating the balloons' explosives, and the balloons will sail on around the world in the jet stream, in a week or so passing right back over Midas. By then, some balloons will already have begun to return to Earth because of gas leakage, and their money will be dumped on the United States of America. And what do you have to say to that, my dear genius?"

McCann had nothing to say. He was stunned. Her logic was impeccable. And Artur Artusov and his thugs were already on their way to Midas. "Floyd," he said to his radioman, "call the surveillance team and get a fix on Artusov and his men."

Floyd busied himself with his circuits. A moment later he reported that Artusov had just arrived in Denver, an hour ahead of the time anticipated by the AYES trackers. The trackers could arrange to slow him up, perhaps, but didn't think it advisable to advertise their presence.

"No," said McCann, thinking out loud, "it's better they don't break cover. If they do, Artusov might find a way to shake them and find his way to Midas before we're ready for him."

"Mr. McCann," said the outside crew chief, whose

men had now fixed the first 200 transceivers and detonators inside the first relay of balloons to be launched, "we're ready to go. Shall we start launching?"

"Just a minute," said Keefe McCann, wishing he could massage his aching head but not daring to remove his helmet. He thought over what Karine Collier had said. He knew that what she said was sound. There had to be another way, safer and surer, for the balloons to be made to discharge their contents over the target area.

Suddenly he had the answer. "Remove all the transceivers and explosive devices."

"*What?*"

"That's right," said McCann calmly. "Take 'em out and start launching. Bare ass. Immediately."

"But if we remove the transceivers and the detonators," the launch chief pointed out reasonably, "how do we get the balloons to dump the money over Russia?"

"We don't. Now, get moving—Artusov's on his way, and if those six thousand balloons aren't in the air before he gets here, I'll personally tie you to one and send you up myself."

26. SHEEP-DIP
19 SEPTEMBER 2016

WHEN ARTUR ARTUSOV AND HIS ADVANCE TEAM OF FIVE arrived in Denver, having traced Keefe McCann to that city from Minot Air Force Base in North Dakota by combining reports of Russian satellite surveillance with agent reports from the Rocky Mountain states, McCann's objective had been almost immediately apparent. Denver Central had informed Artusov on their chief's arrival that something funny was going on in the Federal Reserve Bank: several people, including police officers and federal agents investigating reports that FRB employees had not returned home from work, had entered the building but not reappeared. The FRB telephone switchboard was not answering, and the building was under police siege. Nobody came out, and nobody was allowed in.

Artusov stretched out on the couch in the office of the director of Denver Central and listened as his operatives made their reports. When they were finished, he allowed himself to drop off to sleep. Experience had taught him that when his body demanded rest it was futile to try to reason things out. On the contrary, often when he napped with a problem on his mind, his subconscious took over to such a degree that more than once he awakened with the problem resolved.

And so it was now. After half an hour of slumber he awoke refreshed, with the pieces off the puzzle dropping, one after another, neatly into place.

Why had Keefe McCann come to Denver? Because Denver had the Federal Reserve Bank nearest Minot, North Dakota.

Why had McCann come to a bank in the first place? Because he wanted money, and the FRB had more than any other nearby bank.

So he wanted money, and in very large quantities. To get it from the Federal Reserve Bank would require government consent, which in a "democratic" country like the United States would take months of bureaucratic and congressional wrangling likely to end in absolute refusal no matter what the motive. The alternative was daylight robbery. To accomplish this a powerful, unique weapon would be needed to breach the formidable defenses of a bank system which had never before in history been compromised. McCann had that weapon—F^3, which he had stolen from Gland Junction. Proof was that everybody who went into the bank during the previous twenty-four hours was still there, and Artusov himself could testify that what kept them there was too powerful for human will to resist.

Artusov's mind inexorably wandered to Carmelita de los Angeles. The F^3 neutralizing agent was obviously weakening, for he found it hard to tear his mind away from concupiscent thoughts about the lovely, passionate Latin. He told himself that he would have to move fast: another day and his mind would be quite filled with thoughts of the seductive female, driving out all others; and the day after that, he knew, he would be unable to resist the desire to commandeer an airplane and fly back to West Virginia to immolate himself in that volcano of sexual desire.

He wrenched his thoughts back to the subject of the

moment. McCann had obviously used the pheromone for the purpose of robbing the bank. He had made off with a large quantity of currency and gold, for what purpose he could not yet divine, unless McCann had abandoned public service for private enterprise. That much money would have to be hauled away in a truck—several trucks, in fact. For security the trucks would have to travel in convoy. And they would have been on the road shortly before the bank was due to close, according to the scenario he had worked out.

Artusov sat up and addressed the director, Denver Central, who had been quietly working on papers at his desk as Artusov slept. "Comrade Kedrov, I want Moscow to supply me with satellite analysis of Denver vehicular traffic between the hours of three and five yesterday afternoon. The analysis is to center on traffic arriving and leaving the Federal Reserve Bank service entrance between those hours. There may—probably will—be a number of vehicles entering singly. What I am looking for is several large vehicles, such as trailer trucks, entering and leaving together. Once that aggregation of vehicles is spotted, I want a trace put on them."

The report came in an hour later. Three large trailer trucks had pulled up at the delivery dock at 3:32 the previous afternoon, and left at 4:29. They had driven to an abandoned airstrip at Arco, Colorado, an hour due east of Denver. The trucks had, apparently, off-loaded their cargo into four helicopters. The helicopters took off on a course of 348 degrees true, but the satellite lost them fifteen minutes later under cloud cover and the failing light of approaching night.

Artusov strode to the chart table, picked up a protractor, and on an aerial map of the Rocky Mountain states drew a line running 348 degrees from Arco. The line intersected no major towns or cities. If he initiated a search along that line by reconnaissance aircraft or satellite, it might take hours to reveal the presence of McCann and his men and the gold and currency. And of course, if McCann's motives were strictly mercenary, and represented no threat to the Soviet Union, it would all be work wasted. But Artusov was sure that McCann had not changed his stripes: he had during the previous twenty-four hours made one attempt to contaminate the Soviet Union with F³ during an overflight in a Dekko Delta scramjet, and Artusov was convinced he would try again.

How?

Ruminating for the first time about McCann's operating *method*, instead of where he might be found, Artusov was not long in arriving at the only theory that fit all the facts: McCann was planning to impregnate the currency he had stolen from the Federal Reserve Bank, and somehow scatter it over Russia. The hunger of the Russian people for hard currency would do the rest. There would be a mad scramble, and before the sun set the hands of every able-bodied Russian would have touched the tainted bills—with predictable and catastrophic results.

Very well. The means of distribution of so many millions of bills would be limited.

Rockets? Impossible. The first sign of a rocket launch from America and Russia would put up its ICBMs—and the United States knew it.

Airplanes, then? No, the Americans had the right of aerial surveillance, but dumping doctored bills from their aircraft would contravene inspection protocols, and the Russians would be within their rights to shoot them down immediately.

That left the single possibility of aerial delivery of another sort, the only plausible way of distributing a huge number of bits of paper over Russia in a short space of time: balloons. And not hot-air balloons, which wouldn't have the range and would have to have human crew. Nor

dirigibles, which also needed air crews and would be
shot down the moment they entered Russian airspace.
Smaller balloons. Many balloons. Balloons launched into
the jet stream which overflew both the American and
Asian continents at latitudes which would allow dispersal over all of the Soviet Union. Radiosonde balloons, off the shelf, the only balloons that would not
have to be made for the purpose.

"Determine the location of all depots in the United
States," he instructed the director, "which stock radiosonde balloons for the U.S. Meteorological Service.
Concentrate first on those in the western states. Then
have our satellite research center log all flights since yesterday noon which took off from those depots, or airports in the near vicinity, on a course which intersects
the line from Arco to the north-northwest at a single
point."

Forty-five minutes later the coordinates he requested
were plotted. All the lines intersected at a pinpoint on
the map: Midas, Wyoming.

From his seat in the jet's cockpit, Artusov saw them
through his field glasses from ten miles away: inverted
teardrops from the sorrowful prairie lands of northwest-
ern Wyoming, mocking gravity, ascending into the sky.
Hundreds of them were visible before they disappeared
into the banks of gray cumulonimbus clouds rolling in
from the west. Artunov had been convinced back in
Denver that this was only feasible delivery system available to Keefe McCann on such short notice, but he knew
the Kremlin wouldn't be satisfied with his surmises.
They would want solid fact. Now he had it.

He turned to his signalman, acting as copilot of the
tilt-wing jet that was skimming the ground at twenty-five
feet to maintain radar invisibility. "Inform Moscow Central on the SSB that we have Midas, Wyoming in

sight, that McCann is launching radiosonde balloons into the jet stream, that these balloons will begin appearing over western Russia within forty-eight hours, that once there they will drop many millions of dollars in American currency on Russian soil, that the bills are highly poisonous, and that death will result from the slightest contact with them."

"Yes, sir," said the signalman, who had pressed the button on his recorder at the first word and would transmit the message in Artusov's own voice to prevent any possible misunderstanding. He flipped on the SSB transmitter, punched in the Moscow frequency, and hit the automatic test button.

The red light on the navcom panel blinked at him. A signal was being transmitted, but it wasn't being received by Moscow and retransmitted as confirmation. He immediately cranked in a standby frequency. The red light blinked on again.

"I'm afraid we're not getting through, sir."

"Keep trying," said Artusov, who had reduced speed and activated the automatic landing mode. Behind him four other tilt-jets flying in formation would also be preparing to land. MIT's Western Region had been drained dry to fill the five aircraft. But the men were the best. All seventy-five were trained in *spetsnaz* commando tactics, all were in fighting trim, all were armed with assault rifles and grenade launchers and rigged out in camouflage uniforms. And they had surprise on their side.

The planes settled to the earth as gently as a falling maple leaf. The hatches opened and men began to run swiftly and silently in two directions. Midas was more than a mile away, behind a smooth bare hill. The two lines of skirmishers would encircle the village and then crawl forward. When each was in place, under cover, and as close as he could come to the enemy without exposing himself, he would report in by pressing once on the transmit key on his radio. When all men were in their assigned positions, Artusov would give the signal for the rush. They would overwhelm the Americans and kill them without mercy.

"You stay here," said Artusov to his signalman, "and keep trying. If you can't get through on any emergency frequency, try broadcasting in the clear. The main thing is, get through."

"I'll do my best, sir."

Artusov joined his deputy, who carried the electronic roster to tally the men in position. When the roster showed all were in place, Artusov would give the order to advance. Together, the two men moved straight ahead toward the brow of the hill. As they neared the crest they dropped to their bellies and crawled. Artusov's camouflaged field hat rose slowly a fraction of an inch at a time until he could put binoculars to his eyes and survey the scene before him.

He need not have taken the precaution. The men in the village, clad in fire suits, were too busy filling balloons, tying on white sacks presumably filled with F^3-impregnated currency, and letting them float free into the sky, to be able to note the infinitesimal distortion of the horizon four hundred meters away, even if they had been looking in his direction.

And, in fact, nobody was.

Keefe McCann was watching a screen in a makeshift command post in what had once been the town hall. Forrest, the AYES technician, had set up the screen and finished testing the acoustic and magnetic sensors more than an hour before Artusov and his planes settled on the prairie. Since then they had been waiting.

"They're getting close," said Forrest.

"How do you know?"

"Well, according to the geophone arrays we planted,

they've approached about as far as they can without giving their positions away. This is confirmed by the magnetic array. Those blips circling Midas on the screen represent the actual positions of enemies with a two-foot CEP. As you can see, they are moving in toward Midas, but very slowly, very cautiously."

"And you say you can tell which is Artusov?"

"Yes, sir. At least I can if Artusov is in command, and you say he is."

"Yes," said McCann. "He'd run this operation personally. No question about that."

"Well then, look—each of these points on the screen shows you the position of a man. Each one will probably be carrying a standard army transceiver, or maybe even the Russian version—they're hard to tell apart. To minimize radio traffic, he'll probably signal he's in position by keying his transmitter. When he does, this will cause the LED corresponding to his position on our screen, indicated by a black spot, to blink off."

"And all men will transmit except Artusov."

"Exactly," Forrest said. "The light that doesn't blink —that's your man."

They watched as the black dots drew closer and stopped. Then, one by one, the lights began to vanish from the display.

"He's behind that knoll southeast of town," said Forrest when all the lights except two had flashed off.

"Artusov and somebody else—probably his deputy."

"Yes, sir."

"Are all the weapons armed?"

"Armed and ready to go."

"Then you may fire when ready, Gridley."

Artusov was raising the hand-held transmitter to give the signal to advance when suddenly a curtain of flame erupted halfway down the slope ahead of him. It ex-

tended as far as he could see and, presumably, circled
the town. No man could pass through that alive, and for
a moment he had the wild thought that the Americans
had laid a pipeline around the village and filled it with
inflammable liquid. He dismissed the thought immediately and shouted the order to commence firing, even
though he knew that his advance had been detected, and
even though he could be sure that the instant the curtain
of flame appeared, McCann's men would have dived for
cover.

The roar of automatic weapons broke the prairie still-
ness, but the Russians were firing blindly. The wall of
flame had quickly given way to dense clouds of roiling
smoke through which nothing at all could be seen. Firing
in the blind was futile. They'd have to breach that wall of
smoke and come to grips with the enemy. Then their
superior training and Russian valor would turn the tide.
"*Attack*," he yelled into his transmitter. "Take no prisoners. Kill them all!"

His men rose as one from their positions and took off
at a dead run through the curtain of smoke. As Artusov
surmised, it had been made by a circle of smoke grenades set off simultaneously by remote control. The wall
of darkness gave way after half a dozen strides to bright
sunlight, with the encircled village laying helpless dead
ahead. His men, whooping triumphantly, bore down
upon it, firing from the hip at the buildings.

In one of them, Forrest kept his eyes on the two dots
which represented the positions of Artusov and his deputy, his fingers poised over the keyboard which controlled the thousands of trip-wired pencil-bombs buried
in half a dozen concentric belts around the village. If an
attacker managed to miss one, he would certainly detonate another on his path toward the village.

The mines were exploding with increasing frequency.

In the space of less than half a minute McCann counted forty-five, but still the Russians kept coming. He wasn't worried that they might reach the town center: snipers were posted in sandbagged positions on roofs, just like in Western movies, and would shoot down—on McCann's explicit instructions only—any man who managed by some miracle to penetrate the cordons of land mines.

Forrest wasn't counting casualties. He was tracking the two dots on the screen. As they moved forward, somewhat slower than the others, as befits the prudent commander, Forrest's fingers touched the keys which disarmed the land mines that lay in their paths.

Suddenly, as abruptly as it began, the battle was over. The bodies of sixty-two dead Russians sprawled on Wyoming soil, taking their final rest. Others had sustained wounds ranging from light to mortal. Only two Russians were unscathed: Artusov and his deputy.

McCann had briefed his men that at all costs Artusov must be spared. Thus it was that the two men, advancing shoulder to shoulder against what seemed to them a veritable hail of fire that somehow left them untouched—for the fire was aimed well around them—pressed on, firing at phantoms, until their ammunition was exhausted. They were standing in the middle of the main street, surrounded by 9-mm brass casings, faces blackened, utterly bewildered to find themselves alive.

In the sudden silence, men dressed in fire fighter's suits emerged from the derelict dwellings and shops on both sides of the street. Artusov tried to run, but somebody's leg shot out and tripped him up. He fell heavily to the ground, where three men pinned him. Rough hands hauled him to his feet, and he heard a strange voice, but one he knew must belong to Keefe McCann.

"Welcome to Midas, *tovarich*," said Keefe McCann.

Artur Artusov nodded but remained silent; a prisoner never improved his lot by talking to his captors. Besides,

the longer he held out the better the chances that his
signalman would get through to Moscow to warn them of
the impending danger. And the danger was compounded
as McCann's men had resumed filling and releasing radiosonde balloons with their evil cargo.

"I hate to be a spoilsport, Comrade," said McCann
amiably, "but I wouldn't want you to entertain any false
hopes about your radioman getting Moscow on the line.
We've mobilized some of the best jamming equipment in
the nation for this exercise, and his chances of raising
Moscow are about as good as your chances of raising
your former helpers here from the dead. Also, our men
have doubtless roped in your radioman by now."

"If you're going to kill me," Artusov snapped, "get on
with it. I'm not afraid to die."

"Well, *I* am," McCann assured him, "and I don't want
an innocent lamb's blood on my hands when I do. And
speaking of lambs, what was that sound I just heard?"
He put a gloved hand to the side of his helmet in panto-
mime of intent listening.

From somewhere came a faint bleating.

"You see?" smiled McCann. "I was sure I heard
something. Shall we go see what it is?" He moved off
toward the row of buildings from which the sound
seemed to come. Behind him, secure in the grip of two
former Marines, came Artusov. It was true that he didn't
fear death, yet he knew that something very unpleasant
was about to happen to him. He knew well the procedures and devices used by the KBG to bend citizens to
the state's will, and felt he could expect something along
the same lines from his captors, who would want to
squeeze information out of him before they slaughtered
him as remorselessly as they had slaughtered his men.
The knowledge did nothing to brighten what he knew
were going to be his last hours on Earth.

McCann tried the door to a derelict barbershop, but the dusty interior was devoid of life. He tried the next door, which belonged to a general store with sagging shelves empty but for the dust of ages. The next door was that of the village's sole hotel. McCann pushed the door open. Standing in the middle of the lobby was a large woolly member of the *ovis aries* species, glaring at them balefully.

"Ah, a sheep!" said Keefe McCann, who had been raised in the city.

That was close, thought Artusov, but no cigar: it was actually a ram. A large ram, moreover, with long, competent-looking horns, an irascible eye, and doubtless a dispositon to match.

"Well, Comrade," said McCann, "now we shall leave you, as you and Sylvester here will have a great deal to talk about."

The men released their grip and left the room.

Artusov, alone with man and beast, felt a sudden panic.

McCann, smiling broadly, moved across the room and sprayed Sylvester full in the face with something from a small vial. Then he waved cheerily and followed his men out the door.

Artusov experienced a startling transformation in his attitudes. That ram Sylvester, for instance. Artusov had always thought the ram an ugly, smelly, and brutish member of the species. But now he realized that he had done the animal an injustice. It was, in fact, a noble beast, with a proud, finely chiseled head, and an air of strength, poise, and dignity. No, that was not quite correct. Sylvester—a lovely name, that!—was not merely noble, but actually, well . . . *beautiful*. Why had he never realized until now the depth of his feeling for the species? Tears welled in his eyes. He had been wrong, but he would make it up, and prayed he might be forgiven.

He took a tentative step forward, his arms outstretched in tender supplication. His voice choked as he voiced that word, simple but pregnant with desire: "Darling!"

27. GREEN SNOW
21 SEPTEMBER 2016

THE PLASTIC BAGS STUFFED WITH GREENBACKS, AND the teardrop nylon balloons which carried them, were invisible to radar. The helium-filled balloons had thus ascended into Wyoming's upper atmosphere to altitudes between 28,000 and 46,000 feet, undetected by electronic observation. Even though each balloon could have comfortably enveloped a modest ranch house, even the most powerful telescopes on the ground would have been hard-pressed to pick them up once they reached altitude and were camouflaged against the pale blue sky.

And so, caught by the westerly jet stream, six thousand balloons and their billion-dollar cargo glided silently across the United States, across the north Atlantic, across England and Germany, Poland and the Balkans, toward the Russian frontier. They moved fast. The average transit time was forty-seven hours, and because they had been released over a six-hour period, the vanguard of the balloon armada was more than a thousand miles ahead of the rear. By the time they reached Russia the jet stream's eddies had spread them out across the landscape so that they were advancing along a front of more than two thousand miles, a stealthy invading aerial army that had as yet triggered no alarms in the Soviet Union. Indeed, there was no reason why they should. Without human intervention they would circle the northern latitudes of the Earth for weeks, perhaps months, until the helium slowly leaked out of the balloons and they descended to be snagged by tall trees or came gently to rest on mountain slopes.

To avert such a fate, Keefe McCann's plan had called for destruction by radio of each balloon as it passed over a Russian population center. That was no longer possible. Yet McCann realized that there might be another way to distribute those greenbacks more or less evenly across the broad face of Russia. So long as Artusov was alive and aware of the threat the balloons and their tainted currency presented to Russia, there was a chance that McCann could subtly persuade the KGB man to do the job that he himself was unable to accomplish.

Artusov wasn't thinking about balloons for the forty-eight-odd hours after McCann sprayed Sylvester with the limited-potency F^3 he had acquired from Dr. Caldwell. His thoughts were absorbed with Sylvester, the bad-tempered ram. The love affair had been quite one-sided, with Sylvester resisting Artusov's amorous advances with horns and hooves, and if the earth didn't move, the walls of the town hall shook with passionate persuasion on the one hand, and stubborn resistance on the other. Artusov was ardent. When Sylvester wasn't chasing him, head down and horns pointing toward his posterior, the horny Artusov was chasing Sylvester, with the same end in view. Victories were about evenly divided with defeats. But on both sides the tempestuous pursuit took its toll of energy, and at intervals after passion was spent Artusov would collapse in an unconscious heap upon the floor, there to slumber until his reviving hormones prodded him awake for another round of fun and frolic.

It was during such an interval that Keefe McCann slipped through the doorway into the lobby of the abandoned hotel. Sylvester eyed him warily, perhaps believing that his tormentor had called in reinforcements, but otherwise didn't stir from the bed of straw where he was husbanding his strength for the next frantic encounter.

McCann walked to where Artusov lay, breathing stertorously through his nose. The ramifications of his ordeal were all too evident: his clothing was ripped into shreds, his arms and legs were bloody ruins from repeated gashings and proddings, and his face was puffy and streaked with sweat-caked dirt. He stank worse than Sylvester. McCann nudged him with his foot. Artusov didn't stir. McCann reached down and removed Artusov's watch. He set the date back one day, and replaced the watch on the Russian's wrist.

Artusov awakened with a start from feverish slumber. He remembered, with disgusting clarity, everything that had passed, but the irresistible urge to couple with Sylvester had faded while he slept. He looked across the lobby at Sylvester, standing defiantly with his back to a corner, braced to renew battle. But Sylvester's virtue was no longer threatened. Indeed, as he examined the shaggy, foul-smelling beast, Artusov couldn't for the life of him understand what he had ever seen in him to begin with. He hitched up his trousers and staggered out of the derelict hotel.

Enough daylight remained for Artusov to discern that the Americans had finished their evil work and, as usual, had left a mess behind. In typically wasteful capitalist fashion, they had abandoned the trailer trucks and the tractors that pulled them. White plastic bags pirouetted in the wind, empty helium tanks were scattered far and wide, and two all-terrain vehicles shot up during the Russians' assault lay bare and blackened from the fire which consumed them. The Americans had even left behind the electrical generator, which was thumping away somewhere behind the buildings. He picked up an assault rifle lying in the dust and walked stealthily from one building to another, seeking signs of life. There weren't any. The ghost town of Midas was uninhabited except for him—and of course that wretched Sylvester.

Behind the counter in what had once been Midas's bank, Artusov discovered the American command post, complete with a small but powerful SSB transceiver. He flipped on the switch and the monitor screen came alive with the words "Please enter your transmission frequency." Artusov couldn't believe his luck, but didn't question it. He punched in the frequency of Section K in Moscow, followed by the code for Acting Director Liam O'Shaughnessy Konev.

A moment later a voice came from the loudspeaker: "Kubelsky here. Please supply your countersign."

"Issur Danielovich."

"Identity confirmed. Kindly transmit on scrambler code ROR."

"Scrambler not available," Artusov replied. "Listen closely, for this channel is very likely to be jammed within a few seconds. The Presidium must be warned immediately of the great danger from balloon-borne..." He debated whether to explain the nature of the menace, then decided that the Americans were likely to jam his transmission before he could get the important part of the message across, namely, that they *had to shoot the balloons down at once*, while they were still over the Atlantic and Western Europe. He went on: "...great danger from balloon-borne sabotage materials which have been deployed in the jet stream moving toward the Soviet Union from the west. Several thousand of these balloons have been launched, and all our antiaircraft defense forces must be mobilized immediately to shoot them down..." Artusov glanced at his watch to check the elapsed time, then made a rapid mental calculation. "Their present position is above . . ."

"*Now!*" ordered Keefe McCann.

Forrest threw a switch, simultaneously cutting the RF output of the SSB transceiver and activating two megawatt jammers borrowed at short notice from electronics warfare stores maintained at China Lake. The jammers would, of course, foul up TV reception all over the Northwest. But McCann figured that the world would probably survive *one* night without *I Love Lucy* reruns.

As Artusov spoke, the effect of the F^3-suppressive drug Dr. Caldwell had administered to him just three days before was beginning to wear off. He was having trouble concentrating on what he was saying, as thoughts of the voluptuous body of Carmelita de los Angeles intruded, calling him back to Gland Junction. As he began to describe to the unhearing Konev the specific effects the F^3 would cause, he could not suppress the urge to relive his own intensely erotic experiences. Memories of those golden moments in Carmelita's arms overwhelmed him, and soon he was babbling incoherently, like a bilingual with his mind unhinged, parts of his utterances fragments of admonition to the Soviet authorities, and parts repetition of the expressions of endearance he had muttered while in Carmelita's softly smothering scissor's grip. Gradually he became aware that he was mouthing gibberish. "Ah . . . the hell with it," he finally said in disgust, switching off the transmitter and wondering where he could steal an airplane to take him back to Gland Junction.

In Moscow, his fragmentary message was received with consternation. High-flying Polish air force jets on training exercises over the Baltic and eastern Poland had already reported seeing an extraordinary number of radiosonde balloons, confirming what Artusov had said before his transmission had been jammed. All Warsaw Pact antiaircraft defense systems were alerted to shoot down any balloon sighted. The same measures were taken by all Soviet PVO units, and within the hour hundreds of fighter aircraft were airborne over European Russia.

Free-floating balloons were not all that the weather was carrying into Russia. During the night, thick banks of altocumulus clouds had moved in on a long front from the Gulf of Finland to the Ukraine. They effectively camouflaged the balloons drifting at lower altitudes, which continued their steady progress toward the east, unmolested. Those programmed to cruise at higher levels had a different fate. Squadron after squadron attacked them with blazing machine-gun fire, sending one after another plummeting to earth in a shower of green, as the deflation of each balloon triggered the release of the suspended plastic bag of money beneath. The bills, driven by the swirling tropospheric winds, were distributed over the hundreds of thousands of square miles which lay in their path.

But balloons shot down during those first hours were exceeded in number by those not yet seen, for their small size and neutral color made them difficult to spot. Relay after relay of fighter craft were sent to chase them down, but not until the last surviving balloons had reached the Ural Mountains east of Moscow and the other major population centers did the pace of the hunt slacken.

But that hunt was for those balloons the pilots could see. The cloud-shrouded balloons, meanwhile, floated on undetected, unhindered, toward Siberia. Only then the clouds which had protected them dropped their load of moisture over the Urals did these lower-level balloons become visible; then they too were attacked and brought down in a running one-sided battle that stretched from the western frontier of the Soviet Union all the way to the Pacific Ocean.

The aerial chase lasted, all in all, nearly thirty-five hours, with time off during the hours of darkness when pursuit was impossible.

On the ground, the chase was even more frantic. Apartment buildings and offices, shops and railroad stations, barracks and football stadiums emptied of their millions as the bills floated down. In the classless society which had destroyed its last monarch a century earlier the dollar had long since become king. With the dollar, the wage earner of rubles—moderately worthless because the local economy produced little worth buying—could patronize the hard currency shops which were stocked with exotic foreign goods such as blue jeans, razor blades, soap that actually sudsed, frameless eye glasses, tinned ham, suits that fit, and real Scotch whiskey.

The Russians were witnessing a phenomenon more miraculous than the victory at Stalingrad: the sky was raining dollars. Not only single dollars, but fives, tens, twenties, fifties, and even hundreds. The suspicion that they might be counterfeit was quickly discounted when Moscow Radio declared them to be so shortly after the first bills fluttered to earth. In fact, the radio announcement alerted millions of Russians who otherwise might not have known of the heavenly deluge, and sent them rushing pell-mell into the streets and fields and onto rooftops to get their share of manna.

Russians with hard currency in hand do not hoard it. Bitter experience had taught them that worthwhile goods have a very short shelf life. So the moment man, woman, or child snatched enough American money out of the air to satisfy his greed at least temporarily, he went pounding off to the nearest hard currency shop, clutching his money in a hand sweaty from excitement and expectation. Very few Russians were spared the pleasure of anticipation, for the largess from above was bountiful. The streets swarmed with people showing miles of stainless steel teeth, most of them with something to smile and joke about for the first time in their drab lives.

The human skin easily absorbed the F^3 with which the bills were saturated, but it typically took an hour or more before the bloodstream picked up the pheronome molecules and carried them to the pituitary gland and other organs responsible for the release of the hormones governing sexual arousal and activity. Nevertheless, it was not long before male looked at female, sensed there a rapturous readiness, and without further ado the two, oblivious to the shock and dismay of onlookers not yet seized by sexual frenzy themselves, proceeded to the pleasures of the wedding night, even if it happened to be midday in Red Square. A wave of sudden and instantly requited desire rolled across Russia. Few were immune, among them the sick and aged who were too weak to grasp the bills that littered the hallways of hospitals and nursing homes, as physicians and nurses happily succumbed to the epidemic of venery raging throughout the land. The more robust ailing, who had the strength to retrieve a bill or two, soon experienced the thrill of a lifetime destined, considering their frail condition, to be as short as it was merry.

Business soon ground to a standstill, as did transportation, telephone and radio communications, and other services. Nobody had any clear idea of what was happening, but it was plain that whatever it was, everybody was reveling in it. Barracks, parade grounds, missile sites, ships in harbor, airfields, supply depots, and other military installations emptied as servicemen followed the sensible example set by the civilians. By nightfall of the day it rained dollars, virtually every Russian above the age of puberty was engaged in a mass orgy, to the de-

DANIEL DA CRUZ 279

gree that had an invading army been marching upon Moscow, no defense would have been offered.

Here and there were islands of calm. Some distant collective farms and military outposts had not received a drop of green rain. They went about their daily routine undisturbed, happy that the usual stream of instructions and requests for reports from Moscow had, for some unexplained reason, been interrupted. They didn't question their good fortune: so long as no demands came from the capital, they could slack off and enjoy that extra store of vodka they had saved for just such a day as this.

All was not calm in the Kremlin. There, isolated from the man in the street, the Presidium debated the sudden, almost general, breakdown in communications. Word had been received from informants that the sky had snowed green over many population centers—indeed, they themselves had seen the scramble for bills floating down upon Red Square below their office windows—and then, as the word spread, their switchboards went dead.

But Red Square was alive—alive with writhing, bare bodies. General Secretary Radzhov himself viewed the horrifying spectacle through field glasses and personally gave the order to the KGB to quell the disturbance and haul the offenders away to prison. He watched as the KGB busses rolled up with screaming sirens, scooped up hundreds of the depraved and crammed them into trucks, and sped off. But others even more wanton replaced them in Red Square, tearing their clothes off to couple in a mounting frenzy, like rabbits in springtime. It reminded him of some ghastly medieval plague that once swept whole countries at a time. Obviously, the phenomenon had something to do with the money that had descended from the sky.

"Svetlana," he said to his secretary at the corner desk, who was trying fruitlessly to get KGB headquarters back on the line, "I want you to go down to the square and bring me some of those bills. But be very careful—they are contaminated. Wear gloves, and put them in a plastic bag."

"Yes, Comrade General Secretary," said the young woman, getting a pair of leather gloves from the recesses of her desk and hurrying from the office.

He watched her through his binoculars as she went out the big doors with a large plastic bag, threaded her way between couples in frantic embrace on the cold paving stones, and picked up half a dozen bills with gloved hands and dropped them in the plastic bag. Five minutes later she came through the door to his office.

Wearing rubber surgical gloves, General Secretary Radzhov motioned to her to dump the bills on the conference table. With tweezers, he picked up one and inspected it under the desk lamp. He had seen American money. This was genuine. Or, if counterfeit, its workmanship was superb. He was puzzled. Obviously the bill had been impregnated with some sort of quick-acting poison or aphrodisiac, but what it was he could not guess. What was certain was that he must not, on any account, allow his skin to come into contact with the bill. Still holding it with the tweezers, he brought his nose close and sniffed it cautiously for a clue as to the nature of the poison.

"It has a familiar odor," he said, his brow furrowed in thought, "but I can't place it."

"Maybe I can," said Svetlana, approaching and taking the tweezers. She sniffed. Her upper lip curled in what biologists call the Flehmen Response, instinctively directing the current of air into her nostrils, and then she sniffed again. Her face suddenly sobered.

She put the bill on the table. The fingers of her left hand began to unbutton the buttons on her blouse, those of the right to unzip the zipper of her skirt. In five seconds she was standing in her stockings, garter belt, and shoes. It wasn't much but, as she looked down, she observed it was more than General Secretary Radzhov was wearing...

At Spassky House, the residence of the American ambassador, Chief of Mission Jerry Hathon was viewing the spectacle with high-powered glasses from behind the French windows, appropriately enough, of his salon. Like the Russians themselves, he was not quite sure what was going on, but he knew that it had something to do with the sudden shower of money from the skies. The broad avenue in front of the residence was littered, as he presumed was every other street in Moscow and perhaps all of the Soviet Union, with workers of the world, uniting, having nothing to choose but their janes.

The coded message the day before from his old shipmate Ricardo Rivera Handy—they had made vice-admiral on the same promotion list—had been very explicit. The chief of AYES had warned him, as of receipt of the message, that he was to impose an absolute embargo on all movement to and from the embassy until further notice. No one in, no one out. All would be made clear in due time, but until it was Ambassador Jerry Hathon was not to allow a single door or window in Spassky House to be opened by so much as a millimeter. Looking down at the festivities in progress, the amazing sight of masses of Muscovites literally having a ball for the first time in their drab lives, the silver-haired ambassador wondered wistfully whether obeying orders to the letter was such a good policy after all.

As he mulled over the question, the words of an old Beatles classic came back to him, something about "money can't buy you love."

Liars.

28. NOODLE
24 SEPTEMBER 2016

"LOOKS PRETTY GOOD SO FAR, RICK," SAID AMBASSADOR Jerry Hathon, in answer to the question from the chief of the Atomic Yields Estimates Service on the embassy's secure line. "But it could be too early to tell."

"Nonsense," growled Admiral Ricardo Rivera Handy. "The Soviet Union's radio traffic—incoming and outgoing, foreign and domestic—has come to a standstill during the past fifteen hours. Our satellites show only a few planes aloft. They show nothing moving on the roads, rails, or waterways. Russia is in the grip of total paralysis. It's totally impotent."

"Wrong choice of words, Rick," observed Ambassador Hathon, looking out the window at the action in the street—coming again to a boil at the early morning hour of seven Moscow time as the combatants revived after a few hours of slumber—"but I get your drift. What's next?"

"The Marines are on their way. Also the army, navy, and air force. Every man in uniform we can put in the air or shove onto a ship or cram into a truck is heading toward the Soviet Union. Within twelve hours the troops we're stripping from Germany will be landing at Moscow's airports, and I expect by then you'll have shifted your base of operations to GenSec Radzhov's office in the Kremlin, from which you can establish contact with the various units as they arrive."

"I hope they've been well briefed about not touching anything green?"

"They have. But boys will be boys, and if they decide to sniff the local flowers from time to time, I shouldn't be too hard on them if I were you. After all, considering the past sorry century of Russo-American relations, it's only poetic justice that we should be screwing *them* for a change."

"But what about the Warsaw Pact countries? What about all those Russian divisions based in Poland and Czechoslovakia and East Germany?"

"That's taken care of. The president summoned the ambassadors from Pact countries to the White House and explained the situation. Without support from the homeland, Soviet divisions couldn't advance fifty miles —not that they'd ever try without specific orders from the Kremlin. Besides, the populations of those countries are uniformly hostile to the Russians. Soviet occupation forces know that better than we do. So the president's pitch was 'promise the Russians you'll protect them from the locals, providing they behave.'"

Ambassador Hathon's fears subsided. It seemed that the Washington planners, for once, had thought the situation through. On the other hand, no profound thought had been required. The enemy was disarmed and emasculated as thoroughly as if by a surgeon's knife, but without the tears. The main problem would not be taking control of the country—Jerry Hathon and the embassy's Marine security guard could do that practically by themselves—but to feed the people.

According to Admiral Handy, the potency of the F^3 that had impregnated the bills still swirling through the streets of Moscow would gradually decline during the next fortnight. By June 22, Russia's population would be

drained, exhausted, relaxed, and happy with fate for the
first time in their lives. The release of centuries of state-
enforced rectitude would purge the complex-ridden Russians of their repressions—maybe. The presence of the
Americans would relieve them of the intolerable pressures of an oppressive, self-perpetuating, bureaucratic
government—certainly.

For a while, anyway. Looking down the road, Admiral Ricardo Rivera Handy could see the dim outlines of
U.S.-installed American-style bureaucracy replacing the
Muscovite model. There would be a lot of "free enterprise"—dominated by the General Motors and IBMs
of Russia which would soon take root. The American-
sponsored government, like the old, would continue to
snoop into the affairs of its citizens, using the KGB apparatus already in place rather than the IRS, credit
unions, labor unions, religious fringe groups, pollsters,
and other guardians of conformity in the United States.
Education would decline as Russia replaced intellectual
rigor in mathematics and the sciences with electives, il-
literacy would soar, crime would flourish as judges
turned felons loose on a society which they would blame
for youth's delinquency, and the arts would see 'socialist
realism' wiped out to make way for nonrepresentational
daubs. In a decade or two, Russia would have a 50 percent divorce rate, a 60 percent bastardy rate, a rocketing
crime rate, and psychiatric hospitals burgeoning with
real psychotics instead of political dissidents. Well,
thought Handy, it would serve them right.

Meanwhile, American soldiers would proceed with
the peaceful invasion of Russia. They would come bearing gifts, in the traditional American manner of dealing
with backward nations—fast-food shops, eight-lane
highways, Coca-Cola, television sets, a bicameral legis-
lature, singles' bars, drag racing, credit cards, narcotics,
protest demonstrations, soap operas, homosexual en-

counter groups, weight watchers' clubs, strikes, political action committees, shopping malls, welfare, professional football, movie celebrities, disposable automobiles, and other amenities without which life is a joyless wilderness. They would destroy Russian nuclear armaments, their tanks, aircraft, and warships; and they would make it impossible for Russia ever again to wage war, crushing their fighting machine forever, as the Allies did that of Germany after World War I. Admiral Handy grew misty-eyed just thinking about it all.

In a rush of events, he had spared few thoughts for Keefe McCann, the man whose imagination and daring action had been responsible for the dramatic and timely victory over Russia. Now that the Russian menace had been defused, the weight of his guilt was borne upon him by his secretary, who reported that McCann was on the line, wanting to say good-bye.

"Good-bye?" said the admiral, bemused. "Where is he going?"

"*Really*, Admiral Handy!" said Mrs. Biggs severely. "How can you be so unfeeling? Have you already forgotten about Dr. Semm and his delayed action shots? Keefe McCann is knocking at death's door and is about to be invited in."

"Give me that phone...McCann? This is Admiral Handy."

"Didn't want to bother you, Admiral," said Keefe McCann, his voice somber and lifeless, "but I was just wondering how everything turned out."

"Perfectly, my boy, thanks to you. If it hadn't been for you, well..."

"I guess that means we beat the Russians to the punch."

"How do you mean?"

"That Russian secret weapon your Dr. Pollock devised, the one you sent me to Russia to get the formula for."

"Oh, *that* one," laughed the admiral. "As a matter of fact, they did launch it. Fifty-five hours ago, to be exact, but it turned out to be a dud."

"How so?"

"Well, it hasn't hurt anybody, and our chemists assure me that while they haven't figured out the chemical structure, it is not life-threatening. And we are assured of that fact from reliable sources, what's more."

"A dud, huh?"

"In a sense. You see, the substance—a pinkish liquid —was contained in a rocket that was launched a little over two days ago from a new range in Tbilisi, Georgia. Our AYES inspection team got a prelaunch specimen— some kind of catalyst designed to break up atmospheric carbon dioxide and nitric oxide to reduce the greenhouse effect, it was—and our Moscow labs gave it a clean bill of health as a nonlethal substance."

"The Russians aren't dummies," objected McCann. "Maybe they switched specimens on your people."

"Hell, we always consider that possibility. Before the rocket could make a second pass over the continental United States, we launched a vehicle to collect a sample of their catalyst. We ran it through electrophoresis, paper chomatography, emission spectrography and every other analysis we could think of. Every single one confirmed that this pink cloud is indeed nonlethal. But just to make sure, since my reputation and that of my agency was riding on it, I tested the stuff myself."

"How do you mean—yourself?"

"I sniffed it. Smelled a little like petunia blossoms, but that's all. I'm seventy-seven years old and a bit unsteady on my pins, and God knows if the stuff was going to kill anybody, it would be me."

"So you must have got bum dope about that 'secret weapon'?"

"Sort of looks that way. That satellite has made 36 passes so far over the United States transiting east to west. Haven't had any adverse reports so far."

"Well, I guess congratulations are in order," said McCann, his voice dry and bitter. "Too bad I won't be able to help you celebrate."

"I guess you're referring to that injection Dr. Semm gave you?"

"What else?"

"Now, look, McCann, there's something I've got to tell you that—"

"Thanks, Admiral," McCann broke in, "but I'd just as soon not drown in your crocodile tears. I threw the dice of my own free will, and I crapped out. I only regret that..."

"You have but one life to give for your country?"

"That I can't take you along with me, you canting old son-of-a-bitch," said McCann, suddenly furious that everybody was going to live happily ever after—everybody but Keefe McCann. "Now that I've finished your operation and have my own life to think about again, I have no life to think about. According to Dr. Semm, I should have been dead by now. I guess it's all those push-ups I did in my jail cell that got me this far. But it'll take more than push-ups to cure what ails me."

"You mean you're not feeling well?" said the admiral, truly alarmed.

McCann laughed hollowly. "That's a joke. I'm calling from a hospital bed at Lowry Air Force Base. The doctors tell me my vital signs are going steadily downhill. They're hoping I'll last another day."

"Then they're idiots, like most doctors I've met with. There's nothing wrong with you, man—nothing at all."

McCann laughed again, weakly.

"I mean it. That whole business with Dr. Semm was a put-up job. The needle contained nothing but distilled water. I filled it myself. I only did it to make you cooperate. I never thought..." His voice trailed off.

There was a long silence.

"Are you on the level?" said McCann finally.

"Absolutely."

"Then why do I feel so rotten? Why do I feel like I'm going to die? Why are my vital signs..."

"Vital signs, my ass. It's all in your mind, my boy. Dr. Semm said you would die if you didn't get chelation in time, and the time has passed, and now you think you're dying. There's nothing to it."

"Next you're going to tell me that Dr. Semm didn't get killed in a shoot-out."

"That's what I'm going to tell you. There *was* no shoot-out. I just made up that yarn to jolt you into action. It was cruel, I know, but I'd run out of options. Semm's no traitor. In fact, at the moment he's bent over a microscope in his office right down the hall, and if you have your nurse hook up a videotel, I'll put him on so you can see for yourself. He'll..."

But Keefe McCann wasn't listening. He pressed the bell pinned to his pillow.

A middle-aged woman in starched white came in. "Yes, Mr. McCann?" she said, with the gentle voice of one addressing a patient for whom hope has gone. Indeed, when she saw him ten minutes earlier he didn't look as though he was long for this world. His eyes were dull and sunken and his yellow skin was drawn tightly over his cheekbones. And he was being fed intravenously, since on the two occasions his grieving wife put her cool hand on his fevered brow he had gone into convulsions of vomiting; obviously he was incapable of holding down food. A terminal case if she ever saw one. "Tell me what I can do for you," she said tenderly.

McCann sat up in bed. He reached across with his left hand and pulled the IV needle from his arm. "Two things, beautiful: a bottle of the oldest Scotch whiskey you can find, and my lovely lady. In that order."

Karine Collier had been crying. It was all so unjust. How could Keefe be dying, when their life together had not even started? As she opened the door to his room, she paused to dab at her eyes with a handkerchief and tried to smile. The end must be near, for the message from the nurse's station said that there had been a sudden change in his condition and that she had better hurry. She pushed open the door.

"Come right in," said McCann, waving at her cheerily with a glass filled with amber liquid. "And kindly lock the door behind you."

In a trance, she obeyed. She was wearing a dress of clinging navy blue silk, a compromise between a funereal black and a more autumnal color, which she considered inappropriate for the occasion. "Are you all right?" she said, and was immediately ashamed of her indelicacy.

"Couldn't be better. I'm not sick. I'm not going to die—well, at least not tonight and for the foreseeable future."

"But . . . I don't understand."

"Neither, my pet, did I, until I talked a moment ago with that conniving bastard Handy. I was conned—I, the king of con men. That needle old Doc Semm jabbed in my arm was filled with tap water. Semm didn't die, and neither am I going to. I never was intended to. And as for that Russian secret weapon—that apparently was another hoax. The satellite that was supposed to contain that horrible killer is circling the Earth now, even as we talk, emitting a pink cloud with no ill effects. So both killer substances—the Russians' and Handy's—turned out to be frauds. He had me injected with his little dandy just to keep me humping. And speaking of humping, wouldn't you like a little drink before we get down to it?" He waved the bottle invitingly.

In a daze, she nodded. He poured, and handed her the glass, which she took gingerly, avoiding contact with his skin.

He gently took her other hand in his and pressed his lips to her palm. He didn't throw up.

"You used the antirape pheromone neutralizer?" she said, her eyes sparkling.

"That I did, my love, but after I've finished with you tonight you'll wish I hadn't. Ever make love in a hospital bed?"

"Never. Is it fun?" she asked. She took a quick sip of her drink, put it on the table, and peeled off her dress in one swift, efficient motion. She unhooked her bra and threw it to one side. She slid out of her bikini panties and left them where they lay. She took two languorous steps and was beside him.

McCann encircled her legs with one strong arm and lifted her upon him. With the other arm he pulled down the sheet until their bare bodies touched. Their lips were inches apart. And then they were simply—apart.

There was no hurry. They had the rest of their lives for this. He kissed her ears, her neck, the small of her back. He caressed one leg, then the other, then both. She was breathing hard.

"Now," she said.

"Now," he replied, shifting his position ever so marginally.

"Hurry!" she said impatiently. "I can't wait much longer."

But something was wrong—seriously wrong. McCann couldn't put his finger on it. Or rather, he could —just barely.

And that, of course, was the whole trouble. Try as he might, try as *she* might, try as they *both* might—and they did try, mightily, until they both collapsed from sheer fatigue—he couldn't get it up.

Small consolation, that across the length and breadth of the land, *nobody* could.

ABOUT THE AUTHOR

For 30 years Daniel da Cruz has lived and worked—as a diplomat, teacher, businessman, and journalist—in Europe, Asia, and Africa.

He spent six World War II years as a U.S. Marine volunteer, serving ashore, afloat (in 1941 aboard the *Texas*), and aloft in the three war theaters. A *magna cum laude* graduate of Georgetown University's School of Foreign Service, da Cruz has been variously a census enumerator, magazine editor and editorial consultant, judo master—he holds a second degree Black Belt of the Kodokan Judo Institute, Tokyo—taxi driver, farmer, public relations officer for an oil company, salesman, foreign correspondent, publishers' representative, vice-president of a New York advertising agency, slaughterhouse skinner, captain of a Texas security organization, American Embassy press attaché in Baghdad, copper miner and Adjunct Professor of Anthropology at Miami University.

Da Cruz has published twelve books, among them an American history text, a monograph on Amerindian linguistics, and three suspense novels for Ballantine Books, the most recent of which, *The Captive City*, was awarded a special "Edgar." He has written three other science-fiction novels, *The Grotto of the Formigans* (Del Rey, 1980), *The Ayes of Texas* (Del Rey, 1982), and *Texas on the Rocks* (Del Rey, 1986).